DARK SOMMER

NORA SOMMER CARIBBEAN SUSPENSE - BOOK THREE

NICHOLAS HARVEY

Printed in the United States of America

First Printing, 2022

ISBN: 979-8352746035 (Amazon only)
ISBN: 978-1-959627-15-9 (IngramSparks)

Cover design: Covered by Melinda

Cover photograph of model: Drew McArthur

Cover model: Lucinda Gray

Mermaid illustration: Tracie Cotta

Editor: Andrew Chapman at Prepare to Publish

Proofreader: Gretchen Douglas

Author photograph: Lift Your Eyes Photography

DEDICATION

This book is for my incredible wife, Cheryl.
Here we go again my love;
the adventures continue...

PROLOGUE

Grand Cayman - 2:00am Tuesday

The lights from the monitor beside her bed cast a multicolour glow across the walls on which Kendra struggled to focus. Nothing stayed still in her vision, yet the room was calm and quiet. She held up her hand and knew she was wiggling her fingers, but her blurred vision was out of sync somehow. Her soft, light brown skin swirled before her eyes and her aching body screamed for sleep, but an instinct deep inside drove her to move.

The effort of swinging her legs to the edge of the bed was exhausting, and she paused to rest when her foot knocked against something firm. A line tugged on the back of her left hand, so Kendra clawed and pulled, feeling the tether release with a sharp pain and a trickle of something warm down her arm. A nauseous feeling ebbed and flowed, threatening to empty her stomach at any moment. More details slowly took shape, but her brain failed to complete her thoughts. She touched her swollen chest and felt wires underneath her shirt. A blouse without any buttons.

She tried swinging her legs again, but the barrier halted any movement. Aided by both hands, she lifted her left leg and cleared the barrier, which now dug into the back of her thigh, tipping her body off balance until she lay on the bed once more. She fought the urge to give up and close her eyes. Dragging her leg back over, Kendra reached out and took hold of the tubular bar she could now see in the faint light of an LCD screen. Pulling with all her might, she rolled her torso and right leg over the bar and felt a moment of weightlessness before her fall was arrested with a violent thud.

Groaning, she touched a finger to her face and felt blood trickling from her misshapen nose. Struggling to all fours, Kendra willed herself to stand. The pain seemed to bring more clarity, and damn, she thought, there's plenty of pain. As she shuffled a foot in the direction of the door, the wires on her chest tugged and something clattered loudly to the tile floor. Staying stock still, she listened over the sound of her own heavy breathing. Above her, the air conditioning softly droned as it pushed cooled air through the ceiling vents. Somewhere outside the room, she could hear voices and tried to make out what they were saying. Whatever it was made a lot of people laugh. *Why were there so many people here?*

Kendra reached down and fumbled in the dim light for whatever lay at her feet. It was some kind of box with a strap which she looped over her neck without thinking. Something told her that was where it belonged, and the strain on the wires went away. Shuffling once more, she headed for the thin line of light bordering the door. She rested a hand on the doorknob and caught her breath for a moment, listening carefully. The voices were a little louder, and her befuddled brain finally realised it was a television show.

Slowly opening the door, Kendra peeked outside, looking both ways down the hallway. The doors to every room in sight were closed, but to her right, at the end of the corridor, the nurses' station was brightly lit. Someone sat in an office chair facing a television playing an old American rerun show she didn't recognise. Kendra began moving barefooted down the hallway towards the bright light, driven by a gut feeling more than conscious thoughts or decisions.

The last door on the right was open, so she slipped inside the room, banging the box hanging from her neck against the door jamb as she did so. Holding her breath once more, she heard the chair creak and footsteps approaching. Kendra staggered two steps farther into the room and sank to the floor, crawling behind a pair of rolling carts. The tile was cool and inviting.

"Who's causin' a ruckus in here?" came the nurse's voice, sounding irritated in a thick Caymanian accent. After a moment, the woman grunted, mumbled something, and Kendra heard her footfalls fading as she returned to her chair.

Letting out a long sigh, Kendra struggled to her feet and looked around the room. A dozen rolling carts held clear plastic cribs, five of which contained infants swaddled in blankets. Each crib was labelled but she couldn't make out the words. Stepping to her right, Kendra leaned over the tub and stared at the sleeping child. Her heart skipped a beat, and she immediately knew it was her daughter, despite never having held the baby. Picking up the blanketed bundle, she clutched it to her chest and gently rocked back and forth. The child stirred, gurgled, then fell back asleep in her mother's arms.

A heavy fog still clouded Kendra's mind, and while she struggled to know where she was or what was happening, a powerful urge drove her to leave the building. Returning to the hallway, she stared at the back of the nurse's head while the woman chuckled at the television show, swivelling side to side in the chair. Kendra turned and trudged away from the nurses' station, eventually reaching the end of the hall where a fire door led outside. She hesitated, unsure whether to continue or… *do what?* A moment later, her hip shoved the bar on the door, which slowly opened, its return spring resisting her meagre size.

Heat and humidity swamped her as the door swung closed behind her and a stiff breeze brought the smell of the ocean through the night to meet her like an old friend. It all felt comfortingly familiar, and a smile creased her face, causing a jab of pain in her broken nose. She licked the blood from her upper lip and frowned at the metallic taste. Each new sensory experience pulling her from her last thought, leaving her confused.

Slowly, she made her way down the metal steps, holding the railing with one hand and cradling her baby with the other. To her left, a car engine started, and she guessed there was a road not far from where she stood, although trees and the darkness of night blocked her view. Kendra stepped away from the sound, her throat turning dry in fear. The box slapped against her side, then clattered to the ground as the strap slipped from her petite shoulder. It hung once again from the wires, which she pulled with all her strength. This time, they came free, so she left the box behind and moved on.

Her feet dragged across concrete, then the gravel and rough ground of an unpaved pathway. Kendra headed away from the building, away from the cars, away from the people. She had no idea why, but those three things seemed vitally important. She clutched her baby tightly in her arms and trudged farther away from the fear, pushing tree branches aside and ignoring the pain in the soles of her bare feet.

She had no sense of time. It was dark, so it was night-time, but beyond that, it was impossible to tell. Late at night, she decided, as she'd only heard one car on the road. Kendra looked up to the sky through overhanging branches where a half moon was allowing her to see the trail. Her head was slowly clearing and a feeling of relief came with it. In her arms, her baby stirred in the blanket, so she found a fallen log by the edge of the pathway and sat down.

Resting her baby on the ground, she fought with the strange blouse, finally standing, and pulling it over her head. Naked, she sat back down and lifted her daughter to her breast. The infant struggled at first, having only been fed by bottle in her short lifetime, but soon she suckled, and Kendra smiled again, despite the discomfort.

Tears ran down her cheeks as she looked at the precious bundle in her arms while she gently rocked her daughter back and forth. She was crying for the time they'd been apart, for the now inconceivable notion they might never have been together, and for the uncertainty which lay ahead.

When her baby had taken her fill, Kendra swaddled her once more and set her down. Turning her attention to the blouse, she finally concluded it was actually a hospital gown with the buttons in the rear. Standing, she slipped it on over her head, this time with the buttons on the front. Scooping up her baby, she resumed her walk, sharp pain causing her to limp from the growing number of scrapes on her feet.

A name? It dawned on Kendra that her baby didn't have a name. At least she couldn't remember giving her one. Many people named their children after relatives, but she didn't have any relatives as best she could remember. Except for her mother. The woman who'd raised her alone, that much her addled brain recalled. Until she'd stepped in front of a construction lorry on Town Hall Road and left Kendra alone at seventeen years old. She looked down at the tiny person she'd brought into the world a few days ago and moaned as the tears came again. She'd been about to do the same thing to her own child. Leave her alone in a cruel and heartless world. Kendra couldn't pull her own mother's name from her tired mind, but she was damn well sure her baby wouldn't share her moniker.

She staggered, limped, and dragged her feet along the pathway, unsure where she was going, except it was away from where she'd been. The trail veered right, and through trees on either side she saw the moonlight glistening on water. Perfectly still, calm water. It's a beautiful night, she thought, continuing along the trail as trees closed around her once more. In the distance ahead, pinpricks of light marked civilisation, finally feeling like a welcoming beacon of safety for her and Eve Marie.

"Oh!" she squealed. "Maybe I had you a name in mind after all."

She stroked her daughter's head and plodded slowly on, the crunch of the marl underfoot echoing after each step. That's weird, she thought. I didn't hear that echo earlier.

1

FASHION STATEMENT

Tuesday 10:00am

Waiting sucks. There's always something better to do than sit around in limbo, but you can't do any of it when you're stuck waiting. My partner, Jacob, is much better at it than I am. He's a native islander and by nature, they're far more laid back and relaxed. Unless he thinks I'm about to break a rule, and then he gets really agitated. Jacob doesn't like breaking rules. As police constables, we are supposed to stick to a ridiculous number of procedures, regulations, and laws, which all give the advantage to the criminals. By definition, the criminals don't burden themselves with such restrictions. So I cheat one or two sometimes. By sometimes, I mean Jacob gets nervous quite often.

He hadn't asked for another partner, so I guess he didn't mind working with me. Or they'd told him no. I'd heard a rumour that all the other constables in West Bay refused to partner with me, but I knew that wasn't true. I knew for a fact there were two blokes who wanted to get in my knickers, so they would have jumped at the chance to sit next to me all day. They'd also be disappointed.

Screwing guys at work causes too much drama, and if there's one thing I hate, it's drama. There are actually lots of things I hate, but drama is definitely one of them. Waiting is also high on the list.

"He's not coming today."

Jacob looked at me and grinned. "It's only been an hour or so. Give him time."

"It's been an hour and fifty-two minutes. He's not coming." If I'd been behind the wheel, I'd have started the engine and ended the debate, but it was Jacob's day to drive.

"Teach me anudder Norway word. It'll pass da time."

"You've had your word for the day."

"Give me anudder one. We got nuttin' better to do while we're sittin' here."

"One a day is the rule. I know how you like your rules."

He chuckled. Jacob was a curious fellow, and he'd bombard me with questions all day if I didn't set parameters. Needless to say, I'm allowed to set rules.

We sat in silence for a while. Shaded by the trees we were hiding behind, it was still steamy hot in the patrol car. I wouldn't let him run the engine, so we had no air conditioning beyond the breeze through the open windows. I'd give up a little sweat instead of needlessly burning petrol and pumping shit out of the exhaust for two hours.

We'd seen this skinny kid on and off for a few weeks, hanging out in the dirt car park for Undra's Take Out on Birch Tree Hill Road. It was opposite Kellys Bar, which wasn't the classiest establishment on the island. It was possible the kid was handing out business cards for his gardening services, but he was targeting the drunks wandering across the street for a bite to eat, which suggested otherwise. We needed to catch him in the act to see exactly what he was peddling. If it was weed, the Royal Cayman Islands Police Service considered it a serious offence, but I didn't give a shit. Pills, or more serious drugs, and I'd happily arrest the kid.

I called him a kid, but it was hard to tell his age. I'd turned twenty a few months back, and he could be my age or older, but he was small and wiry, so he appeared younger. Every time we'd seen him, he'd been wearing loose trousers hanging down his bony arse and a black hoodie with the sleeves cut off. Anyone wearing a hooded sweatshirt with no sleeves deserves to be arrested for stupidity. The summer days were hotter than the surface of the sun, with humidity that left you dripping wet the moment you stepped outside. Sleeveless made sense, but the hoodie part was a giveaway that he was hiding something.

"Two hours. Let's go," I told Jacob.

He started the car, and hot air blasted from the vents. I turned the fan switch to low while the system expelled the scorching air from the ducts. Jacob drove slowly to the end of Birch Tree Hill Road and signalled left.

"Go right."

"I was going to make a loop, head out Batabano," he replied, sitting at the stop sign.

I sighed. I wasn't sure why I wanted to turn right. We had a coin toss we used every day to decide our patrol, which kept our route and direction of travel random. He was following today's plan, but sometimes you just get a feeling.

"Go right. We'll take Town Hall and come back to Batabano on Church."

Jacob shrugged his shoulders and turned right on Reverend Blackman Road. I looked around, curious what might have triggered my radar. The first lane on our right was Dill, which ran a few hundred metres to a dead end.

"Stop!"

Jacob hit the brakes and pulled to the verge just past Dill.

"What da hell? You scared me ta death."

"He's down there," I said. "Maybe that's his house."

Jacob started to put the patrol car in reverse, but I opened my door and jumped out.

"Where da hell you goin'?"

"I'll text you," I said, closing the door and peering through the open window. "Turn around and stay out of sight out here. When I text you, drive up Dill."

"What was he doing?" Jacob asked, and I could tell by the urgency in his tone he was getting worried.

I didn't have time to explain. "Get the registration of anyone driving out of Dill and wait for my signal."

I heard him shouting after me, but I didn't have much time to get into position. Behind Dill was the Jimmy Powell cricket oval, the clubhouse, and farther on was a baseball field. Using the GPS map on my mobile, I ran down the driveway of a nearby home, across their back garden, and ducked through some trees until I faced the rear of the little old cottage I'd seen. At five foot nine and pretty athletic, it didn't take me long. I texted 'now' to Jacob and waited, catching my breath.

Between the cottage and the neighbour's house, I saw our patrol car on Dill and heard a panicked voice shouting. I dashed across the unkept garden of the cottage and stood next to the back door, staying clear of a window. Another car engine revved and spun its tyres on the gravel road, then abruptly stopped. A woman bellowed from inside the home, then the back door burst open and the skinny kid came bolting out. I reached over and wrenched his baggy trousers down.

The kid went sprawling down the concrete steps and tumbled in a heap in the dirt. I strolled over and hauled him to his feet. He held a hand to his cheek where apparently his face had brought him to a stop. He moaned and looked at the blood on his fingers from the graze.

"What da fuck you doin'? You done busted up my pretty face."

"Pull your trousers up," I replied.

The door burst open again, and a large woman wielding a switch broom lumbered down the steps.

"What on God's wonderful earth is goin' on, Minnow?"

She halted at the bottom of the steps and looked at her son, then at me. I saw the broom coming and stepped clear as it whistled past me.

"What you done to my boy? His face all messed up," she yelled, drawing back for another swing.

"He's selling drugs right outside your house," I protested.

The woman froze, her eyes shifting to the kid. "What dis lady just say?"

Minnow decided not to stick around and face his mama's wrath. He turned and tried to run, but I tugged on his trousers again and he tripped to the dirt. His mother pounced, swatting at him on the ground with her broom. I stood back and grinned. I figured she was a big lady and would tire herself out in short order.

The back door opened more sedately and Jacob stood at the top of the steps, by which time Mama had run out of steam and was catching her breath. She turned and looked at my partner, then at me.

"You takin' him to jail?"

"Depends what he's selling," I replied.

She looked at her son, who was now nursing a graze on his arm from his second tumble. If he'd had sleeves on his hoodie, he'd have probably saved himself the extra wounds.

"Empty out yo pockets, Minnow," his mother demanded.

"Come on, Ma, they makin' dis shit up."

"Then empty out yo pockets and prove dem wrong, boy."

Minnow began getting to his feet, his eyes flicking between me, Jacob, his mother, and possible escape routes.

"Don't run. You'll just trip over your trousers again."

He glared at me, then pulled his dusty trousers up.

"Pockets!" his mother ordered.

Minnow raised his hands. He knew he was screwed and chose not to hand over the incriminating evidence himself. His mother huffed and shoved her free hand in his pocket. Her face shifted from anger to a look of disappointment. Minnow hung his head as she handed me a bundle of tiny Ziploc bags containing pills. I just had time to take them from her before she was swinging the broom again. Minnow yelped as the stiff bristles whacked his bloodied cheek.

I was happy letting her dish out all the punishment she cared to give, but Jacob came to his rescue. It was hard not to feel bad for her. I didn't know their story, but I knew that look on her face. She was angry at her son, perhaps angry at their circumstances, but most of all, she was feeling guilty. The woman would always question whether there was something more or different she should have done.

Her son would most likely serve prison time for dealing pills. In prison he would be surrounded by equally hard-done-by innocent men, who claimed to be victims of this, that, or the other. They were all guilty of making poor decisions, and that's the influence that would consume him. I didn't have a better answer for the system, but if this kid ever had a chance in life, it would be pushed farther out of reach the moment he went behind bars.

Our radios buzzed. "Whiskey Three, Whiskey Three, we have an unresponsive person reported by Jackson's Pond. Over."

Jacob and I looked at each other. "Man," he mumbled.

I keyed my mic. "Central, this is Whiskey Three. We can respond. ETA three minutes. Over."

Jacob fished the remaining bags from Minnow's pockets and shepherded him around the house towards our patrol car. I paused and looked at his mother. She stood forlornly in her back garden, leaning on the broom with a tear running down her cheek.

"I'll see what I can do," I said, with no idea what I thought I might do to help the kid.

She nodded, and I ran to catch up with Jacob, opening the back door for him. Already in the back seat was another dark-skinned man who I guessed to be the buyer. Jacob bundled Minnow in the car and I ran around the other side, opening the rear door.

"Get out," I ordered the man.

Jacob looked across the roof as the man quickly wriggled out of the car, holding his cuffed hands towards me.

"He da udder guy, Nora. He da buyer."

I unlocked the cuffs. "Get out of here and get some help. I'm busting you next time."

"Nora?" Jacob hissed. "What you doin'?"

We both closed the rear doors on our side and I jumped into the passenger seat. Jacob got in the driver's side and started the car.

"Possession, okay?" I said in a low voice.

Jacob shook his head. "Jeez, Nora. Why you gotta always make tings difficult?"

"Just giving a kid a chance," I replied.

Jacob shook his head again. "Fine," he groaned.

I switched on the siren and lights as he turned onto Reverend Blackman Road.

2

LUCA

Tuesday 10:30am

Within minutes, Jacob drove down the marl road at the north end of Jackson's Pond and parked where the trail became impassable in the patrol car. At least, according to Jacob. My Jeep would have made it no problem, and I would have given it a try in the car, but he had the keys. We got out and looked around. On the south side of the pond I saw a man with a dog. He was waving in our direction.

Jackson's Pond was a rounded, triangular-shaped area of naturally low-lying land less than a kilometre in length. Next to it, a quarry had been dug for limestone, forming a second pond with a narrow dike between the two. Esterly Tibbetts Highway bordered Jackson's Pond to the east, homes limited the quarry's reach to the north, and woods separated them both from West Bay Road to the south and west.

As Jacob had chickened out on the off-road trail across the dike, we walked briskly along the rough terrain to where the man stood patiently waiting with his Dobermann by his side. The dog was panting in the heat.

"You called the police, sir?" I asked. "An unresponsive person?"

The man had grey hair which blew around in the breeze and wore lightweight grey trousers and a loose cotton shirt. By the lines on his face, I guessed he was at least sixty, but he appeared fit and healthy for his age.

"I did indeed," he replied in a polished English accent. "Although I called it in as a body, but unresponsive is accurate."

He pointed into the water where a naked body lay face down. Jacob ran along the rocky edge and knelt beside the water.

"When did you discover the body?" I asked, flipping open my notebook.

"Probably one minute before I called. Ten-twenty or thereabouts," he responded in a soft but confident voice. He was remarkably calm and relaxed considering a dead person lay a few metres away.

"Did you touch the body or pick up anything in the area?"

"I was going to pull her out and try CPR, but she was cold to the touch, so I knew it was pointless. Luca here spotted her first."

The dog looked up at the mention of his name. I reached down and he nudged my hand with his nose, guiding it to the top of his head. When I scratched behind his ears the dog closed his eyes and leaned against my leg. I heard Jacob calling Central to make sure a scene of crime officer was being sent, along with a detective.

"She? You determined the body is female?" I continued.

"Shape of the figure. No hair on the legs," he replied.

"That's quite observant."

"Former police in the UK. Old habits and all that."

"Your name, sir?"

"Andrews, Jeremy Andrews. I live over there on Hillard," he said, pointing to the homes beyond the quarry.

"Thank you, Mr Andrews. If you wouldn't mind waiting, we may have some more questions."

He nodded and Luca looked disappointed I was walking away.

"I'm Constable Sommers and this is Constable Tibbetts," I said, realising I hadn't introduced ourselves.

Andrews nodded again. "I know who you are."

I paused. I was a private person who preferred to remain anonymous, so it always jarred me when people I'd never met knew me. My first major case on the force had been a kidnapping broadcast across the internet, with me as a central character, so being recognised happened far more often than I liked. I forced a smile and continued towards the body.

"She's been murdered," Andrews said.

I stopped again and was about to ask for his reasoning, but decided I'd rather get my initial observations for myself before discussing anything. As a former police officer, he could be more useful than the average witness, but first, I had to make sure he wasn't a suspect. Or that the woman hadn't gone skinny dipping drunk off her arse and accidentally drowned herself.

I stood over the body, and Jacob joined me. Well, she hadn't drowned herself, unless she'd fallen backwards against something solid, then managed to stumble face first into the water. She had a large, bloody wound to the back of her head. Andrews was also right about her being a woman. I could see the edge of her breast in the clear water. She'd probably had light brown skin, but the grey hue of death was now turning her flesh a depressing shade of taupe. The water would have hastened her drop in body temperature.

I wanted to lift her head and see her face, but I knew the SOCO would want that left to them. There were no other obvious marks on her back or legs, but her bare feet were a mess. Her soles looked like they'd been sandpapered raw. I stepped back and crouched down, looking around the rocky shore of the pond for signs of a struggle, her clothes, or anything which might provide clues. Small clumps of hardy seaside oxeye added a touch of green to the dusty limestone terrain, the combination making it easy to spot the reddish brown of dried blood.

"Come away from the edge," I said, pointing to several stains in the dirt.

Jacob moved back and began his own sweep of the immediate vicinity. I stood and walked to the main trail, staying to one side of the footworn path. I noticed Mr Andrews had also kept himself clear of the trail, standing by the trees in the shade.

"What do you think?" he asked me.

I squinted in the bright sunshine reflecting off the pale ground and wished I'd brought my sunglasses with me. "You're right. She's female and dead."

He raised an eyebrow and tried to hide a slight grin.

"What police department were you with?" I asked.

"I retired as a DCI for the Met. Major Investigation Team for the last ten years or so."

I grunted an acknowledgement and scanned the view in either direction of the pathway. I was curious to ask the man more questions, but not before I'd completed my own inspection. Sirens wailed in the distance as the other support services approached. If they drove an ambulance all the way in to the scene, I'd never let Jacob live it down.

To the north was the neighbourhood where Andrews said he lived. South-east led to an underpass below Esterly Tibbetts Highway which, if I remembered correctly, fed a bunch more gravel trails through woods. To the west, a thin screen of trees shielded another natural pond, much smaller than Jackson. A leg of the trail appeared to continue around the water's edge.

"Which direction did you come from?" I asked, and Luca looked at me expectantly. Apparently, he thought I was addressing him and wanted to scratch his ears again. I obliged.

"Same way you approached," Andrews replied. "We walk back around the quarry side."

The trail across the dike led straight to the path he was talking about. He would have to turn left and walk 100 metres to reach where we stood.

"When did Luca see the body?" The dog shoved my idle hand with his snout. I'd absent-mindedly stopped fussing him.

"We were ten or twenty yards from here when something caught his eye and he tugged on the lead."

I glanced at the point on the trail he'd described and figured it was possible to see the woman from there.

"He likes to do his business around here," Andrews added with a knowing smirk. "We detour into this wider area where there's a bit more grass." He held up a small green plastic bag of shit for emphasis.

Satisfied his story was legit for now, I moved on. A police car, ambulance, and unmarked SUV pulled up next to our patrol car and shut off their sirens. There were no other vehicles present when we arrived, so the woman was either brought here or did some walking. Her feet suggested the latter had at least been a part of her evening.

Walking to the dike, I turned left and followed the trail around the corner of the quarry until it ran straighter towards the homes in the distance. I found nothing of note and turned back. The man responsible for me joining the Royal Cayman Islands Police Service, and my mentor - if I didn't screw up too badly again - was Detective Roy Whittaker. We met as I reached the dike.

"Good morning, Constable Sommer," he greeted me in his warm but firm tone. "I understand we have a body."

He was tall and thin with short, neat, greying hair and a goatee. He always dressed immaculately in a suit and seemed immune to the balmy island heat. The man had taken an enormous risk supporting a foreign runaway with a dubious past, and I'd repaid him by crossing a line six months ago in my last major case. Fortunately, he didn't know quite how far I'd taken things, but I'd been on unofficial probation since, and my detective training had been on hold.

We walked together towards the scene and I filled him in on the basics of what I knew. "This is the gentleman who found the body,"

I said as we neared Andrews. "Mr Andrews, this is Detective Whittaker."

Both policemen extended their hands. "Hello Jeremy, it's good to see you, although I'm sure we'd both prefer different circumstances."

"Indeed, Roy. Fortunately, things like this don't happen as often on the island as they did on my beat."

Whittaker's forehead creased. "Happening more frequently than I care for these days."

"One is too many, right?" Andrews responded.

"Very true," the detective said, turning to me. "Do we have an ID?"

He must have seen me glance at Andrews, as he added, "Jeremy consults from time to time. We can speak freely in his presence, Nora."

I guessed I could strike Andrews from my suspect list. "She's naked and we haven't found her clothes or a purse so far, so no driver's licence. No tattoos or obvious features, and it's hard to tell age until she's turned over. We should have a diver search the immediate area in case anything useful was dropped or thrown into the water."

Whittaker pulled out his mobile and typed a quick text before looking at me once more. "I've requested a diver. What else have you concluded so far?"

This was part of his mentoring. He loved challenging me, and while it usually irritated me, it had been a while, so I hoped my doghouse days were over. I would have preferred it wasn't in front of another detective, even if this guy was retired, but resuming my training was more important.

"When SOCO gets here, we can flip her over and see what other injuries she might have, but right now I'd say the wound to the back of her head was likely the cause of death."

"You don't think it could be accidental?" Whittaker interjected.

I looked at Andrews and hoped he wasn't thinking I was simply going by what he said. "Doubtful. There are small traces of blood by the shoreline, but I don't think she received the wound here. There'd be a bigger mess. It's a serious injury. Pretty sure her skull is fractured. I could see…" I stopped myself. Giving them the ugly details didn't sound professional. "Anyway, her feet are chewed up like she's walked some distance barefooted, but I couldn't find blood on the trail nearby. She's a small woman, so my first guess is that she was killed somewhere else, and carried here."

Andrews went to speak, then stopped himself, looking at Whittaker.

"Go ahead, Jeremy."

Andrews smiled. "Brought by vehicle, perhaps?"

"There are no tyre tracks leading to this spot and it would be hard to reach without a 4x4," I replied, now glad Jacob hadn't attempted the dike in our patrol car. "It's possible the perp carried her from where we parked, or from the highway, but both would run the risk of being seen, even in the middle of the night as the highway's lit."

"Next steps?" Whittaker asked.

"See what SOCO comes up with, and I'd carefully search the other pathways leading here. She's naked, so there's a good chance she was sexually assaulted, which means there might be three crime scenes. The attack, the murder – which may have happened somewhere else – and here," I said, pointing towards the body.

"What do you think, Jeremy?" Whittaker asked his friend.

"Solid start," he replied, giving me a nod as Luca nudged my hand again.

"Dogs," I blurted, interrupting whatever Andrews was about to say. "Sorry, sir. I would have our K9 unit search the trails for blood."

"That's all I was about to add," Andrews said, winking at Whittaker.

"Okay, thank you both," Whittaker said, turning to walk towards the body. "Oh, Nora," he said, stopping for a moment. "Who's in the back of your patrol car?"

"Oh, shit!" I blurted, and looked around for Jacob.

3

DENTAL WORK

Tuesday 11:30am

Jacob offered to take our young drug dealer into the station alone so I could remain on scene. At first I told him I'd come too, as it didn't seem fair on him, but he insisted. Jacob's not real keen on seeing blood and I don't think he wanted to be there when they turned the body over in case she'd been further assaulted. I made him promise to process Minnow for possession… if the kid hadn't died from heat exhaustion already, locked in the back of our car.

Rasha, our lead scene of crime officer, arrived and began examining the woman's body. Whittaker had assigned two other constables to walk the pathways north and south, so I took the final option, which led into the woods. I didn't have to go far.

"Sir!" I called out from the narrow marl trail between thick groves of sea grape, popnut, and ironwood trees.

I stayed still until Whittaker arrived, with Andrews and Luca following.

"Something happened here," I said, pointing to large patches of blood along the edge of the path and more spots on the leaves of low shrubs. "They've dragged the trail with something to cover up the tracks and hid most of the blood." I pointed in the direction we'd all arrived from. "The brush marks lead that way and then stop where the trail gets more use and isn't so dusty."

The detective carefully looked around, paying attention to the area beyond where we stood. The trail disappeared to the right before a row of trees along the edge of the smaller pond. "Looks like they swept the path in that direction as well."

"I think I can circle around and look on the other side of the turn," I offered, trotting past Andrews towards Jackson's Pond. Luca looked at me expectantly, but I didn't have time to stop.

Earlier, when I'd followed the trail in the direction of the homes, I'd noticed the path we were inspecting ran behind a few trees where the corners of the quarry and small pond were only 15 metres apart. Jogging along the rough terrain, I stayed central to the pathway. Enough people had now walked the area, and the killer - if this was indeed a murder - appeared to have cleared the obvious tracks.

I pushed through the shrubs and bushes until I stood by the side of the path which wound around the pond before heading west. I saw no signs of brush marks. Moving along the trail, I carefully watched where I made every step, making sure I wasn't treading on another print. At the corner, I found the point where someone had either started or finished covering their tracks.

Taking two more steps, I could see the detective. "Starts back here," I told him. "This trail leads west. It doesn't look like it gets much use."

It was actually a T-junction, with the trail continuing along the border of the pond to the south-east. Where Detective Whittaker stood was a turn off the main path, but that spur towards Jackson's Pond appeared to get all the traffic. The main path alongside the small pond was overgrown with weeds and overhanging branches, but in the distance, I could make out the roof of a home.

"There's more blood here," I said, seeing spots on the shrubs to my left.

Whittaker made his way towards me, inspecting both sides of the path as he delicately placed each step. Once he reached me, I pointed out the blood which had a distinct spatter pattern if I looked from the right angle. The detective stood next to me, taking in the same perspective. We both turned and studied the bushes and trees on the other side of the path.

"Conclusion?" Whittaker asked.

"We know which way the killer swung, but we don't know the direction he or the victim were facing," I replied, thinking aloud. "If we can determine the direction, we'll know if the killer was right or left-handed."

"Agreed," Whittaker said quietly, stroking his goatee. "We can assume both were standing by the height of the spatter."

"Maybe the first blow didn't kill her," I wondered. "And she made it five metres up the path before he hit her again."

"He?" Whittaker said with a raised eyebrow.

I shrugged my shoulders. "Unless it was a tall woman, or she stood on a box. The spatter is below the victim's head height, so the blow came from slightly above."

"All true," he responded. "But the victim may have ducked, or the killer could have swung in an arc, so the blow came from higher. Too soon to make the assumption the killer was male."

I nodded, although we both knew nearly all acts of violence like this were performed by men. We walked back towards Andrews and his enthusiastic dog sitting impatiently beside him. Luca's bum quivered a centimetre above the ground as his short tail furiously wagged, throwing up dust.

"Sorry," Andrews said. "Luca seems to be besotted with your constable. I'll wait in the clearing."

Whittaker smiled. "I think you're both fine where you are, Jeremy – seems the attack took place over here. I imagine the poor young lady was dead and being carried beyond this point."

I knelt down and looked at some bloody marks on a rock

protruding from the coarse ground cover. I held my hand over the rock and lined up the stains with my fingers. The victim was petite, and I had long fingers to go with my long arms and legs, but it was still clear the marks had been made by a hand.

"I think she was on the ground here."

Looking amongst the leaves and twigs, I spotted something small and white. "*Fy faen.*"

Whittaker knelt next to me. "Is that what I think it is?"

I tore a page from my notebook and folded it in half, placing a marker next to a tooth, hoping the stiff breeze wouldn't blow the paper away.

Whittaker stood. "Let's see what progress Rasha has made. She needs to process this scene when she's done at the water."

I followed him back towards Jackson's Pond, dreading what our SOCO might have found when she pulled the woman from the water. Andrews tagged along, and Luca brushed against my leg as we walked. He was tall enough I could scratch behind his ears without bending down.

The K9 unit had arrived and Luca decided the Alsatian required his attention more than me. He didn't strain at his lead, but his eyes stayed firmly on the police dog. Andrews quietly ordered "heel", and Luca obediently stayed at his side as the former detective moved away to his spot in the shade of the trees.

Whittaker explained the scene and the areas for the sniffer dog to explore, keeping them clear of the site where we believed the actual attack took place. The handler left with the Alsatian's nose already on the ground, searching for blood.

A pop-up tent had been erected by the water and Rasha stood by a gurney under the shade, examining the body they'd already pulled from the water. Two paramedics stood close by, waiting to wheel the victim away.

Our SOCO was medium height with a curvy figure, which was currently hidden beneath a pale blue disposable, hooded oversuit. A face mask, nitrile gloves, and shoe coverings completed her unflattering outfit. We stopped short of the tent to avoid any contamination.

I looked at the young woman now laid on her back. Rasha had covered the body, leaving her head exposed. The victim's lifeless, milky eyes stared blankly at the roof of the tent. As I feared, her lower jaw had suffered a crushing blow in the killer's attempt to remove her teeth.

"It's safe to say this is now officially a murder investigation," Whittaker said solemnly.

"No doubt," Rasha agreed, her soft English voice in stark contrast to the violence laid before her. She briefly looked up from examining the victim's decimated mouth. "I'll have a better idea when I do the full autopsy, but I'd say the blow to the back of the head was fatal, and the crude dental work was post mortem."

"Any identifying marks?" Whittaker asked. "I'd like to figure out who she was."

"Nothing of note," Rasha replied. "No tattoos or obvious birth marks. No jewellery, and I don't see any sign she wore a wedding ring."

"Would the bash to the head have been instantly fatal?" I asked.

Rasha thought for a moment. "Let me answer that question after autopsy. Her skull is fractured, but I need to see the extent of the damage before saying for certain."

I nodded, but I'd already decided the poor woman had probably staggered down the trail before collapsing, her hand falling on the rock I'd seen. The killer then flipped her over and bashed her teeth out to hide the dental evidence. He — or she — didn't want anyone to know the victim's identity. I hoped she was indeed dead before that point.

"But she didn't drown, correct?" Whittaker asked.

"Again, I'll confirm after autopsy, but I've seen no evidence of drowning. She was probably dead before being placed in the water."

"Okay, thanks," he responded. "We believe we've found the murder scene over there along the trail," Whittaker continued, pointing towards the path through the woods. "I'll have the section of interest marked off. K9 are looking for more blood evidence and we're sweeping all the trails."

"I'll look when I'm done here," Rasha replied.

"Murder weapon?" I asked.

The SOCO paused and looked at me. It was hard to tell behind the mask, but I suspected she'd had enough of our questions. "I've found traces of wood in both wounds, but if she was killed along the trail, they could be from contact with debris on the ground. Let me do the full autopsy, and I'll be able to tell you with more certainty."

"Thank you, Rasha," Whittaker said. "Please keep me informed as you learn more."

We left the tent, leaving Rasha to go about her work.

"Let's assume for the moment that the killer used a piece of wood found along the trail," Whittaker said. "Where would the weapon be now?"

I paused and looked from the trail to the water. "If they carried the body, it's unlikely they'd keep hold of the stick they used."

"True, but we know they returned to the scene to attempt a clean-up. They could have taken the weapon with them when they left."

I stared at the dense mass of trees, shrubs, and bushes. "The whole thing feels rushed and sloppy. Nothing about it appears premeditated," I ventured. "I think the weapon is either in the woods or the smaller pond beyond the trail. Somewhere they could have easily thrown it from the scene."

Whittaker looked in dismay at the impenetrable woods. "I'll have a drone flown over the area. Maybe we'll get lucky and it'll spot something on top of the canopy."

"Roy," Rasha called out from behind us. We both turned. "I believe she may have recently had a baby."

The sheet covering the victim's body was neatly folded down, revealing her breasts and abdomen.

"A baby?" Whittaker repeated.

"She's lactating," Rasha added.

The detective's shoulders dropped, but he waved his thanks. "This keeps getting worse," he said under his breath.

"We need an ID," I voiced as we resumed our walk. "This has all the signs of a jealous boyfriend."

Whittaker nodded. "Agreed."

4

SUGARY BREAKFAST BARS

Wednesday 1:00pm

I'd noticed that in most cases the crime and guilty party were either obvious or, like in this situation, completely unknown. In the latter, things tended to move frustratingly slowly. Everything took time. Autopsies, DNA results, SOCO reports, they all took what felt like forever. Rasha was one of only four people in her department, and I knew they were working their arses off, but I hated waiting.

When Jacob had returned, we'd spent yesterday afternoon knocking on doors in the nearby neighbourhoods fruitlessly asking if anyone had seen or heard anything. Today, we were back on patrol and weren't sure if we'd be further involved in the investigation or not, but I couldn't stop thinking about the young woman. In all probability, she was one of the many poor locals who fell between the cracks. Her fingerprints hadn't been in the system, facial recognition – although compromised by her disfiguration – yielded nothing, and her description didn't match any missing persons.

"She must be a local," I concluded out loud.

"What's dat now?" Jacob responded, looking at me sideways from the passenger seat.

"The woman. She must be a local or lived here a while at least."

"We done wit dat case now, I betcha. Detectives will take it from here. Not much point fussin' over it." He pointed to a car coming from the other direction, clearly speeding. "Let's give dat fella a warnin'. Turn us around, Nora."

I carried on down the road and Jacob slumped in his seat.

"Fine. Why you say she has to be local?"

"Dental records," I replied curtly.

"I thought da killer done made dem no use?"

"Why would he bother doing that?" I countered.

Jacob thought for a moment. "Right. Because she likely have dental records here." He fidgeted a bit before continuing. "Maybe he just all crazy and happened to hit her in da mouth. Could be da man didn't know much where he was beatin' her."

"How many teeth were found?"

"Only tree or four, right?"

"Three," I confirmed. Whittaker had told me that much before we left the scene. "Either the woman only had three teeth or the killer took the time to pick them up. That sound like bad aiming to you?"

Jacob squirmed in his seat again. He didn't have a strong stomach when it came to the ugly details.

"Dat takes some cold-hearted man to beat on da woman dat way."

I kept driving along Bonneville Drive. We'd used our coin toss system, which today had produced heads for clockwise direction, then we'd both flipped tails, which was route pattern number two. At Batabano, I made a right, and we rode in silence for a while. Batabano became Church Street, where I slowed, pulling into One Stop Mini Market on the left.

"Get me one of those coffee energy drink things," I told Jacob, who opened his door as I came to a halt. My friend AJ had me hooked on coffee, and lately she'd discovered these tasty coffee-flavoured cold drinks in a can. We both ate healthily most of the time, but these cans of artificial flavours, caffeine, and chemicals had become our guilty afternoon pleasure. I'd also had to stop giving Jacob shit about drinking soda pops.

He paused in front of the car to say hello to an old timer who was sitting in a chair reading the newspaper in the shade. There were over sixty thousand people on the island, but Jacob Tibbetts seemed to know half of them. Out of the corner of my eye, I noticed someone flit quickly from the double door at the end of the building. There was something familiar about them. I jumped from the car, startling Jacob, who was about to enter the store.

"Did you see her?" I shouted.

"See who?" he replied, looking at me in confusion.

I ran around the end of the building, but couldn't see anyone. I kept going and checked the back. Nothing. The convenience store was on one end of a short row of shops next to a driveway leading to a home behind. Whoever it was hadn't had time to reach the house, but she'd vanished into thin air. Jacob walked around the corner behind me.

"What's got ya all stirred up now?"

"I saw her."

"Saw who?"

"That girl I told you I've seen a few times now. Damn, she's quick."

"Maybe dat energy drink'll help you keep up," he said, grinning at me.

I turned back towards the patrol car. "It won't if you don't take your smart arse into the shop and buy me one."

Jacob's laugh finally faded as he entered the store, and I returned to the car. That was probably the third time I'd seen this young girl, and each time she'd evaporated before my eyes. This was the second time in West Bay, but the first time I'd seen her was in George Town. She couldn't be more than thirteen or fourteen, petite, with frizzy dark hair and a pretty face from the little I'd been able to see.

She reminded me of another friend, Hallie, who I'd met at the International Fellowship of Lions. We'd both been recruited to accompany wealthy clients at the private membership resort. Hallie was new when I'd almost completed my one-year contract. A deal which, it turned out, meant I wouldn't get paid or given a new life and identity as promised, but thrown in the ocean with a weight around my ankles. Detective Whittaker, AJ Bailey, and Hallie's distant cousin, Thomas, who works with AJ, saved us and brought down the human trafficking ring.

Hallie was now living with Thomas's parents and doing really well in college. Before the resort, she'd been living on the streets, and I feared this teenager was doing the same. I hadn't seen her break any laws, but I wanted to find out her story and make sure she had a home. Every kid deserves a home. Well, almost every kid.

I got back out of the patrol car and marched into the store, nearly bowling Jacob over who was walking out.

"Where you goin' now, Nora?"

The man at the counter looked up and smiled. He was used to seeing me every other day we worked. Passenger bought. That was our system.

"Do you know the young girl who just left?" I asked without preamble.

The man frowned. "What girl ya talking about?"

I looked around the small store. Rows of chest-high shelving held merchandise and groceries, with cool storage behind glass doors lining the back wall. I spotted several security cameras mounted in the corners of the room, just below the ceiling.

"Do you record the camera feed?" I asked.

The owner looked at me and shrugged his shoulders. "Not during da day. They're just for show, really. Dere's a live feed back here," he said, pointing to a screen behind the counter. "I have dem set to record when da alarm is on."

"And you didn't see a young girl in here a few minutes ago?"

He shook his head. "I was serving Jacob. Can't say I saw anyone else in da place."

"Just before Jacob came in, she was inside. I watched her leave."

He looked apologetic and shrugged his shoulders again. "Sorry. Maybe she just looked in da door den left?"

I was pretty sure that wasn't the case. I suspected she saw us pull up outside and bolted. Walking to the front doors, I looked down the farthest aisle. Cereals, baked goods, bread, and breakfast bars.

"Can you see me in your cameras?" I asked, looking across the store at the owner.

He looked at his monitor screen. "Sure. I can see you in two of da cameras."

"Tell me if I go out of view," I said, and walked down the aisle. I stopped by the shelves loaded with Pop-Tarts, packaged sweet rolls, and other breakfast themed items of varying types and nutritional benefits.

"I still have you on da one camera," the owner told me.

I crouched down.

"Can't see you now."

I stayed low and shuffled back towards the door.

"I see you again," he announced.

I was no more than two steps from the double doors, which remained open during business. He had one of those air screens which supposedly kept the cool air conditioning inside by blasting a curtain of air from above the door. I'd learnt to take my cap off before entering or I'd be picking it up off the floor.

"Thanks," I said, and waved as I walked out.

Getting back in the car, Jacob handed me my energy drink.

"Get it figured out, Miss Sherlock?" he jibed, chuckling at his own joke.

"I think she's enjoying a tasty treat right now, watching us."

Jacob looked around. We had the building in front of us, another business across the driveway, and a handful of vehicles in the car park. "Perhaps she's laid on da roof over dere wit a pair of binoculars," Jacob said, continuing his jovial ribbing.

I scowled at him. "Believe me, she's watching. She knows I saw her and wants to see what we'll do."

"Probably just a neighbourhood kid tryin' to pinch some sweets," Jacob responded as I backed out and turned around.

I let him have the last word, but I knew he was wrong. It was the same girl I'd seen before and she was covering too much ground to be a regular kid. Besides, she'd been wearing the same dark blue summer dress each time, and the same white trainers. The local kids wore flip-flops or sandals. This girl was ready to run.

My mobile ringing interrupted my thoughts, and I dug it out of my pocket. It was Whittaker. I answered the call, letting it play through the car's speakers.

"Sir."

"Hello Constable, is Tibbetts with you?"

"Yes sir," Jacob answered.

I waited at the exit of the car park and checked the mirror to make sure I wasn't holding anyone up.

"Do you know the maternity clinic in West Bay?" Whittaker asked.

"Dat small place on Hell Road?" Jacob replied.

"That's the one. Run over there and see if they've had a patient fitting our young woman's description lately. I'll text Nora more details from Rasha's report when we hang up. She believes the woman gave birth within the last few days, certainly no longer than a week ago. I'm on my way to George Town Hospital now. Let me know what you find out."

"Yes, sir," I replied, and hung up.

Turning left on West Church, something caught my attention in a tree lining the car park. I didn't have time to stop, but I was sure I saw a flash of dark blue as we left.

5

UNDER THE WEATHER

Wednesday 2:00pm

How would you like to be born in Hell? I thought it would be pretty cool, but I was born in a hospital in Oslo, so it wasn't difficult to find something more exciting. Grand Cayman's version of Hell is an area of black limestone the size of a football pitch. It's jagged, menacing, and black due to some kind of weird algae attacking the ironshore, which is usually dirty white in colour.

Supposedly, somebody once claimed it must be what hell looks like, so they built a fence around it, made platforms to view from, and opened a gift shop including a tiny post office. Now cruise shippers are bussed in to stare at the ancient rocks, and send a postcard from Hell. Personally, being stuck on a large ship with thousands of people is more like my idea of Hell.

Naturally, they named the street by the tourist trap Hell Road, and we parked in front of an inauspicious building a few hundred metres down the road on the opposite side. It was simple, pale yellow, and identified by a sign over the glass entry doors which read 'West Bay Maternity Clinic'.

Jacob and I walked inside to a small reception area. I'm not sure what I was expecting, but something more elaborate I suppose. The place reminded me more of a dentist's than a mini hospital. A lady appeared from an office beyond the reception desk. She smiled and didn't seem surprised to see the police in her lobby.

"Hello dere, how may I help you?" she asked in the musical accent of the local people.

"I'm Constable Tibbetts and dis is my partner, Constable Sommer," Jacob replied politely. "We were checking to see if you've had a patient in da last week who fit a description we have."

"Dat may fall under our patient confidentiality, you understand? We can't give out dat info just any old how."

"She won't complain," I assured her. "She's dead."

The woman frowned and looked me up and down.

"Nora!" Jacob hissed under his breath.

People are too fucking sensitive. The English word for no longer alive is dead. That's what the young woman we found was. Dead. Was I supposed to start by saying she's under the weather? Give everyone time to adjust to that idea before moving on to 'not doing well at all'.

"She's five feet two inches, 128 pounds, with black hair, brown eyes, and gave birth within the past week," I continued, ignoring their reactions. "No distinguishing marks and we believe her to be between 19 and 25 years old."

The room fell silent, disturbed only by a telephone ringing in the office.

"May I ask your name, ma'am?" Jacob said, succumbing to the awkwardness.

"Bee," the lady replied, her eyes finally leaving me and looking at my partner. "Sorry, Belinda Ebanks, but everyone call me Bee."

"Okay dere, Bee," Jacob continued. "Unfortunately, we found dis young lady, but she didn't have any identification, so we're trying to figure out who she is and track down da family."

Bee nodded slowly. "Hold on just a minute. Let me get da doctor. I tink it best you talk wit him."

She disappeared into the building, and Jacob turned to me. "Why you gotta be so rude all da time? You gone and upset dis nice lady."

I rolled my eyes. "Maybe you should go ask the girl if it's okay if we find out who she is... oh, that's right, you can't ask her. She's dead."

Jacob put his hands on his hips and shook his head. He was about to give me more shit when the door opened from the patients' area into the lobby. A tall, good-looking man in a doctor's coat approached us and held out a hand.

"I'm Doctor Conroy Kirkconnell," he said. His skin tone was light brown and his features suggested mixed heritage, common in the Cayman Islands, but his accent was slight like Whittaker's. As he firmly shook hands, his eyes looked straight into mine as he introduced himself; hazel eyes which exuded kindness and empathy. I was slightly taken aback.

He released my hand and greeted Jacob. "I hear you're trying to ID a victim and you believe she may have recently had a child?"

The doctor looked back and forth between us.

"We are," I began. "We found a young woman yesterday and believe she gave birth within the last week."

"Where's the child?" he asked, keeping his captivating eyes on me.

"We don't know, but if we can ID her, maybe we can find her family."

"Hopefully den we can make sure da child is okay," Jacob added.

The doctor thought for a brief moment. "Okay, let's do this. Give me your description, and I'll tell you if we've had anyone in the clinic who matches. If we haven't, then there's no need to disclose any names."

I repeated the details we knew about the victim, and the doctor looked thoughtful again. "A local, you think?"

"We have reason to believe she was either Caymanian or lived on the island for a while," I replied.

"Do you have a picture?" he asked.

Jacob and I looked at each other. I don't know why I hesitated; the man was a doctor, but Jacob had the same look on his face. Somehow, it felt disrespectful to show anyone a photograph of the girl in the state we'd found her. I took out my mobile and opened the picture Whittaker had sent me, holding it up for Kirkconnell to see.

He visibly winced, then shook his head. "She's not been a patient here," he said softly. "At least, not recently." The doctor continued looking at the picture, so I let him take his time. "There was a young woman who came by here a while back. She was seeking an abortion. We examined her, if I recall correctly, but she and her baby were both healthy. Without a legitimate medical reason, we couldn't help her. I can't be sure, but this may be the same woman."

It seemed archaic and naïve to me that abortions were illegal, but many islanders had strong religious beliefs. Of course, they were quick with their opinions about someone else's body, but nowhere to be found when the destitute mother couldn't feed her kid. I'm all about personal responsibility, but sometimes shit happens.

"Do you have a record of her visit?" I asked, bringing my thoughts back to our current problem.

"Of course, but without a name, it might take some time to find." He looked at Bee, who'd been loitering behind the reception counter. "Do you remember the young lady I'm talking about, Bee?"

"I tink so. Let me take a look. Maybe if I see da name, it will jog da memory," she replied, and made her way to the office.

Kirkconnell turned back to me. "One of our nurses spent most of the time with her. I can ask them too. We're a small facility, as you can see, so we don't see that many patients, but they add up over time."

"Are you part of the hospital in George Town?" I asked, purely out of curiosity. It didn't seem cost effective to have a satellite clinic in West Bay if it could only help a handful of patients.

"No, they have a small West Bay facility, but we're an independent non-profit," the doctor explained. "We take the cases which inevitably slip through the cracks." He leaned against the counter and as I maintained my attention on him, he continued. "As I'm sure you're aware, the Islands used to have free healthcare for its citizens, but a few years ago the government adopted mandatory health insurance. There's a low-cost minimum insurance available, but for many locals, especially single parents, it's still out of reach. Sadly, we have to turn some mothers away as we only have four beds, but most of the time we can handle those in need."

"Do you recall which nurse helped dis young woman?" Jacob asked.

Kirkconnell's eyes diverted to my partner once more, and I felt a tinge of annoyance.

"We only have four full-time nurses and a couple of part-timers who fill in sometimes, so it won't be too hard to figure out," the doctor replied. "It'll be in the file, of course, but let me ask the two who are here today."

He left the lobby, and the front door opened behind us. A very pregnant woman stopped when she saw the police uniforms, a look of concern taking over her face.

I grabbed the door and held it for her. "Please, come in."

For a second I thought she was going to bolt, which would have been comical to watch in her condition, but she came inside and hurried to the counter. "Miss Bee?"

The woman reappeared from the office and the two conversed in heavily accented English, which I couldn't follow. I noticed Jacob grinning, so I presumed it was entertaining for him. The pregnant woman waddled through the door into the main part of the building and I heard the doctor tell her he'd be with her shortly. He returned through the door with two other people in tow.

"Let me introduce you to two of my nurses," Kirkconnell said, gesturing to an Indian woman I guessed to be in her mid-thirties.

"This is Sarika Kumari. She's our head nurse. And this is Ian Belfrey, another experienced nurse we couldn't manage without." Everybody politely nodded greetings, and the doctor continued. "They both recall the young lady I spoke about, so I thought it best for you to ask them your questions directly."

"Do either of you recall her name?" I immediately asked.

They both shook their heads.

"I didn't spend a lot of time with her, I'm afraid," Nurse Kumari said. Her accent was English with a hint of her native Indian thrown in.

"I examined her, but I don't think she gave her name. She was in and out pretty quick," the male nurse offered. He spoke with what I thought was an English Brummie accent, but I was often confused with the regional differences. "She was in good shape, so I told her we'd be happy to help her through full term, but we couldn't terminate the pregnancy. She left pretty smartish after that."

I held up my mobile and showed them both the photograph of the woman on the autopsy table.

"Blimey," Ian muttered. "Poor thing."

Sarika's brow creased, but she closely examined the picture. "That's her though, isn't it, Ian?"

"Maybe, yeah, but hard to say for sure. It's been a while, and that's not seeing her at her best."

"Did you take a blood sample?" I asked.

Ian shook his head. "Like I said, she didn't stick around, so she never actually became a patient."

"Anyting else you tink we should know, or would help us find her family?" Jacob asked.

Both nurses said no, and we thanked them for their time.

"Sorry we can't be more help," the doctor said sympathetically. "I wish we'd been able to assist her more back then. Maybe things would have turned out differently. I assume by the photograph she was murdered?"

"We can't say at dis time," Jacob responded.

Kirkconnell caught my eye for a moment. I figured it was a rhetorical question. No one bashes their own jaw to pieces.

"I'll look again when da phone quietens down," Bee said, appearing from the office. "But I don't see a matching file anywhere and I'm sure we made one. Everybody goes through dere gets a file," she added, pointing to the door into the building. "It must be around somewhere."

I had a feeling Miss Bee kept tight reins on the filing system, so she'd make it a personal quest to find the paperwork.

"Please let us know if you come up with anything," I said, more to the doctor than to Bee.

"We will," he replied. "Please stop by any time we can be of further help. I hope you're able to figure out what happened to this poor woman."

I nodded, took one more glance into those hazel eyes, then Jacob and I left.

"He really wants you to come by again," Jacob ribbed as we walked to the car. "I tink he wants him a little Constable Nora."

I rolled my eyes. "Shut up, Jacob, and get in."

6

———

TRUMPET-PLAYING PUFFINS

Wednesday - 6:00pm

Most days after work, I had plenty of energy left and I usually freedived the reef by my shack, or went for a run. Today hadn't been physically taxing, but I still felt completely drained by the time I walked through my front door. It was hard to push the young woman's image from my mind. I was about to take a shower when my mobile rang. My friend AJ talked me into meeting her for a drink.

I grabbed my keys and trudged back through the woods to the road where I park my Jeep. My shack, which was generously given to me by a wonderful man named Archie Winters, is on the waterfront on the north side of West Bay with no direct access. It used to be part of the Spanish Bay Reef Resort, which had been torn down years ago, but was on its own lot, which Archie owned. An easement had allowed access through the resort grounds, but the current owner was a douchebag who tried to have Archie kicked out. The owner's now tied up in a legal mess from his douchebagness, and Archie had to find somewhere else to hide from his somewhat dubious past. Before he left, Archie signed the property over to me to make sure it didn't wind up in court too.

Starting the straight-six engine, I turned around and headed west. The CJ-7 was my boyfriend's project, which he'd been close to completing before he'd been murdered. That was over a year ago. I still thought about him every day, but life had a way of shoving new thoughts, problems, and even joys into my mind, saving me from drowning in grief. People say time helps. I don't think it's time itself; it's the distractions which accumulate, given time. If I'd sat in my house and stared at the walls for the past year, I'd still be consumed by the loss.

Detective Whittaker had taken a tremendous gamble. He'd offered me a chance to join the police force, an entity I'd carefully avoided crossing paths with since I'd run away from home at sixteen. He knew some of my prior transgressions, but fortunately not all, and he chose to overlook my past, giving me a way to move forward. I've surprised myself by how much I enjoy police work. It's frustrating at times, but getting idiots and lowlifes off the street was rewarding. Plus, sometimes I got to taser the shit out of them.

I pulled into the car park at Macabuca and found a spot next to AJ's Ducati motorcycle. The sun was beginning to set and the sky to the west was already winding into its nightly display of rich colour. As I walked towards the outdoor bar, which was shaded under a thatched roof overlooking the ocean, AJ waved from a bar stool.

She's a little shorter than average, fit and lean, but with more feminine curves than I have, shoulder-length blonde hair with purple streaks, and full-sleeve tattoos on both arms. AJ is the coolest chick I've ever met, and she has no idea how much people respect and admire her. She thinks she's a short, goofy, English nerd who's okay looking.

We hugged, and I sat on the stool next to her. Her hair was wet.

"You've been diving," I said.

"Yeah, first open water dives of a class, so we went out here," she replied, nodding towards the sheltered inlet in the ironshore coastline where steps led into the water. It was a great spot for shore dives and for teaching.

"I saw your bike."

She grinned. "Yeah. Thomas drove the van and dropped the people off on his way home. I decided to ride, but I need to dry off before I put my gear on to leave."

She looked like a stormtrooper from *Star Wars* in her armoured bike clothes and helmet. She's so cool.

"Been busy?" she asked.

I wasn't supposed to discuss cases with anyone, but AJ didn't count in my mind. First of all, she and Reg Moore worked for the police whenever the RCIPS had difficult or technical dives, and secondly, I trusted her completely.

"Did they call you to dive Jackson's Pond today?"

AJ frowned. "No, thank goodness. Sod diving in there. I dread to think what's been tossed in over the years."

"A young woman," I said bluntly.

AJ's eyes got wider. "Bugger! You had a body recovery?"

"Not really. The body was by the edge, but Whittaker was sending divers in to look around."

"Was she… you know…" Even AJ had trouble saying sad words.

"She was very dead. Murdered."

"Bugger," she muttered again. "How long had she been in the pond?"

"Not long. We think someone dumped her there last night."

AJ made a face like she'd smelt something bad. "At least it wasn't a gooey one."

"No goo," I responded, "but some *drittsekk* had beaten the shit out of her."

We both sat up straighter and paused our conversation as the bartender approached.

"Strongbow, AJ?" he asked.

"Please," she replied, and they both looked at me.

I shrugged my shoulders. "Same." There was no run in my

future tonight. "And water, please." I wasn't much of a drinker and I figured with all the charging around today in the heat, I probably hadn't hydrated enough. Maybe that was part of why I felt so tired. The crash on the back side of the energy drink wasn't helping either.

"Have you seen a teenage girl around lately? Looks a little like Hallie, but younger," I asked, moving away from the murder victim. Telling AJ about my day always felt good, but I didn't want to dwell on the woman in the water. Her image was already haunting me.

"That's pretty vague, Nora. Does she do something I should notice?"

"Like what?" I asked, not really understanding her question.

"Well, I presume you're asking because something about her has caught your attention. Is she in trouble? Or missing?"

"Oh, I see. I thought you were asking if she walked around playing a trumpet, or carried a puffin on her head."

"A puffin?" AJ laughed. "I don't think we have many puffins in the Cayman Islands."

"Not to my knowledge," I confirmed.

"But you have puffins in Norway, don't you?"

"We do, but they're elusive little buggers."

"Then it would certainly be noteworthy to see one on a local girl's head around here. Especially playing a trumpet."

"Norwegian puffins don't play trumpets."

The bartender set our drinks down and looked at me with a puzzled expression.

"Have you seen a young girl with a trumpet-playing puffin on her head?" I asked, as straight faced as I could manage.

"Not lately," he replied without missing a beat. "Had a three-legged boy with a pet llama the other day. Served him a Tom Collins."

"The llama?" AJ asked with a chuckle.

"Of course, the llama," the bartender replied with an indignant look. "The three-legged boy was underage."

We both laughed as he walked away, grinning.

"Now, what were you saying about puffin girl?" AJ asked.

"I think she's living on the streets. I've seen her in West Bay and in George Town, but I can't get near. She literally vanishes. I spotted her coming out of One Stop Mini Market this afternoon, and by the time I reached the corner of the shop, she was gone."

"She's not Puffin Girl. She's Sue Storm," AJ said, looking pleased with herself.

"You know her?" I asked, unable to hide my surprise.

AJ rolled her eyes. "Sue Storm is the Invisible Woman in Marvel comics."

I stared blankly at my friend.

"I've seen the films," she said defensively. "You know, the *Fantastic Four* movies."

My expression didn't change.

AJ grinned. "I'll add those to the films we can watch on a rainy day."

She had a personal mission to show me films she thought were cool, funny, sad, or exciting. I usually fell asleep. Except in the *Dragon Tattoo* movies. The original Swedish version was my favourite. That chick was cool, too. Really messed up, but cool.

"I prefer Puffin Girl. Anyway, the point is I'd like to speak with her, so if you see the kid, let me know."

AJ nodded and took a swig of her cider. After a beat, she turned to me. "Have Hallie talk to her."

I hadn't thought of that. The idea made sense.

"She might even know the kid," AJ added. "Or the kid might recognise Hallie."

"The problem is finding Puffin Girl. I can't have Hallie with me all day in the patrol car."

"When have you seen her?"

I thought for a moment. Three sightings weren't enough to see a pattern, but it might be a start. "Today, just after 1:00pm in West Bay. A few days ago by Foster's market, but that was mid-morning.

And the first time was downtown George Town after work. Probably six or seven o'clock."

We both took a pull on our drinks and thought it through.

"If you're right, and she's living on the streets, then she could be transient, moving wherever she sees opportunity."

"Or, she has a place she stays in West Bay, then works the evening crowd downtown," I said, thinking aloud.

"She could take the bus back and forth," AJ suggested.

We looked at each other and I'm pretty sure she had the same idea as me. We called them buses, but they were really just large passenger vans. If you were anywhere along their route, they'd stop and pick you up. "We could watch the bus," I said. "We could try at different times until we see her."

"Or just ride the bus until she gets on," AJ said. "There's only a handful which run along Seven Mile Beach. They go to George Town and back all day."

I liked the idea. If I had to bet, I was sure the girl would take the busy bus after 5:00pm. She'd be lost in the crowd and arrive in George Town while the place was still full of cruise shippers, plus the local crowd eating and drinking after work. I'd run the idea by Hallie and see what she thought. If I was right about Puffin Girl and she was fending for herself, between us, Hallie and I had plenty of experience living that life.

7

THE ONE THAT GOT AWAY

Thursday 6:45am

I sleep better than I used to, but still not well. My mind doesn't like to switch off at night, and as soon as I'm awake in the morning, it's ready to go again. That doesn't mean I'm clever first thing in the morning; it just means I can't go back to sleep. I view my mind as a separate creature from the rest of me. Sure, it's located in my brain, which allows me to walk and talk, but that's just a teaser it gives me to make me think it's on my side. It's not. My mind is my nemesis.

When I sleep, my mind is in a cage where all it can do is whisper to me and project awful images into my head. But as soon as my eyes open, so is the cage, and my evil mind is ready to pounce. It knows exactly what will keep me awake. This morning it was the young woman in Jackson's Pond. At 5:30am I gave up on getting any more rest and had coffee and breakfast. At sunrise I was already swimming to the reef, and by 6:45am I was back from freediving and showering under the outdoor tap.

The West Bay police station was small and had none of the

hustle and bustle of the main branch in downtown George Town. At 7:15am, forty-five minutes before the day shift started, the place was deserted. I logged into one of the computers and began searching the database for missing persons. I knew Whittaker would have had someone already run this process for the woman in the water, but my search was about Puffin Girl.

I filtered the search going back seventeen years, well past what I guessed her age to be, and selected female, unsolved. The result contained thirty-one hits. A city in America probably has that many a month or worse, but on our little island, that number seemed excessive to me. On average, almost two young women each year disappeared, never to be found. I wondered how many had chosen to drop off the radar, and how many were buried on the island, or at the bottom of the sea. The thought was chilling.

Sorting through the list, I narrowed down the names by age on the date they went missing. That left me with three likely individuals. One was an infant who was last seen eight years ago, so that couldn't be Puffin Girl. How does a baby just vanish? I shivered at the thought. That left me with two names.

Four years ago, Elizabeth Ebanks went missing from school when she was nine years old. I enlarged the photograph on file. It was one of those school pictures they take every year and sell to your parents. She was a cute kid with a gap-toothed smile. I tried to imagine the girl as a teenager, but it didn't really matter as I'd only caught glimpses of Puffin Girl and probably couldn't pick her out of a line-up.

The last possibility was Jasmine Holder. She'd been in foster care but didn't come home from a sleepover at a friend's house nearly three years ago. The family she was staying with lived in East End. There would have been a pretty big fuss all over the news when she went missing. Six months later was the pandemic lockdown, which would have made moving around difficult without drawing attention. Her picture was a casual shot of the young girl on a swing in a garden. Her hair was cut short and she could easily be mistaken for a boy.

"Good mornin' sunshine," Jacob declared from the doorway, making me jump. "What you up to in dere?"

I hit print on the two files and stood up. "Research," I replied, walking to the printer.

"Dat girl you think you keep seein'?"

I nodded, folding the sheets of paper. "Puffin Girl."

"What did you call her, now?"

"Sue Storm," I said, deciding not to explain how I'd come about her nickname.

Jacob laughed. "That's perfect! Like da Invisible Woman, huh?"

Everyone watches too much television, I thought, slipping past Jacob and heading down the hallway.

We both flipped heads, which meant route one, then Jacob came up tails so we'd be going anticlockwise. He was back behind the wheel and turned left out of the station to start our patrol when my mobile rang. It was Whittaker.

"Sir," I answered, putting the call through the vehicle's hands-free system.

"Good morning. I have a few updates if this is a good time?"

"Of course," I replied. "We're just leaving the station."

"Perfect," the detective said. "Go by the clinic again and see if they've found the file. I presume you haven't heard from them?"

"No," I replied, and Jacob looked at me with a grin. He was dying to give me shit about the doctor, but he couldn't with our boss on the phone. I smacked his arm and told him to turn around.

"The divers found nothing useful, I'm afraid," Whittaker continued. "Same with the drone, although we're still going over the footage more closely. Maybe we'll get lucky and spot something."

"No missing persons match?" I asked.

"No one similar from the past few years, and no report of a friend or family member missing."

I thought about bringing up Puffin Girl as we were on the

subject of missing women, but I had so little to go on it seemed premature. Plus, I didn't want him to think I wasn't focused on the current case, which I was glad he was keeping us involved in.

"No one has come forward from the door-to-door, sir?" I asked.

"I'm afraid not. We released the story to the media this morning. I'm hoping someone will step forward who knew her. I can't believe she was completely alone here."

"She met at least one person, sir."

The line went quiet for a moment.

"She'd been pregnant," I added.

"Of course," Whittaker said, with a hint of amusement in his voice. "Unless we're witnessing a historical moment, I suppose she knew one man. But that's not to say conception didn't happen elsewhere."

"Immigration doesn't have her fingerprints or matching photograph, correct?" I asked, and sensed Jacob fidgeting in the driver's seat. It made him uncomfortable when I asked pointed questions, especially of the detective. And I often forgot to throw the appropriate 'sirs' in when I was thinking things through.

"No, but fingerprints aren't required for a non-visa entry and I don't think we can rely too heavily on facial recognition software with her being in the condition we found her," Whittaker responded, not appearing to mind my query.

"She could be a Cuban or Haitian refugee for all we know," I mused. "Sir."

"All true. I'm heading over to meet with Rasha now. She's completed her full autopsy, so let's touch base later this morning."

"Yes, sir," Jacob quickly replied, and Whittaker hung up. Jacob was always eager to get off the line. I wasn't big on chatting over the phone; well, I wasn't big on chatting, period, but I was keen to be back in the detective's good graces, so if he wanted to talk about the case, I was more than willing.

"Why are you scared of him?" I asked.

Jacob looked offended. "I'm not scared of da man."

"You avoid talking to him whenever you can."

"Don't mean I'm scared," he replied, pulling into the car park of the clinic.

"Then why?" I persisted.

"I don't want to mess up is all."

"How are you going to mess up talking to the bloke? You think you'll suddenly blurt out that he has a big nose, or his wife is ugly?"

Jacob frowned. "What da hell you talkin' about? I tink I can manage not to insult da man. Besides, he don't have a big nose, and I never met his wife."

"She's a nice lady," I said, getting out of the car. "She's got some curves."

Jacob grinned at me over the roof of the car. "I like a woman wit curves."

"So you fancy the boss's wife? That's pretty ballsy," I said, striding over to the front door.

"Damn, Nora. Why you gotta say a ting like dat?"

I pulled open the door and looked back over my shoulder. "So you didn't have time to bring up the doctor before we got here."

I walked inside and heard him muttering to himself as he followed me in.

"Good morning, Bee," I called out and saw her head pop up from the desk in the office.

"I'll be right dere, miss," she responded, and shuffled out of the office, slipping her glasses from her face and letting them hang from a sparkly chain around her neck. "Don't know what's happened, but dat file is nowhere to be found. I searched all over last night and come in early dis mornin' and did da same again."

"Does that happen sometimes?" I asked. "A file gets misplaced?"

The woman stared at me as though I'd insulted every member of her family. "It don't never happen in dis office, young lady."

Well, it's happened now, I thought, but stayed silent. AJ would call that progress, but I didn't think so. The only difference was volume. I still thought the same way, I just kept the sound off.

"Da file couldn't be in da clinic somewhere?" Jacob asked politely. "Perhaps one of the udder staff members has it?"

Bee shook her head. "Only files out dere are for da patients in da rooms, or doctor has for upcoming appointments. Dey all know I'll beat dem wit a switch if they mess wit my files."

I believed the woman. Not about someone having the file as it was clearly missing, meaning somebody had it somewhere. But I was sure she'd whip the shit out of anyone messing with her filing. If we caught the killer and he indeed had the missing paperwork, I figured we could save the taxpayers a fortune by letting Bee have ten minutes alone with the bloke. We could shovel his carcass into a box and call it case closed.

"And the file wouldn't have been transferred to another facility?" I dared to ask.

"If dey request it and all, sure. But den I make a note of dat so every file number is accounted for. Anyway, request would come to me and I'd remember dat."

"Is anything kept electronically?" I asked, and received another glare.

"Can't rely on dose damn computer machines. I always keep my files in order and ain't never let me down."

Once again, I held my tongue about the inaccuracy of her statement. The door to the rest of the building opened and Doctor Kirkconnell appeared. He looked straight at me and I noted his piercing eyes hadn't faded since yesterday.

"I thought I heard your voices," he said. "Good morning to you both. I'm so sorry we can't help you further. I presume Bee has explained the missing file?"

I nodded.

"I can vouch for Bee's diligence with the paperwork. I can only imagine one of us messed up somewhere along the line and lost it."

"We appreciate you makin' a thorough search," Jacob said. "Please let us know if you do find it at any point."

"We certainly will," the doctor replied. "Of course, we can't be certain this is the same woman who was…" He faltered for a moment. "The poor woman you found."

"Be nice to find out though," I said, and the doctor glanced at Bee. They both glowed red with embarrassment.

"Of course. I apologise again," Kirkconnell said.

Jacob opened the front door, and I turned to follow him out.

"Miss Sommer?" the doctor said softly.

I paused and wondered what he'd forgotten to tell us. He walked over to the door and continued in a hushed voice. "Would it be out of place for me to ask you to dinner sometime?"

"Probably," I answered without much thought, as it probably was against some rule or another. I was taken aback. I hadn't been on so much as a date since Ridley, and I found myself torn. Kirkconnell seemed like a really nice guy, and he was certainly pleasant to look at, but I still felt like I was being disloyal to my soulmate.

"I'm sorry, I certainly didn't mean to break any rules or cause you trouble," I realised he was saying.

"I'll pick you up from here. Tomorrow evening at 5:30," were the words that came out of my mouth. I let the door close behind me and walked in bewilderment to the car.

8

MR SQUISHY

Thursday 9:00am

I sat down in the car, and Jacob stared at me like a cat chewing a canary. Or some expression like that. I heard AJ say the phrase once, but I may have got it wrong. He had a shit-eating grin. That one I'd heard a lot of Americans use, but no way would I say it. If I was eating shit, I wouldn't be smiling in any way. It made no sense. A cat would probably smile if it caught a canary.

"What did I miss in dere?" Jacob asked in amusement as he backed out of the parking spot.

"The doctor wanted to make sure Bee had a contact number for us."

"That was it?" Jacob muttered despondently.

"Yup."

He was so trusting.

Jacob pulled up to Hell Road and waited for traffic to pass. I glanced in the side mirror.

"Wait," I snapped. "Back up."

"You forget someting?" he asked as he slowly reversed. I reached over and pushed on the steering wheel, so the car turned.

"Stop. Now pull straight ahead."

"Want to tell me what you're up to here, Nora?" Jacob complained, but drove forward to where a marl lane ran alongside the maternity clinic and disappeared into a wooded area.

"Drive up here," I said, not willing to share my thoughts just yet.

Jacob turned onto the gravel road and drove slowly so he didn't stir up too much dust. He gave up asking questions. He'd learnt over time that I'd fill him in when I had something complete to say. I knew he didn't like the arrangement, but he'd realised pummelling me with questions didn't get him anywhere and annoyed the crap out of me.

The lane curved left then right, and after 100 metres we passed an opening leading to an old cottage. It was hit and miss whether it was occupied or derelict. I waved Jacob on to the end where tall wild grass and weeds had swamped any path that may once have gone farther. Various pieces of junk lay around in the undergrowth. A rusty washing machine, several bald tyres, and something that could once have been a child's swing set, or perhaps farm equipment. It all looked undisturbed, including the grass and weeds.

There wasn't enough room to turn around, so Jacob backed up and used the cottage entrance to make a three-point turn. I looked over my shoulder out of the back window and still couldn't decide if the dwelling was habitable. I guessed that was always a matter of opinion, depending on your circumstances.

We turned left to leave the way we came, but I stopped Jacob again at the first curve. To our right, another old trail disappeared into the trees. I got out of the car and hadn't made it three steps before I heard the high-pitched whining buzz of mosquito wings. They sprayed insecticides all over the island with aeroplanes and trucks, but it was impossible to keep the little blood-sucking bastards at bay completely. I'd discovered they liked Nordic blood.

Pushing through the first row of low-hanging branches, the path opened up to a narrow walking trail. If we were in Norway, I'd suspect it was a game trail, but the Cayman Islands didn't have any deer or larger mammals. It could have been stray dogs or simply a neighbourhood kid's shortcut to school. Regardless, there were no signs of recent footprints or disturbed undergrowth.

I walked back to the car and swatted three bugs on my arms, each leaving a bloody splodge as evidence she'd had her last meal from me. Dropping into the passenger seat, I quickly closed the door.

"You get bitten some?" Jacob asked.

"You could have gone to look," I retorted. Jacob was invisible to mosquitoes and other flying, biting insects. He never got bitten, especially if I was around for them to feast on.

"Maybe I would have if my partner told me what da hell we're doing out here."

He made a good point. My reluctance came from the fact I wasn't ready to admit the clinic run by Mr Gorgeous Eyes should be on our suspect list. Maybe it was because of his charm, but usually I was wary of everyone involved in a case until the facts proved their innocence. For some reason, I'd seen him as a peripheral witness.

"The young woman had her feet torn up from walking barefoot across a rough marl trail, and here's a marl trail right next to the only place we've connected her to so far."

Jacob looked puzzled as he eased the patrol car along the bumps towards the road. "We got dese roads like dis all over da island. If da woman ran from da parking at Jackson's Pond to where she died, her feet would be all torn to shreds."

"I know. I'm just saying I'd not considered the doctor a suspect until now, and I think we should," I said, leaving out the going on a date tomorrow night part.

"Dat movie-star-lookin' doctor gonna be right disappointed when he finds out you're tinkin' he's up to no good," Jacob ribbed. "I'm tellin' you, he wanna be da Nora bobo."

My partner took a full minute to stop laughing, and I let him have his fun. It was better than admitting I might have screwed up two days after Whittaker seemed to be trusting me again. I'd call the clinic later and cancel. That was the best thing I could do and nobody needed to be any wiser.

Jacob turned left on Hell Road, and I quickly told him to turn the other way.

"We going dis way from da coin toss," he complained, but he was already slowing and swinging the car around in the road.

"We will after this," I said, pointing out the front window at a silver Mercedes moving west on Hell Road.

He accelerated after the car and as we closed, a grin crept across his face. "Well spotted," he chuckled, seeing the fluffy head of a dog leaning out the driver's side window.

I flicked the flashing lights on as we caught the Mercedes, but I could see the back of the driver's head and not once did it turn to check a mirror.

"How long you want to keep dis up?" Jacob asked.

"Until I've run the registration," I replied, tapping the figures into our dash mounted laptop.

The car stopped at the T-junction with Watercourse Road, and without ever using indicator, turned left towards the south-facing coastline of West Bay.

"We better pull dem over soon or we'll run out o' room to write on da ticket."

"Six outstanding parking fines. Four of them are now 'failure to appears'."

I reached over and flicked the siren on for a short burst. The Mercedes veered back and forth in the lane as we surprised the driver. Their head was now bobbing around, checking every mirror, and the dog nearly fell out of the window. The car pulled over to the side of the two-lane road and stopped. We parked behind the Mercedes and I checked for traffic before getting out. The dog turned its attention to me and yipped in a frenzy as I approached; it bounced around, hanging half out of the window.

"Mr Snuggles!" I heard the driver yip, nearly as annoyingly as her dog. "Stop barking."

"Good morning, ma'am," I said, not raising my voice to be heard over the noise.

"I'm in an awful hurry," the woman said in an East European accent. "What can I help you with? Mr Snuggles, calm down."

"You can start by subduing your dog and putting it in the back."

"You made him go crazy with siren," she replied, attempting to gather up the writhing ball of fluff. If it didn't sound like a dog, I'd swear it was an oversized, long-haired rat.

"Stay!" the woman told the dog as she placed him on the back seat. "Stay!" she repeated as he completely ignored her, continued to yip, and attempted to jump upfront. Her left hand blocked the gap between the front seats, imprisoning Mr Rat Snuggles in the back.

"Driver's licence please," I ordered, remaining as civil as I could manage. "Is this your car, ma'am?"

"Of course it my car," she muttered while shuffling one handed through her Louis Vuitton handbag. "What is this about? I did nothing wrong."

She finally handed me her licence. Irina Westinghouse, which matched the name that had come up on the computer. "It's illegal and dangerous to have an animal in the front of a moving vehicle, ma'am."

Irina looked at me with a frown. "Mr Snuggles is not dangerous, he good dog and like to ride with me."

"Ma'am, if you were to have an accident, what would happen to the ra... to the dog?"

"This *fignya*, I never have accident."

It was clear that English was not either of our first languages, but I was pretty certain the definition of accident involved the words 'unplanned' and 'unexpected'. I reached over the roof and slapped the top of the Mercedes with my open palm. The sudden noise made the woman jump, and the startled noise generator in the back fell off the seat and landed on the floor with a grunt. I reached in the open window and slapped my hand against Irina's store-bought chest and she flinched again.

"When you hit something, the airbag goes off and punches you in the face and chest, preventing you from coming forward and hitting the dashboard. If your mutt is between you and the airbag, what do you think happens to him?"

She looked at me with a startled expression. "You hit me!"

"Correct answer," I responded. "Mr Squishy gets shoved into you by the force of the airbag. They'll be picking little doggy bones out of your expensively sculptured face for weeks. That's why it's illegal and dangerous."

"*Fignya*," she muttered again, and I made a mental note to look up what I presumed was a swear word. "You can't hit driver. My husband sue you."

"Sounds fun," I replied as I wrote out her ticket. "You have six outstanding parking tickets, four of which are FTAWs…"

"What is this F…A… whatever?"

"Failure to appear warrants, ma'am. It means you neither paid your fine nor showed up at your court date. I can arrest you and take you to the station."

"*Der'mo*! Not possible! I'm late for appointment. My maid sometime use car, she must get ticket. Not mine."

"The car is in your name, Mrs Westinghouse. Therefore, the paperwork was sent to you, and you're responsible for the tickets. If you'd like to get out of the car, you can accompany us to the station and pay what you owe."

"I pay you. No station," she snapped, revealing a wad of banknotes in her matching Louis Vuitton wallet.

"I'll add attempted bribe to the ticket," I said, and continued writing.

"Not bribe!" she squealed. "I pay ticket!"

Pausing, I tapped my pen on my pad of citations. "I'll cut you a break," I said, looking at the yapping rat in the backseat. "I'll spare you the embarrassment of handcuffs and a ride in the back of the patrol car if you go straight to West Bay Station and pay your outstanding fines. All six of them. The desk clerk will also be happy to note any complaints you may have."

"I have appointment," she whined.

"For what? Massage? Nails? Botox?"

Irina let loose a stream of profanity in her native tongue. I waited for her to stop. "Handcuffs then?"

"Give to me. I go pay others now," she relented and snatched the ticket I handed her. "What this? Not use turn signal?"

"You didn't use your indicator at the stop sign, or to pull over here."

"*Fignya!*"

I couldn't wait to look that up. "You'll see I left off the attempted bribe."

The power window began going up as I heard her hiss, "*Suka.*" There was more, but it was drowned out by the barking rat.

9

BREAKFAST FOR LUNCH

Thursday 11:45am

We called the station and warned them an angry lady was coming by to pay her fines, then finally started our patrol. We took our time as the police radio was quiet, and it was nearing lunchtime when my mobile rang. It was Whittaker again.

"Sir?" I answered over the car's hands-free system.

"Nothing useful from the clinic?" he asked.

I'd texted him earlier and told him they still couldn't find the missing file, but I hadn't expanded on any further details.

"Not really," I replied.

"Alright. I'm holding a briefing at Central if you two would please attend as 'first on scene' officers. It's at 1:00pm."

"Of course, sir," I replied.

"Good. I'll message West Bay station and let them know I'm borrowing you for a few hours. See you then."

"One question, sir, before you go," I said, hoping he hadn't hung up.

"Yes, Constable?"

"Is the marl from different parts of the island identifiable?"

"Hmmm. Interesting question." he replied, then thought a moment. "I seem to recall an old case where that did, in fact, come into play. Rasha will be at the briefing. Why don't you ask her? She'll have a more complete answer than I do. If I remember correctly, the case I'm talking about had oil from where someone had serviced their engine on the trail next to their house. We found oil residue in the gravel on the plaintiff's boots, which placed him near the house."

"Okay, thank you, sir," I responded, not wanting to talk about it further. Jacob was right; there were hundreds of miles of marl trails all over the 26-mile-long island. My suspicion was a crazy long shot.

"Something pertinent to this case, Nora?" Whittaker asked.

"Unlikely, sir. But I'll talk to Rasha."

"See you at one," he replied, and hung up.

I looked over at Jacob. "You didn't want to ask the boss how his wife is doing?"

Jacob groaned and slapped the steering wheel. He was about to say something, but he took a deep breath instead, then wagged his finger at me. "No, no, no. You get me dis way all da time, and I'm learnin'. Da smart fish don't bite on da shiniest lure."

I kept a straight face, but smiled inside. Maybe my friend was learning. That would take some fun out of my day, but I loved a challenge.

"Let's get lunch before we go to the briefing. I'm famished."

"Where d'you feel like today?" Jacob replied.

"You're driving, your choice."

He thought for a minute. "Den I say da Burger King."

"No."

Jacob threw his hand in the air. "If it's my choice, den it's Burger King."

"It's only your choice if you make a good choice. Burger King is never a good choice. I'm not eating that *dritt*."

We had this same conversation once a week, and it always went exactly the same way. Jacob's wife wouldn't let him take the kids to fast-food restaurants, so his only opportunity was at lunch with me. He was persistent, I gave him that, but we still hadn't lunched at a fast-food chain yet.

"The Diner," I said. "They have a burger."

"Fine," he crumbled. "I just don't know why you hate da Burger King so much."

This was the trouble with spending so much time with someone; there were far too many worthless conversations. As a rule, people don't change their minds about things, so explaining my reasoning for hating fast-food chains and why they had no place on the island was probably a waste of words and breath.

Most of the time, people are only looking for something to support their way of thinking, and between the internet and media, there was plenty of bullshit to back up any crackpot idea. It wasn't easy to keep an open mind about something you really wanted to be true. Besides, I was pretty sure I'd explained my position before. And that's another problem with talking so much: you can't remember what you've already said.

"The Diner has breakfast all day," I said. "I can have an omelette."

"Maybe I'll have breakfast for lunch," Jacob responded more cheerily.

"Breakfast is the universal meal that works any time of day," I pointed out.

"Dat's true, I guess," Jacob agreed thoughtfully. "You wouldn't have ribs for breakfast, or chicken pot pie."

"Exactly," I said, happy to engage in a worthwhile conversation.

After breakfast for lunch, we headed south towards George Town with plenty of time to spare. Jacob stayed on West Bay Road instead of cutting over to the Esterly Tibbetts bypass. We both preferred the old two-lane roads to the dual carriageway, which felt out of place on a Caribbean island. Of course, at rush hour, all the roads were jammed up for a few hours each day, which seemed even less like a slice of tropical paradise. I heard a song once by an old guy named Don Henley who described the problem pretty accurately.

As we passed by clusters of older two-storey condo buildings, nestled amongst mature trees and landscaping which blended them into the coastline, I brought up maps on my mobile. Switching to satellite view, I zoomed in to the area that had popped into my mind.

"Slow down," I told Jacob, and he eased off the throttle pedal. "Do you see the apartments ahead on the left?"

"Not yet, but I know where dey are. It's da old Island Dream Motel building."

"Stop just past there."

"What we up to now?" he asked, already signalling left to pull over.

"This is where the trail comes out from Jackson's Pond," I said as he pulled to a stop just beyond a clean but dated looking single-storey building with decorative dormers in the steeply sloped roof. I recalled noticing the place in passing, but had never paid attention to it.

"It's a motel? There's no sign."

"No. Hurricane Ivan messed da place up like so many. Motel went outa business and someone converted da rooms into apartments. Low-income subsidised housing, if I remember right."

I looked across the road at the Silver Sands, where a beachfront condo would set you back well over a million. "Nice location for government housing."

"It ain't government housing, just subsidised by da government," Jacob corrected me. "Owned private I believe."

I got out of the car and walked along the edge of the property, searching for the trail, which was mostly hidden in the satellite aerial view. I heard Jacob's car door and figured he'd decided to take a look as well this time.

The building was long and low, with various design features to make it look like a terraced row of little homes, except they didn't have front doors. A main entrance sat at the south end of the building with a small painted sign above the covered porch which read 'Island Dream Apartments'. Behind, thick woods reached within five to ten metres of the structure. I guessed the apartments didn't have back gardens, but perhaps a very small common area and pathway.

As I neared the trees, I spotted a narrow band of marl overgrown with weeds leading east, and after pushing a few branches aside, it opened onto a clear trail.

"Dis goes back to da pond?" Jacob asked, arriving behind me.

"That's what the map shows. I think I stood at the next corner when I was circling behind where our lady was attacked."

We both looked down the trail but low, stray branches and overgrown weeds blocked our view after 10 or 15 metres.

"You tink she came from dis direction?"

I shrugged my shoulders. "It's possible." I turned around and shoved my way back through the foliage until I could see the road. "Unless she walked all the way down West Bay Road, there's nowhere around here she's likely to have come from," I added, turning my attention to the apartments. "Except that place."

We still knew nothing about our victim, but for some reason, I couldn't imagine her coming from the expensive condos along the other side of West Bay Road. Perhaps it was because I'd convinced myself she was local, and the condos were almost exclusively owned by part-time residents and rented out to visitors.

"Dey must have canvassed dose apartments," Jacob pointed out. "Besides, da dog din't find nuttin' down dis trail."

"The dog found nothing except the blood between the area where she was attacked and the edge of the pond where she was dumped. It rained Tuesday night, so any faint traces the dog may have picked up would have been gone."

"I suppose," Jacob said, getting back in the car.

Once we were heading south again on the road to George Town, I thought through the options of how the young woman could have arrived at the place where she'd been attacked. Five trails led to the spot, and we didn't know in which direction she'd been heading before someone had struck her down. I decided I'd ask about the apartments, but I was sure Jacob was right. Whittaker would have had someone check them out.

It was two and a half kilometres on foot from the clinic on Hell Road to Jackson's Pond. Certainly a manageable distance, and without shoes it would have caused the wounds to the woman's feet. There was also the possibility she'd been brought there by her killer, which meant a car parked at one of the access points. These were all topics I decided to raise if they weren't on the briefing's agenda.

10

SURGICAL PRECISION

Thursday - 1:00pm

I don't know why, but the amount of noise a group makes in a room has always fascinated me. A gathering of individuals takes on a collective vibe, often influenced by the senior or more animated member. Naturally, it's guided by how much trouble is possible. A noisy classroom goes quiet when the teacher walks in. Sometimes. Less so now teachers are powerless over their students.

The briefing room at Central station was not large, but could seat twenty people at the four rows of tables. The dozen officers present chattered in relaxed tones until Detective Whittaker walked into the room and everyone fell silent. In this case, it was not from fear of consequences, but from respect.

"Good afternoon everyone, thank you for attending," he began. "I'll try to keep this a short meeting, but I want everyone present to have a chance to inform the group of what we know so far."

One of the IT group had connected a laptop to a large monitor at the front of the room and a picture of the young woman's body in the water now appeared. Whittaker continued talking, nodding to the tech each time we wanted to show the next slide in the PowerPoint presentation. He covered the few details we'd put together about the scene of the attack, the body being dumped, and the area between the two which had been brushed or swept to cover evidence.

"Our victim was murdered between the hours of 11:00pm Monday evening and 5:00am Tuesday morning. Cause of death was blunt force trauma to the back of the head," he said, accompanied by a bloody picture of the back of her scalp. "Further blows were then made to the lower jaw. We believe to destroy dental record identification." I noticed Jacob looked away when that slide appeared on the screen. "We recovered several teeth at the scene. More were found, along with bone fragments, in the victim's throat during autopsy. None appear to provide us with enough information for a dental match."

I raised my hand. "Constable Sommer?"

"Were the jaw injuries post mortem?"

Whittaker gestured towards Rasha, who stood to the side of the room.

"I found no evidence of defensive wounds, and the blow to the cranium had caused brain trauma, so I suspect the victim was either dead or unconscious when the second set of injuries occurred."

Whittaker continued. "From blood spatter and the location of the teeth we found, we believe the victim was struck from behind, here," he said, pointing to the spot at the corner of the trail from a drone picture of the scene on the next slide. "Then she either stumbled or was moved to the second location, a hundred feet away, where the second set of blows were made."

Detective Weatherford, who was sitting upfront, raised his hand. "Same weapon used?"

Whittaker allowed Rasha to answer again. "We believe so. All injuries to the jaw were made by a piece of wood consistent with a sturdy tree branch. From wood splinters and bark taken from the wounds, as well as blood-stained fragments at the two scenes, we concluded a piece of ironwood was used as the weapon."

"The victim had also suffered a broken nose, but not from the blows to her face. A flatter instrument or surface had caused the injury. Initially, I thought it was from falling to the ground, but there were no traces of marl or dirt consistent with the trail."

Rasha looked at Whittaker, who took his cue to resume. "We've been unable to recover the murder weapon. I suspect it was a broken branch found along the trail which was carried from the scene by the killer, or thrown into the woods. We used a drone to look over the canopy and sent the dog into the woods wherever he could penetrate, but we've yet to find it."

With a nod from the detective, the next slide appeared, which was a digital artist's reconstruction of what the young woman probably looked like before her face was bashed in.

"We need an ID for our victim," Whittaker continued. "Someone must know her. She was late teens to mid-twenties, five foot two, and a hundred and twenty-eight pounds. As you all know by now, she recently gave birth. We believe three or four days before her death. No more than a week. We can't be sure, but all signs point towards a successful pregnancy and delivery. Until we know differently, we must assume her infant is alive and on the island somewhere."

The detective paused and scratched his chin for a moment. "It's rare these days, but some babies are born at home under a midwife's care, and then we have all the medical facilities, including the two sister islands. We have reached out to them all and are in the process of contacting our licensed midwives."

Whittaker turned to Rasha once more. "You have a few more details?"

Rasha stood. "The victim had sedatives and pain medication in her system, both consistent with postnatal care. I also found residue from electrodes on her chest, which suggests she was recently hooked to a monitor in a healthcare facility, although it doesn't preclude home care as they are available for the public to purchase."

Rasha sat down, so Whittaker continued. "So far, one of our only leads is from the private non-profit maternity clinic in West Bay who believe the woman came by a while back seeking termination of her pregnancy. They turned her away, which is their legal obligation, and have not seen her since. Unfortunately, none of the staff can recall her name and their file on her visit is missing."

With another nod, a street view of the clinic appeared on the screen. The marl lane to the right side was just visible. "The clinic is owned by a consortium of people here on the island and managed by a Doctor Conroy Kirkconnell. He's a local man, educated in the UK, has a clear record, and from what we've dug up so far, appears completely committed to the clinic. He attends all their fundraisers, campaigns for political reform to help low-income locals with medical care, et cetera.

"The facility employs four full-time nurses, one office manager, and several part-time nurses who fill in on sick leave and holidays. We've run background checks on all the staff, and outside of the usual speeding and parking tickets, only one of the group raised a flag."

The next slide showed an immigration visa photograph of the Indian woman we'd met at the clinic. "Sarika Kumari is British, born to Indian parents who emigrated to England in the early eighties. Educated in the UK, she worked in hospitals before coming here on a permit under sponsorship from the clinic. She had allegations brought against her for stealing pain management drugs from Highgate Hospital, a private facility where she worked. The hospital dropped the charges, but her employment ended. We can find no record of further employment in the UK. She came here six months later."

Weatherford raised his hand again. "How did she get a permit with a blemished record, sir?"

"That's a good question," Whittaker replied. "We've reached out to the Department of Immigration asking the very same. I'm guessing she had documentation explaining the situation to their satisfaction, but we'll see."

The detective stepped away from the screen and nodded to the IT tech. "Our second lead is a phone call the emergency line received."

The background static of a phone call began playing over the speakers.

"Emergency. Which service?" came a Caymanian female voice.

After a few seconds with the sound of someone taking breaths, another Cayman-accented female responded. Her voice wasn't so calm, and she was trying to speak quietly. "Da woman. Da woman dey say bin found. I know who she is."

"May I have your name, ma'am?"

"Is she really dead like dey say?"

"Ma'am, may I have your name and a number we can reach you on?"

The woman didn't answer, but a muffled sound like feet shuffling kept the room listening closely. A man's voice was unintelligible in the background, then a few grunts and knocks before the line went dead.

Whittaker returned to the front. "Pay-as-you-go phone that we traced to the cell tower in West Bay, but as you know, that covers a large portion of the west end of the island. The woman has not called back. We're combing through the recording for further useful background sounds, but as yet we've been unable to clean it up enough to understand what the man says."

Whittaker began pacing back and forth as he spoke. "Our first priority is to make an identification. From the little information we have, we believe her to be local, and if the phone call was genuine, there's at least one person who knows her. We're also looking for her infant who we can only hope is in safe hands. We've asked for all medical facilities to notify us if a baby is brought to them under any form of suspicious circumstance.

"Next. Why was our victim near Jackson's Pond, and how did she get there? Same questions for the killer. Were they together?

We've requested CCTV from the government cameras in the vicinity, but many of the homes and condo associations also have their own security cameras. We will be assigning areas to canvas and ask you to retrieve any available footage from between 6:00pm Monday and 10:30am Tuesday. That will require extensive time to review, so plan on overtime for the next week."

The mention of times reminded me I'd made a date with someone who was moving closer to our suspect list. I needed to cancel it.

"I'll be speaking with the West Bay Maternity Clinic staff individually, starting this afternoon. We need to tread carefully. The clinic has a stellar reputation on the island, with support from many prominent local figures. The only reason they have our attention is a missing file, and a black mark on one employee's record in another country. If we had any other evidence of substance, the clinic would be a low priority on our list. But we don't."

Whittaker studied the police men and women before him. "Please find us more evidence. We know nothing about this young lady, except one thing. She didn't deserve to be bludgeoned to death in the middle of the night."

The detective let out a sigh. "Any questions?"

No one else raised their hand, so I did. Next to me, Jacob let out a slight groan.

"Constable Sommer?"

"I was going to ask Rasha about the marl, sir."

"Oh yes," he said, turning to face the SOCO. "Nora was asking whether marl from different parts of the island have a distinct element that can be identified."

Rasha thought for a moment. "The marl itself doesn't usually, but the environment it's located in can leave trace elements. Salt spray, for example. Dirt mixed in can sometimes be matched to an area, or at least provide evidence that the marl came from somewhere else."

Whittaker nodded and looked over at me. "Did that answer your question?"

"What about Hell?" I asked.

"Good point," Rasha replied. "Marl is simply a gravel version of the limestone rock, and the limestone in that concentrated area is very distinct because of the algae which turned it black. But we don't take limestone from Hell. Most of the trails have marl gravel brought in from the quarry rather than utilising stone from the trail's location."

She had a point I'd overlooked. Most of the marl used throughout the island came from the few quarries we had. I looked at Jacob in surprise as he raised his hand.

"Constable Tibbetts?" Whittaker said, looking as surprised as I was.

"Is it okay if I ask a question, sir?"

Whittaker smiled. "Of course, Jacob."

"Tank you, sir. Are we tinking dis attack was someone da woman knew? Like a crime of passion, sir?"

Whittaker wagged his finger at my partner. "That's a great point to raise, and one I should have touched on already, Jacob. My answer would be yes. Initial observations of the murder scene and the weapon we know was used suggests this was not premeditated. It does point towards an enraged boyfriend or husband. It takes a good deal of rage to bludgeon someone to death, then continue in a deliberate manner with the intention of disguising their identity."

My hand shot up before I could stop myself.

"Constable Sommer?"

Damn. I didn't really want to express what was on my mind, especially in a room full of far more experienced police officers than me. This was another sabotage by my brain.

"I was thinking those two acts seem to be in conflict with each other, sir."

"How so?" Whittaker asked, not appearing to be as annoyed as I expected.

"Well, I get a jealous lover who tracks her down and loses control, smashing her over the head. But he only hit her once."

Whittaker nodded slowly and scratched at his goatee. "Go on."

"If the guy went mental, why didn't he hit again?"

"You're suggesting it's more likely a jilted boyfriend would continue striking her?"

"We believe she stayed on her feet and staggered down the trail. Why didn't he hit her again?" I noticed every person in the room had turned to stare at me.

"We believe that one blow was enough to kill her," Rasha said.

"Right, but if the guy's in a mad frenzy with enough anger to hit her once, I think he'd hit her again when she remained on her feet." Sod it, I thought, and got up, standing in the aisle down the side of the tables. "He smacks her from behind," I said, swinging my arms as though I were wielding a club, "then lets her stagger down the trail until she collapses face down." I took a few steps, then reached to the floor as though I was rolling a body over. "He then flips her over and with surgical accuracy whacks her in the mouth a few times." Standing back up, I flailed my arms once more, demonstrating the attacker's final blows. "If a nutty boyfriend stopped after one strike to the head, I don't see how he'd work up the balls to carefully beat her teeth out."

"Fuck me," one of the officers muttered under their breath.

Maybe I was a little overzealous in my demonstration.

"I agree it seems opportunistic, and not premeditated," I added. "But I think it was calculated, not passionate."

"Certainly worth considering. Surgical precision with a crude instrument," Whittaker said.

11

HORMONE-DRIVEN TEENS

Thursday - 3:00pm

Whittaker had assigned us the east portion of the neighbourhood north of Jackson's Pond. It was an affluent area, with nice homes on larger lots. Most had a view, or at least a peek, of Jackson's Pond, a smaller pond to the north, or the quarry - which looked like the other ponds. Unsurprisingly, knocking on doors in the middle of the afternoon returned mostly non-responses.

Of those who were home, we had several without security cameras, one lady who was too drunk to converse with, although she tried dragging Jacob inside her house, and only one with a camera, but it covered nothing beyond their own property. We had one more house on Elnathan Road to check.

Jacob stayed in the car making notes on the homes we'd already visited, and it was my turn to see who was home. I rang the door-bell of the sprawling single-storey home and waited. The place fronted the smaller pond, had perfectly manicured landscaping and a modern, sterile feel to the design. Many of the wealthy locals chose locations like this, with more room and a social neighbourhood over a small waterfront condo for the same price.

I was about to give the doorbell another try when a voice came over a speaker.

"Can I help you?"

I looked around for a security camera, figuring I was being viewed, but I couldn't see any. The voice sounded like a teenage boy, so I dreaded to think what I'd just interrupted him doing.

"Police," I replied, holding up my badge in case he could see me. "We're checking with homes in the neighbourhood to see if anyone has security footage from Monday night. It may help us with an ongoing investigation."

There was no reply, and I stood there for a few moments, deciding how annoyed I planned to get at this kid. The lock clicked, and the wide front door swung slowly inwards, accompanied by the faint whirr of an electric motor. I stared inside at polished concrete floors leading through an expansive open space to tall windows overlooking a lush garden and the pond. It was sparsely but artfully furnished in a modern, minimalistic style in keeping with the exterior. What I didn't see was the teenager.

"Please come in," the voice said over the speaker.

I glanced at the car, where Jacob looked up from his notes. It felt uncomfortably weird entering the house from an invitation over a speaker, but at least my partner was watching. I took a step inside.

"Where are you?" I asked.

The reply still came from the speaker. "Please walk forward and turn left. You'll see me."

I had visions of a rampant hormone-driven teenager, freshly inspired by a session of online porn, standing naked swinging his dangly bits around. I bet his dirty movie didn't end with the male lead having his privates tasered by the cop in the sexy uniform, but that was in this kid's future if he didn't have any clothes on.

Everything about the situation told me to be cautious, but curiosity moved my feet and pretty soon I was standing in the living room. To my right was a kitchen which looked like a chef's dream come true, and between the kitchen island and the windows, a long glass dining table. In front of me, twin L-shaped couches filled the lounge. A space between them led directly to a double glass door onto the concrete deck.

I turned to my left. Beyond the couches, a long glass desk held three large computer monitors, and behind the desk was a young man. He was seated in a powered wheelchair, and I was pleased to note he was fully clothed.

"Come in," he said, and I heard the front door close behind me. "I'm sorry I didn't come to the door. I was finishing a test."

I walked closer, and with a nudge of a joystick mounted to the arm of his wheelchair, he turned in my direction. His age was hard to determine. He had a thin face, smooth brown skin, buzzed hair, and inquisitive eyes. His body could have been that of an old man's, his limbs bony and weak. He wore grey tracksuit bottoms and a well-worn white T-shirt with a picture of a green alien on it. I think it's called Yoda and comes from the *Star Wars* films.

"I'm Constable Sommer."

"I know." His voice was tinted with a Caymanian accent, but he spoke eloquently.

I remembered my name was on a badge on my shirt. "Do you have security cameras?"

"Duh," he said, and rolled his eyes. "I don't let just anyone in who claims to be with the police. What's up?" His lips slipped into a cheeky grin.

"What's your name?"

"Robbie. Robbie Barker."

"How old are you?"

"Fifteen."

"Who else lives here?"

"My parents."

"Where are they?"

"Dad's at work, Mum's shopping."

I looked out the windows across the pond to the trees on the other side. There were two gaps where I could see creamy white marl.

"What has any of that to do with camera footage?" Robbie asked.

I turned back to him. "Nothing. I was just curious. Do any of your cameras point away from your property?"

"Like across the pond?"

"Yeah, just like across the pond."

He nudged the joystick and squared up to the computer monitors. He used small, quick movements of his fingertips to control the computer and the screen to his left soon showed an array of camera views.

"Come look," he said, and I walked behind him and peered over his head at the screen. "This about the girl?"

"Yup."

"Pretty sad."

"Yup."

"Got any good leads?"

I pointed to the screen. "Camera twelve. How far back do you keep footage?"

"Two weeks on the local hard drive, six months on the cloud," he replied. "You want Monday night?"

"Start at 6:00pm."

The array disappeared, and a single screen took its place. Within seconds, the view from the camera I'd chosen showed up with 18:00:00 in the upper right corner.

"You're pretty handy with the computer."

"What else am I gonna do all day?"

"You do all your school work online?"

"Yup."

"What else do you like?"

"Gaming."

"The shoot-'em-up shit with heads exploding?"

"I used to, but now mostly mystery-solving on the deep net."

"Deep net? I've heard of the dark web."

"Dark net, or web, is the illegal stuff. Deep net is the majority of information on the worldwide web, but you can't find it through search engines."

This kid was sharp. It was one thing having the time to look up all these things, it was another to retain and understand the information. "How do you control the computer so fast?" I asked.

"Eye-tracking software," Robbie replied, as though it was how everyone used their computer.

"*Dritt.* That's pretty cool."

"My mum doesn't like swearing."

"How do you know I was swearing?"

"I looked it up when you said stuff in Norwegian during that crazy kidnapping live stream."

I wished there was an erase button to wipe that whole thing from everyone's memories.

"You were pretty Lara Croft during the whole thing," he said with a chuckle.

"She has bigger boobs," I replied.

"True, but you're still pretty hot."

"Thank you, Robbie, but let's get back to this case," I said, hiding a smile. I couldn't imagine the challenges this kid faced every hour of every day, yet he had this amazing attitude and sense of humour.

"Okay. What now?" he asked.

"Play the footage at ten times normal speed. You watch the gap in the trees on the left, I'll watch the right. Stop the tape if you see anything move behind the trees."

"It's not tape."

"Huh?"

"The security footage isn't on tape. It's a solid-state hard drive."

"Watch the left gap, smartarse."

Robbie chuckled as I pulled a chair over and sat next to him. He hit play on the solid-state hard drive recording.

We sat in silence watching the sun slowly set on the computer screen. Speeded up, the trees' movements in the breeze made them look slightly blurry. Ripples in the pond from birds landing were V-shaped lines zipping over the water. I figured once it was dark, at the distance the camera was from the treeline, we wouldn't be able to make out a thing. But even at 200 metres away, when the camera shifted into night vision mode, I could still see reasonable detail in the high-contrast green-hued picture. Yet nothing passed by the trees.

I wanted to glance up and check the time code, but I was worried I'd miss something. It was tedious work. Each hour still took six minutes, and if a person walked by the trees, they'd flash past like an Olympic sprinter, so I was scared to blink.

My mobile buzzed, and I asked Robbie to pause, glad of the break. Jacob was wondering what was going on. I texted back, 'Your partner's been chopped up and fed to the tarpon.' A little icon indicated he was typing a reply, and I grinned. Six months ago, he would have been running through the front door and calling in the cavalry.

'I bet she's still telling you what to do,' came his reply. Jacob was definitely learning under my guidance. He got a middle finger emoji for his troubles, and I told Robbie to play on.

After another fifteen boring minutes, I thought I saw something, but before I could say a word, the picture stopped. Robbie rewound until we spotted the movement again, then played it forward at normal speed.

"It's a car," he said as we watched a pale-coloured blob move through both gaps.

I checked the time code. It was 02:36:18. I made a note.

"Again, please."

We watched the footage several more times at regular speed, then slowed down. Outside identifying the vehicle as a relatively small saloon car, there was very little we could tell.

"Let's see when it leaves," I said, getting cross-eyed looking at the fuzzy green image.

Robbie set the playback at ten times normal speed again and we both focused on our gap. It didn't take long for the car to reappear.

He stopped, rewound, and found the moment the vehicle came into view, then paused the playback. I noted the time code. It was 03:02:45.

"Miss Sommer, was she murdered?" Robbie asked. His tone was one of concern more than youthful excitement about dramatic news.

I moved my chair around so he could see me. "You can call me Nora, and I'm not allowed to say," I replied, while slowly nodding my head.

His brow creased. "That makes me sad."

"Me too," I agreed.

I heard a garage door going up on its electric opener.

"We can watch the rest," Robbie said.

"Sounds like you have company, so if you make me a copy, I'll have our tech look through it."

"It's just my mum."

I looked at my watch. It was 5:09pm. *"Fy faen!"*

"That's a really bad word."

"Dritt. Sorry. Yeah," I stammered, standing up as the door from the garage opened.

"Robbie? Why's there a police car outside our house?" came a woman's voice.

"No cause for alarm, ma'am," I said, thinking we'd probably scared her to death.

"I wasn't too alarmed," she replied. "Once I saw the policeman fast asleep inside the car."

"I'm helping the police with a case, mum," Robbie blurted. "Nora and I have been reviewing our security cameras."

"Really?" his mother said, looking at me.

"I'm Constable Sommer, Mrs Barker. Robbie has been most helpful. I think we've found some useful footage."

"The cameras in our house?" she asked, her voice rising in concern.

"No, no, beyond the pond," I quickly explained. "You have a

camera pointed across your garden at the water. We could pick out the trail behind the trees."

"I see," she said, her voice calming. "Then don't let me disturb you. I have groceries to bring in from the car."

"Actually, I have to leave now," I said. "I'm going to be late for an appointment." I'd forgotten to cancel the damn date with the doctor, and now I had twenty minutes to show up and disappoint him in person. There was no way we could go out with Whittaker investigating the clinic.

"It won't take much longer to look through the footage that's left," Robbie said, looking at me hopefully.

I thought it over for a few moments. Sod it. Finding the killer was far more important than politely cancelling a date. "Alright. Let's see if there's any more action."

12

KARMIC BALANCE SHEET

Thursday 6:00pm

I scared the crap out of Jacob when I banged on the driver's side window. By the time I'd walked around the car and got in the passenger seat, he'd wiped the drool from his chin and was wide awake.

"What took so long?" he mumbled at me, checking his watch. I caught the look of surprise when he realised our shift officially ended an hour ago.

I held up the memory stick Robbie had given me with all the footage. "We have a car arriving around 2:30 in the morning and leaving 25 minutes later."

"Could you get da registration number?"

"It's a night vision shot from 200 metres away. I'm assuming it's a car, but it could be a spaceship or a white rhinoceros."

Jacob looked at me with a puzzled expression, so I guessed he wasn't as awake as I'd thought.

"It's really blurry."

"Oh," he replied, and pulled away from the house, turning left to take us out of the neighbourhood. "Who lives at da house? I saw a woman come home while you were inside."

I didn't bother to tell him she'd seen him too - snoozing on the job. "A kid in a wheelchair helped me. That was his mum who came home."

"How old is da kid? He was on his own?"

"Fifteen. He seemed fine by himself."

"Why he in da wheelchair?"

"I didn't ask."

"You didn't ask what's up wit da poor guy?" Jacob said. "He must tink you a strange lady, not askin' after him and all."

"Why?"

Jacob fidgeted in his seat the way he did when he became agitated about something. "'Cos dat's da polite ting, right? Show some concern for da boy."

"Can you imagine how much of the day that kid spends thinking and having to talk about being stuck in that chair?"

My partner thought it over for a while. Several times he started to say something but decided not to. After a minute, he finally spoke again. "He look like he in da chair while someting heals? Or, you tink he always gonna be?"

"He didn't appear to have use of his legs or arms, but he could move his fingertips. He controlled his chair and the computer with a joystick. Oh, and he has this really cool system that uses his eye movement like a computer mouse. I think he moves the mouse with his eyes, then clicks with his fingertips. We talked about that."

While Jacob pondered that concept, I looked up the number for the clinic from the internet using my mobile. I called, keeping the phone to my ear, expecting to hear a voicemail greeting.

"West Bay Maternity Clinic, Doctor Kirkconnell speaking."

"Ummm... Hi, this is Constable Sommer," I stammered, taken by surprise. I'd planned on being able to say I'd called but got voicemail. I hadn't intended on leaving a message, or worse still, speaking to the doctor.

"Hey," he said in a relaxed tone. "I'm guessing plans have changed?"

"Yeah, sorry," I bumbled. I really didn't want Jacob, or anyone else for that matter, knowing a date was ever on the cards.

"No, I'm sorry," he said quietly, and I presumed he was hiding his side of the conversation from someone. "I put you in a difficult position."

"Thanks for understanding," I replied. "I need to go."

I hung up and took a deep breath. The guy was frustratingly nice to go along with his good looks. Just my luck, the one man I've had any interest in since Ridley, and he's a witness - or maybe suspect - in a case.

I connected my mobile to the hands-free system and called the detective.

"Whittaker," he promptly answered.

"Sir, we have footage of a car going in and out of the parking area north of Jackson's Pond at 2:30am Tuesday."

"Really? How clear?"

"It's pretty shit."

The line went quiet.

"I mean, it's rather blurry, sir."

"Where are you now?" Whittaker asked.

"Heading to West Bay station, sir."

"Okay, I'll meet you there," he replied. "I'm at the maternity clinic, so I'm only a few minutes away."

"Sir," I mumbled and hung up.

Fy faen. The person Kirkconnell had been shielding our conversation from was none other than my boss. I felt like a kid caught behind the bike shed with a dirty magazine... smoking... with a pocketful of stolen sweets. For a few moments I couldn't breathe, a knot formed in my stomach, and it all felt like the worst possible situation.

Slowly, I began placing the pieces together and calming my nerves. Usually, awkward situations didn't bother me, but this was different. I was on the verge of being back in Whittaker's good graces, so I didn't want to ruin it over something as meaningless as a first date.

The other part was the Ridley factor. I didn't much believe in fate, but I did believe in karma, which scared the shit out of me. I'd done enough bad things in my time to accrue a karmic debt that would be tough to pay back in ten lifetimes.

I didn't know if it was Ridley not ready to let me go, or my monthly karma bill was due, but something was not only stopping this date from happening, but punishing me for even trying.

By the time we reached the station, I'd settled myself down. The detective's expression when he saw me would tell me whether or not we had an issue, and I reminded myself I had done nothing wrong. I'd tried, but hadn't actually committed a rule violation.

Whittaker was waiting for us in the lobby, and I held up the USB stick as we entered.

"Great, let's take a look," he said, and led us straight towards an office in the back. To my relief, he seemed fine.

"That was all," I said, after showing the detective and Jacob the footage. "I've watched until sunrise and there's no other movement."

Whittaker produced a USB stick of his own and inserted it into the computer.

"This is the CCTV footage we requested," he explained, opening a PDF file.

A map of the island appeared on the screen with reference codes next to dots marking the cameras' locations. He jotted down a few of the codes, then found the first video file matching the code. It took a few moments to fast-forward through the recording and find the correct time period.

We were looking at a roundabout on Esterly Tibbetts Highway, which was the first junction to the north of Jackson's Pond and the neighbourhood we'd visited. The camera was mounted on the east side of the roundabout. It caught all the traffic passing through the highway, or taking the only exit west, which was a road leading to Willie Farrington Drive on the south-east side of town.

Whittaker played the footage. The night vision wasn't the same quality as Robbie's, but it had the benefit of street lights along the highway. A pair of headlights approached from the west before slowly turning across the road and disappearing. Briefly, we had a side view of the pale-coloured car, but it was too far from the roundabout lights to make out any detail.

Whittaker fast-forwarded until headlights appeared again, returning to the road and turning away from the camera in the direction the car had arrived from. He froze the footage and zoomed in. It was hopeless. The car was little more than a blur behind two red tail lights. There was no way we could make out the registration plate, never mind the letters and numbers.

"What other cameras do we have?" I asked.

He returned to the map. "If he turned left, we have one at Foster's market and then the crossroads beyond that. If he turned right, we don't have coverage along Willie Farrington. Next is Batabano if he made the next right, or the station here if he went left."

I looked at all the small lanes and driveways between the camera locations. The driver had endless possibilities that expanded exponentially the farther he went. We spent the next fifteen minutes searching through the recordings, to no avail.

"Maybe he lives on Willie Farrington," Jacob suggested.

"Or knows where the cameras are," I pointed out.

"We could canvas da street and see," Jacob added.

"Agreed. We should certainly do that," Whittaker said thoughtfully. "But I also agree that's a long shot."

I studied the map again. The road leading from the roundabout wasn't named and was relatively new. Apart from the old trail leading to the pond, there was only one other place of note. With a quick search on my mobile, I came up with a number and called.

"19 North. How may I help you?" came a perky female voice.

"This is Constable Sommer with the RCIPS. Do you have CCTV at your property?"

There was a brief silence before the woman gathered her thoughts. "Oh, umm, yes, I think we do. I mean, I know we do."

"Do you have access to the recordings?"

"I've no idea. I've never been asked before…"

"Do you have security on site?"

"Umm, no, in fact, I'm not actually on site. I'm with the developer. We monitor this line twelve hours a day while we're still in the selling phase. We have several entry units available at amazing prices for the Seven Mile Beach Corridor."

"I'm investigating a crime, not buying one of your overpriced rabbit hutches. Who handles the security cameras?"

I felt Whittaker nudge my arm, and he raised his eyebrows at me.

"I can call my boss and find out. May I have a number to call you back?"

"Why don't you give me your boss's number and that'll cut out all the bull… it will save time. Ma'am. Thank you." It was a bit late, but I threw in some extra words which people used to sound nice.

She gave me the number and while I was dialling, I sensed the detective's eyes burning into the side of my skull. "I know, be nice," I said, before he could beat me to it.

"Carson Ross," a man answered with an American accent.

"Hello, this is Constable Sommer with the RCIPS. I was hoping you could help me with security camera footage from your property at 19 North?"

Whittaker gave me a thumbs up, so apparently I was being acceptably pleasant.

"May I ask what this is in regard to?"

"It's an ongoing investigation, sir, so I'm afraid I can't share the details, but we're looking for any footage showing the road passing by the property."

"I see. That shouldn't be an issue as it doesn't affect any residents' units," Carson replied. "We have two cameras facing the parking lot and you can see the road. Can you call back in the morning and I'll arrange for the security company to release what you need?"

"Tonight would be better, sir."

"I was just heading out to dinner with my girlfriend," he said, sounding mightily inconvenienced. What a *drittsekk*.

"When we find the dead girl's family, I'll let them know we would have found the killer sooner, but some pin-dick named Carson didn't want to be late for his date."

I'm not sure what he said in reply as Whittaker took the phone from my hands and kissed the guy's arse until he agreed to overlook my 'forwardness' and put us in touch with the security company.

13

A POLITE BOLLOCKING

Thursday 7:00pm

Detective Whittaker sent Jacob home and called the company Pin-dick had given him the name of. He actually called the personal mobile of their office manager, who we'd dealt with during a previous case. We'd worn out our welcome with her back then, so I was surprised when she answered the call. Patti Weaver reluctantly agreed to meet us at the Caribbean Security Systems office in George Town, once she'd verified with Pin-dick that he'd indeed given us permission.

It was dark when we came out of West Bay station, which I hoped hid the look of trepidation on my face. As we left the car park, the lecture began. I knew I had no defence, so the best way to handle the verbal reprimand was to take it on the chin and say nothing except apologies. I made sure not to utter the words 'it won't happen again', because we both knew it would.

"Promise me you'll make an effort to be nicer, Nora," Whittaker said, as he pulled his SUV into the car park at Caribbean Security Systems.

"I promise I'll try harder, sir," I responded.

Pin-dicks would still be pin-dicks, but I felt I could honestly attempt to inform less of them about their condition.

"Thank you," he said, and we got out of his SUV.

One of the many things I respected about the detective was his ability to move on. He wouldn't prod and poke and hint about the issue in the days and weeks ahead. He'd given me a polite bollocking, now he expected me to respond with actions, and he wouldn't bring it up again until the next time I screwed up. Well, the next time he heard, or heard about, me screwing up.

Patti Weaver was already at her desk, and she frowned at us when we entered her office. She spoke with the musical local accent but with perfect diction, similar to the detective, which generally meant they'd been educated overseas, or were used to dealing with English and American customers.

"Mr Ross says I can provide you with security footage from the two cameras facing the road. No others."

"That's all we're interested in, thank you," Whittaker replied in a charming tone.

"Time frame?"

"From 6:00pm Monday until 6:00am Tuesday, please," the detective replied.

"Could we look at a short clip now?" I asked.

Patti sighed and looked at me expectantly.

"Beginning at 2:34am Tuesday morning, ma'am."

She beckoned us behind her desk so we could see her three-monitor array. On the central screen, the footage began to play from the time code I gave her and we watched a grainy view of one of the two entranceways into the condo complex. At 02:34:51, the car passed by on the road.

"Still can't see the reg plate," Whittaker noted.

"Fast-forward until you see the car return, please," I said, knowing there was no other traffic during that time.

Patti did so, then paused and rewound once she saw the blur go by. On its way out, the car was closer to the camera, being on the left-hand side, but the angle stopped us seeing a plate.

"We should be able to get a make and model from the shape," I commented. "It's two-door and I think the colour is white or silver."

"It's an older Honda Civic," Whittaker said confidently. "My wife used to have one many moons ago."

"Do you want to see the other camera view?" Patti asked.

"Yes," I answered, then hurriedly tacked on, "please."

The second camera was mounted farther along the buildings, facing back at an angle towards the two entrances through the decorative knee wall. I was quietly optimistic we'd have better luck. Patti paused as the car entered the frame. Of course, it didn't have a registration plate on the front.

"Move on?" Patti asked.

"Yeah. Let's hope the back plate is on."

It was, but barely readable. Patti zoomed in, but the numbers and letters became more indistinct.

"I think we might have a shot at enhancing that enough to read," Whittaker said. "I'll give it to the tech folks first thing in the morning."

We thanked Patti, whose frosty demeanour had slowly melted as she'd helped us with the footage, and we left with a portable hard drive of video.

"Where's your Jeep?" Whittaker asked as he paused at the road.

"West Bay station," I replied. "I can take the bus."

"No, I'll drop you," he insisted.

I knew it was well out of his way, but I was ready for a shower and something to eat, so I didn't complain. Although it would take a little longer, he drove up West Bay Road, preferring the more scenic route over the bypass. We rode in silence. Whittaker was one of the few people who seemed comfortable not filling every moment with mindless chatter. I'm sure he had just as much to think about as I did.

For once, it was me who spoke first. "Did anything come from your interviews at the clinic?" I asked, realising we hadn't discussed them. He would have brought up the doctor during his earlier scolding if he knew about the date, so I felt bold enough to ask.

He pondered his answer for a moment. "Nothing concrete. They all had glowing things to say about each other, and Kirkconnell vehemently defended Kumari. Told me they'd originally met in the UK and assured me they had accused her of someone else's misconduct. Her only guilt in the affair was not telling the authorities who had stolen the pills."

"Do we keep investigating the clinic?"

"The missing file bothers me," Whittaker replied thoughtfully. "It's too convenient that the one link we have to our victim happens to have gone astray."

"Why would the doctor tell us about the girl if he was hiding the file?" I countered, not because I wanted to defend the man, but because it made little sense to me. "He didn't have to say anything."

"Good point. Perhaps he was worried one of the staff would mention her and make him look like he was hiding something."

"He asked me out," I said, with half a plan of what I was saying.

Whittaker's head turned my way. "He did?"

"*Ja.* I could have coffee or a drink with him if it would help the investigation."

The car was quiet and this time I did feel awkward. I had no idea what was going through the detective's mind.

"I'm not sure that's a good idea at this stage," he finally said. "I'm not sure it's a good idea at any stage, to be honest, but certainly not at the moment."

"Okay," I replied casually.

"If he's guilty of anything, I can't imagine he'd let those details slip over drinks," Whittaker added. "He seems like a smart guy."

"It's surprising what some blokes will reveal when they're trying to impress a woman," I pointed out.

The detective made a noise that was either a scoff or a chuckle, or a mixture of the two. He drummed his fingers on the steering wheel. "I'm sure you're right, Nora. But I can't put you in an uncomfortable situation like that."

I figured he was referring to my time as an escort at the resort, but it wouldn't be anything like that. We'd be out in public and I could choose what happened between us. At the resort, there were expectations the clients had paid a lot of money for.

"It's okay," I said. "I can do it if it helps the case."

I heard Whittaker let out a sigh as he slowed behind a bus pulling to a stop outside Foster's market. "Hopefully it won't be necessary," he said, but I wasn't paying attention any longer.

Stepping from the bus was Puffin Girl. "I'll be just a minute, sir," I mumbled as I shoved the door open and walked briskly towards where the bus was pulling away, leaving several people on the pavement. She was wearing dark leggings and a loose, beige shirt, but I recognised her hair and build.

By the time I reached the dispersing crowd, she was gone. She hadn't come past me, so the only options were the pavement ahead, which I could see, or into the Foster's car park. I jumped through the thin hedge and scoured the area. The market was busy with people shopping after work, so the car park was half filled with vehicles and shopping trolleys being wheeled about.

Had she seen me, or was she always this cautious? I had no idea, but if it was me and I was worried about being followed, I'd cover some distance, then hide to check my tail. I jumped back through the hedge and ran to the middle of the road, hearing a shout from the driver of a car that I must have surprised. Another car, heading south, stopped when they saw the uniform and let me cross the rest of the way. I waved a thank you.

Moving quickly north down the dusty verge, I ran until I was level with the far exit from Foster's, then stopped and studied the car park. Me relocating almost certainly meant she needed to move as well to keep me in view. I still couldn't see her, so I ran back across the road, then slowed to a jog going south, looking up and down each row of cars.

Three rows in, a movement caught my eye, and I watched as Puffin Girl appeared from behind a small van, swiftly crossed the road, and disappeared down a driveway. I could have given chase, but I knew it would be fruitless. She was familiar with every path, road, and trail in West Bay. I stood with my hands on my hips and smiled. I was becoming obsessed with the kid. Something about her captivated me. Perhaps she reminded me of myself when I was a runaway, or maybe I just found her cool. But I knew too well the life she was living, and there was nothing cool about that. I was determined to make it better for her.

A honk of a car horn caught my attention, and I turned to see Whittaker behind the wheel of his SUV. I jogged over and got in.

"What was that about?" he asked, driving towards the car park exit.

"That girl, I'm pretty sure she's homeless," I replied, contemplating how much information I was prepared to share.

"Then report her to the Department of Children and Family Services. That's what they do, Nora."

"They won't catch her. She's too smart," I replied.

He laughed. "For you too, apparently."

I grinned. "This time, but I have a plan."

"Hopefully, your plan involves contacting the Department of Children and Family Services," he reiterated.

"My plan involves riding the bus," I responded, pleased that the bus idea AJ and I had come up with had merit. "Let me speak with her first, then I'll get child services involved."

I took Whittaker's silence as acceptance of my plan.

14

———

ONE GOOD TURN

Friday 6:30am

The coral reef had a different feel first thing in the morning. As the sun rose, the creatures of the night crawled or swam back into their hiding places, and the colourful daytime residents resumed their roles. I dived to 10 metres and gently kicked along a coral finger. Low in the sky, the bright, early light cast long shadows from the sea fans and tube sponges in stark contrast to the yellows and greens of the surrounding reef.

I finned to the sand, where a natural tunnel ran through the coral finger. Switching on the small underwater torch I'd brought with me, I carefully ran the beam inside the opening, trying not to alarm the inhabitants. To my left, backed into the crevices, several lobsters probed the water with their antennae. I reached beyond the first ridge of old limestone and felt around with my bare hand. When my fingers touched something smooth, I left the object in place, and retreated, gliding to the surface for another breath.

My friend Archie Winters had left the urn with me for safe keeping. In theory, it contained his late wife's ashes, but in reality, he'd packed it with diamonds and lead weights to keep it on the bottom of the ocean. He'd be back one day to collect his nest egg. At least, I hoped he would. I thought of him at some point every day. It was hard not to, living in the shack he'd given me. But I enjoyed thinking about him. It brought a warm feeling, and although we hadn't known each other long, I felt a deep bond and connection with Archie.

Swimming to shore, my thoughts switched to Puffin Girl. Was she really Elizabeth Ebanks or Jasmine Holder? The idea of solving a cold case was intriguing, but more importantly, if she was one of the two missing girls, it meant at least one of them was alive. Otherwise, the odds of either child still breathing after such a long time were thin at best.

I stripped out of my bathing suit and washed the salt away under the outdoor shower around the side of the shack. A blue iguana watched me from his perch on a nearby rock, where he basked in the morning sun. It was rare to see the endemic blue, almost driven to extinction in recent years. We stared at each other for several minutes before I remembered I needed to get ready for work. Hoping the sighting was a good omen for the day ahead, I towelled off and went inside.

Edvard. That's the name I decided to give my new blue iguana friend, as I poured coffee into my travel mug. Edvard Munch was the Norwegian painter famous for his work called *The Scream*. He was a recluse, which seemed fitting for the blue. Maybe by naming him I'd get lucky, and he'd hang around the shack.

With coffee in hand and my rucksack thrown over my shoulder, I locked the front door and set a pebble in the door jamb as I did every day. It was my crude security system to let me know if anyone had been inside while I was gone. Edvard was still on his rock and I moved past him slowly, hoping not to scare him away.

Using a towel I left in the Jeep, I wiped the driver's seat clean and climbed into my CJ-7. It started on the first try, as it always did since Ridley had rebuilt everything. His last project would have been the cosmetics, but I liked the faded blue paint. A soft top would save me from getting wet occasionally, but it hadn't bothered me enough to do anything about it yet.

While the six-cylinder engine warmed up, I made a call on my mobile.

"Hey, sis," Hallie Bodden said in way of a greeting.

We joked we were sisters, which was pretty funny when anyone saw the petite brown-skinned island girl next to a tall, pale, blonde Norwegian.

"What are you doing this evening around 5:30?" I asked. She knew me well enough not to expect a preamble.

"No plans. I should be done wit my studies by den. What's up?"

"I need your help with something. I'll come by and pick you up."

"'Kay."

We hung up, I dropped my mobile on the passenger seat, and pulled out onto Conch Point Road. I felt okay about the day. A year ago, I didn't care if I lived through each day, so feeling 'okay' was a vast improvement. Having things to look forward to made a big difference. I was excited at the prospect of helping Puffin Girl, and optimistic about the lead we'd generated from the security footage regarding our murder victim.

As I was pulling into West Bay station, my mobile rang. It was Whittaker. I parked and answered the call. "Sir?"

"Good morning. I had our tech come in early. She pulled a partial registration from the video and we've matched it to a 2002 Honda Civic. The plates haven't been renewed in five years, but the last owner on record is Rashid Bakewell. Williams is signing out a firearm and will meet you and Tibbetts at West Bay station. Please accompany him to the address he has and pick this young fellow up for questioning."

"I'm at the station now, so I'll brief Jacob and find Williams, sir."

"Bakewell has a record, mainly drugs, nothing violent so far, but tread carefully," Whittaker said, before saying goodbye and hanging up.

It was 7:45am and Jacob wouldn't be here for a few more minutes, so I went inside and found Williams. He was an experienced policeman with firearms clearance and tactical training. He'd been tough on me when I'd joined, but had accepted me after a few difficult cases.

"What's up, beanpole?" he said, giving me his cheeky grin. "I hear I get you and Tibbetts for back-up."

"Someone has to make sure you don't screw up," I countered. "Sir."

Williams laughed. He was a stocky, muscular man with buzzed hair. He looked every part the former military trained soldier that he was. The Islands had formed a Cayman Islands Regiment in 2020, officially a battalion under the British Armed Forces, but Williams had previously served four years in the UK. He now helped train the Cayman regiment in his spare time.

"Mornin'," Jacob greeted us as he walked into the lobby. "Someting going on dis morning?" he asked, seeing Williams holding a holstered firearm.

"We have a suspect in the murder case to bring in," I quickly replied. "Sergeant Williams is tagging along to see how it's done."

Jacob shook his head at my blatant disregard of rank, but Williams just laughed again.

"Rashid Bakewell," the sergeant read from a sheet of paper. "House on Dill Lane."

"Dill Lane?" I questioned. "Isn't that where we picked up…"

"Minnow," Jacob said, finishing my thought. "That's his real name."

"You know dis guy?" Williams asked.

I groaned.

"We just nicked him for possession da udder day," Jacob said, giving me a stern look.

I couldn't believe it. It was my fault Jacob went easy on the guy and now we find out he could be the murderer in our case. Still, I couldn't picture that skinny youth clubbing a woman to death, then smashing her face to pieces. But maybe my judgement was flawed now I knew I'd been lenient on a guy that didn't deserve it.

"*Fy faen,*" I mumbled to myself. "He was sitting in the back of our car when we were called to the scene Tuesday morning."

"Where did you pick him up?" Williams asked.

"At da house," Jacob replied while I continued silently scolding myself.

"Did he resist?" Williams inquired.

Jacob snickered. "He tried runnin' but Nora helped da man fall over."

I walked over to the counter. "Hey Clara, got something that seats three of us plus a suspect?" I asked the clerk.

She handed me the keys to one of the SUVs, "Here you go, hon, dis one got plenty of room, but one of you gotta sit in da cage."

"Great," I replied, taking the keys and stomping towards the door.

"Looks like we're leaving, Sarge," Jacob chuckled.

I heard Williams laughing as they both trailed me to the patrol vehicle.

I pulled over to the side on Reverend Blackman Road, just short of Dill Lane, and turned to Jacob. "Wait here. I'll text when we're ready to move in. You'll cover the front."

My partner looked at me, then glanced at our superior officer in the back seat.

Williams shrugged his shoulders. "You know da perp, I'll say if I don't like da plan."

Jacob got out and Williams moved up front. I turned the SUV around, drove back to Birch Tree Hill Road, and turned left.

"This is his patch," I said as we passed by Kellys Bar and Undra's Take Out. The bar was closed this early in the day, but the food shack was open for breakfast. I didn't see Minnow anywhere.

I turned left at the junction where Birch Tree Hill met Stadium, then left again into the marl driveway to the cricket oval.

"Last time, he bolted out the back door," I explained as we trundled down the rough trail. "He'll try something different today. His only options are towards the main road, or this way to the cricket grounds."

We were circling the outside of the oval and I stopped before we reached the turn onto the trail which joined the end of Dill Lane.

"My guess is he'll come out the front and run this way, except he won't want to stay in the open. He'll pick a path through the woods," I said, pointing to the dense stand of trees to our left.

"Okay," Williams responded with a nod. "Text me when we're a go and I'll move around the corner where I can see."

I got out of the SUV and jogged past the turn to Dill, continuing in an arc around the back of the Bakewell property. I stayed behind the cover of some shrubs and texted Jacob and Williams. After hitting send, I jogged to the back door and knocked. Inside, I heard a woman's voice muttering something, and a moment later the door opened.

"What you doing back here?" Mrs Bakewell said, recognising me. "I got a perfectly good door round front for visitors."

"Is Minnow home?" I asked, trying to see past her.

"He ain't," she replied. "What he gone done now?"

"May I come inside?"

"Doubt I'd be stoppin' you if I did mind," she said and stepped out of the way. "I was just boilin' da kettle for some tea. Want one? I have coffee too."

I looked through the door to the living room and didn't see or hear anyone else in the house. "Coffee, please," I responded, and sat at the kitchen table. "Do you know where he is, Mrs Bakewell?"

She shook her head as she poured boiling water into two mugs. "I sure don't. I try my best keepin' up wit dat boy, but he bin a handful since he were small. His brudda do okay in school, but not Minnow."

I wondered if that had anything to do with him being nicknamed after a fish whose sole role in life was being eaten by bigger fish. Hardly a self-esteem builder. But I believed his mother was trying her best. The inside of their home was clean and tidy, despite the awful appearance of the back garden. I assumed there wasn't a Mr Bakewell around to handle the outdoor chores.

"You wit dat fella out dere?" she said, looking through the side window at the street.

"Oh shit," I blurted, and texted the other two.

15

BEAUTY AND THE BEAST

Friday 9:00am

Mrs Bakewell insisted on making coffee for Jacob and Williams, brought out a biscuit tin, and would have kept us there all morning if she didn't have to leave for work. We wanted to know where to find her son, and she was more interested in asking me about Norway and living where it snowed. I felt bad for her. She seemed like a lovely woman, and we were going to be arresting her son on suspicion of a brutal murder. But we didn't tell her that.

"You can't think of anywhere Minnow may have stayed last night?" I asked one last time from the doorstep.

"Guess I should know better what he up to, but he don't tell me much," she replied. "I tink he have a girlfriend, but he won't say."

"What's your udder son's name, ma'am?" Jacob asked.

"Trey. Why you ask?"

"Maybe he knows where Minnow bin getting to," Jacob replied with a smile.

Mrs Bakewell frowned. "S'pose he might, but he at school."

"We appreciate your time, ma'am," Jacob said. "Give us a call if Minnow shows up." She nodded and closed the door.

"Tink she'd call?" Williams asked when we were back in the SUV.

"Maybe," I replied. "After she beats the truth out of him with her broom."

I drove past the house and down Dill Lane to Reverend Blackman Road. Turning left, I began winding my way across to the bypass. This was one of the situations when I couldn't take the extra time on the coast road.

"Does he have a mobile?" Williams asked.

"She swore if he had one, she didn't know the number. Claimed she'd taken him off her plan when he ran up a bunch of charges," I replied, having asked her before they'd come inside the house.

"He have one," Jacob added. "He had it wit him when I charged him."

"Okay, so what now?" Williams asked.

My partner looked at me from the passenger seat, and I gave him a nod.

Jacob turned to Williams. "We're goin' to school."

John Gray High School was on the south side of George Town and served as the only public high school on the west side of the island. All the kids from West Bay bussed down each morning and returned the same way. We parked and walked inside the large main building to the front office. A slender, dark-skinned lady in her sixties greeted us with a frown over her spectacles riding on the end of her nose.

"How can I help you?"

"We'd like to speak with Trey Bakewell," I said, showing her my badge.

"Trey Bakewell?" she said, sounding surprised.

"Yes, ma'am. Is he here?"

"I'm sure he is," she replied, rising from her seat. "Let me page him for you."

The woman used a telephone to page the lad, and we heard her voice echo around the building from various speakers.

"What do you need with Trey?" she asked after hanging up. "Used to be we'd have uniforms come by when his brother attended…" she paused and wrinkled her nose. "Or didn't attend would be more accurate. But Trey never causes any trouble."

"He's not in trouble, ma'am," Jacob reassured her. "We're hoping he can help us with an inquiry."

A teenager appeared from a hallway with a worried look on his face. He wore the school uniform of dark blue trousers and a white, short-sleeved, buttoned shirt. His hair was neatly cropped and glasses perched on his nose. If anyone saw Trey and Minnow next to each other, they'd never believe they were related.

"Trey, the police have some questions for you," the lady said, and the boy stared at us with his mouth slightly open.

"No one has been hurt," I said, and his face immediately relaxed. "I'm Constable Sommer, and this is Tibbetts and Williams. Let's step outside for a moment," I continued, and he followed us out of the front door, much to the lady's dismay.

"Trey, we need to talk to your brother," I asked. "Do you know where he is?"

"What he done now?" the boy asked.

"We believe he can help us with our inquiries," I replied, giving nothing away.

Trey shrugged his shoulders. "He's not at home?"

"No. We just left your mother. She doesn't know where he is."

The teenager nervously nudged a stone with the toe of his trainer and looked at the ground. "I dunno. He didn't come home last night."

"Is that unusual?" I asked.

"How d'you mean?" he responded, looking up at me.

"Is he normally home every night?"

Another shoulder shrug. "He comes and goes."

"Where does he stay when he's not home, Trey?"

He went back to kicking at stones and looking down. "Dunno."

I felt bad for the kid in the same way I had sympathy for his mother, but I was starting to lose the little patience I had.

"Look, we're going to find him, and the faster we do, the faster he can clear himself from our investigation. So tell us where he is."

"He's my brudda," he groaned.

"Then help us find him."

"He screws up all da time, but it's just petty stuff."

"Trey, what we're investigating isn't petty bullshit. We need to talk to him."

He looked up again and met my gaze. His eyes were full of despair.

"Does he have a girlfriend he stays with?"

Trey sighed and finally nodded.

"Who and where?"

"I don't know her real name. She goes by Belle," he said quietly.

"Bell? Like in a church?" I asked.

Trey scoffed. "Don't think she know where to find no church. Belle, you know, like Disney."

Jacob nudged me and nodded, so I assumed he knew what the kid was talking about.

"Where does Bell live?" I asked.

"Red house on Town Hall Road. She live in da garage. I tink her papa live in da house."

"Does she work, or go to school?" I asked, and Trey looked at me as though I was mad. "Okay. Thanks, Trey," I said and handed him a business card.

"Do you have a mobile?" Jacob asked.

Trey nodded.

"Got Minnow's number?"

He shook his head. "He got one of dem prepaid tings. Changes all da time."

"Call us if you hear from your brother. It'll be much better for him if we talk to him," I said.

Trey didn't look convinced, and we watched him head back inside the building.

"Tink he'd call us?" Williams asked.

"No chance," I replied as we walked to the SUV. Trey seemed like the smart kid his mother claimed, but he was worried about his older brother. If Minnow told him not to, he wouldn't contact the police.

I pointed the SUV north once more and began the drive back to West Bay.

"A red house on Town Hall Road..." I said, looking at Jacob. "You know it?"

"No, but we'll find it. Can't be too many painted red."

"Why does she call herself Bell?" I asked, still picturing a noisy brass implement hanging in a church belfry.

"Didn't you watch da Disney movies when you were a kid?" Jacob asked.

"I've never really watched TV or movies."

"Belle is the woman in *Beauty and the Beast,*" Jacob explained enthusiastically. "You haven't heard of her?"

I shook my head. "I know Mickey Mouse and Donald Duck."

Jacob jumped around in the passenger seat, fumbling with his mobile, presumably searching for pictures of Disney characters I didn't give a shit about.

"You two are like a brudda and sista goin' back and forth," Williams complained from the back.

I glanced in the rear view and caught his eye. "I said you'd learn a thing or two with us."

Jacob was right, there were only two houses along Town Hall Road painted red. The street was less than a kilometre long, so it wasn't surprising. One was red with a second building in turquoise. It looked like a business. The second one was set back behind trees with an unkept front garden and a detached single-car garage off to the side. Beyond the garage, I could see a small silver car.

"How do you want to play this one?" Williams asked.

"We'll knock on the side door and see who's home," I replied. "You hang back in case the garage door opens."

We walked through the opening in the waist-high wire fence at the front of the property, and up the crushed limestone driveway, overgrown with weeds. I didn't see any signs of life in the main house, which was a small concrete block single-storey dwelling. The garage had one window on the side and then a wooden door. It was too bright outside to see anything through the window, so I moved quickly to the door and knocked loudly.

"Police, open up."

I took a step back to join Jacob and checked Williams's position to our left. He had stayed out of view of the window and covered the front. I could see the car clearly behind the building, parked at an odd angle in the long grass. The Honda had seen better days. It looked like more money had been spent on a stupid rear spoiler and noisy exhaust than basic maintenance.

I heard movement inside, but no one answered the door. I banged again. "Police."

The movement became more animated, and I heard a door or window creak open.

"Go around the back," I told Jacob, and pulled the Taser from my belt.

A thud and rustling came from behind the garage, and then Jacob yelled, "Stop dere!"

After a few thumps and some more rustling, Williams calmly called out. "I got him."

I was about to join him around front, when the door burst open and someone came charging out, screaming. I quickly dodged out of the way, and what I could now see was a young female lunged past me. She turned and glared, wide eyed and panting.

Probably the same age as Minnow, the woman was scrawny like her boyfriend, had hair of all kinds of colours in clumps of little ponytails all over her head, a ring through her lower lip, and a stud through the bridge of her nose. Her light brown skin was adorned with tattoos, but not the colourful pieces of art like AJ's. These looked more like she'd asked a five-year-old to scribble all over her arms, chest, and throat.

"Fucker!" she yelled, and charged me again. Not her smartest move.

I released the cartridge from the Taser, as I was sure I wouldn't need to zap her again. She was writhing around in the dirt, twitching and jolting, which made it harder to read the crap she had permanently scribed on her body. 'Fuck authority' was one I was able to make out.

"What did you do to her?" Williams asked as he walked up with Minnow in handcuffs.

"Yeah, man, what da hell you do?" Minnow asked.

I gave up trying to decipher the graffiti all over Belle, and looked up at Jacob, who'd arrived from the back. "She doesn't look like any Disney character I remember."

16

____

MINTY FRESH BREATH

Friday 11:00am

I sat across the table from Minnow in the interview room. He was slumped in the chair as though he was imminently going to melt and slide to the floor. Despite their prior failure to aid his escape, he still wore his trousers halfway down his bum. They appeared to have boxer shorts sewn in, which was how they remained somewhat in their intended place.

I'd always wondered which came first. Did rappers decide to dress like gang members, or was it the other way around? Maybe it had something to do with early rappers *being* gang members. Either way, it was a shame so many innocent kids chose to make themselves look like criminals. I wouldn't want to be a cop in a big American city. How do they know who's about to shoot them, and who's on their way to a movie?

Whittaker came in the room and explained to Minnow that our interview would be recorded, and he had the right to counsel if he so chose. Minnow shook his head.

"For the record, Mr Bakewell has declined to have counsel present," Whittaker said, which made Minnow squirm in his seat.

"What dis all about?" he mumbled. "You already stitched me up on da drug charge."

I took a deep breath, resisting the temptation to lunge over the table and smack him up the side of his dumb-arse head. I was so mad at myself for giving him a break. Fortunately, I restrained myself, figuring the detective would consider that fell under the category of being rude to civilians.

"Where were you on Monday night?" Whittaker asked.

"What?" Minnow responded, his entire face contorted into a look of distaste.

"It's a simple question, Mr Bakewell. Where were you Monday night?"

"Why you wanna know dat?"

Whittaker sighed. "Perhaps you're unclear on how this works. I ask you a question, and you answer my question with an honest response."

"Unless you're guilty," I added. "Then you'll refuse to answer and avoid the questions."

Minnow chewed that over for a few moments. "I ain't guilty o' nuttin'"

"Actually, you're certainly guilty of possession," Whittaker pointed out, "as we established earlier this week, and I'm betting our team is finding more interesting items in your girlfriend's place as we speak. Where were you on Monday night?"

Minnow shrugged his shoulders. "I don't know."

"I see," Whittaker said and turned to me. "Constable Sommer, would you mind requesting a psych evaluation for Mr Bakewell? Apparently, he's unaware of his actions and surroundings."

"I ain't crazy!"

"Then you should be able to recall where you were a few days ago."

Minnow crossed his arms, and I was worried he'd snap a spindly rib or two if he squeezed any tighter.

"You weren't at home," Whittaker pressed on. "You and your car are on CCTV from the early hours of Tuesday morning. Does that jog your memory?"

The young man couldn't hide his surprise. His expression betrayed his shock and realisation we were asking questions to which we already knew the answers.

"Hanging by Kellys. Den I may have taken a ride wit da girl."

"Where to?"

Minnow shrugged his shoulders again. "Just around."

"In your car with expired registration," I pointed out.

Whittaker leaned back and looked at me. "I'd say that's the least of his problems."

"True," I played along.

"I just drove around some, clear my head."

"Did you happen to stop anywhere in particular?" Whittaker asked with a slight smirk on his face to let Minnow know the truth was already known.

"I maybe parked up some by Jackson's Pond."

"Did you take a walk while you were there?" Whittaker asked casually.

"No."

"And your girlfriend can corroborate that?"

Minnow looked up, and his eyes narrowed. "You askin' if she say da same ting?"

"I am," Whittaker confirmed.

"Why don't you ask dat den?"

The detective turned to me. "Constable Sommer, would you please begin interviewing Miss Corbin. Let's see what she has to say about Monday night."

Before I could rise from my seat, Minnow waved a hand at me. "She don't know shit."

"You said she was with you," I pointed out.

"She weren't wit me, exactly."

"Where, exactly, was she?"

"Dat's da reason I driving," Minnow admitted, looking crestfallen. "I out lookin' for dat bitch."

"So, let me get this straight," Whittaker responded, tapping the table with his finger. "You were alone by Jackson's Pond at 2:36 in the morning for 26 minutes." Before the kid could stammer out a word, Whittaker pressed on. "What were you doing for 26 minutes, Mr Bakewell?"

"I didn't say nuttin' about how long I dere, you makin' dat shit up, man."

"We have you on CCTV. What were you doing for nearly half an hour?"

Minnow was speechless. His brain couldn't process all the pieces of the puzzle fast enough. We were throwing facts at him and he was trying his best to dovetail them with the lies he was spinning.

Whittaker pulled a copy of the artist's rendition of the victim from a folder and slid it across the table. "Do you know this woman?"

Minnow gave the picture a cursory glance, then shook his head.

"That's odd. She was at Jackson's Pond the same time you were on Monday night."

"Weren't no one else dere," he replied, giving the picture a better look. "Wait! Dat da bitch bin on da news? No way, man!" he yelled, jumping to his feet. "You ain't pinnin' dat shit on me."

"Sit down, Mr Bakewell," Whittaker barked, and I stood with one hand ready on my Taser. I wouldn't need much of an excuse to zap this *drittsekk*.

Minnow took one look at me and sat back down, shaking his head. "Dis is bullshit, man."

"Let me recap a few facts for you," Whittaker continued. "By your own admission, supported by CCTV, you were alone at Jackson's Pond for 26 minutes during the same time this young lady was murdered." He tapped the picture, pushing it closer to Minnow. "We'll be taking a blood and DNA sample from you, which will undoubtedly place you at the murder scene. Our SOCO has your Honda Civic in our lab right now. Have you any idea how thorough they are?"

"I didn't give you no permission to take my wheels, man."

"We had a warrant to search Miss Corbin's property, your mother's house, and your car."

"You told my mudda I'm busted again? Shit, man, she gonna freak."

"How about you start being honest with us, Mr Bakewell?"

Minnow slumped forward with his head in his hands. After a few moments and several grunts, he looked up. "Me and Belle had a bust-up, right? Someone told me she took off wit a dude. When she don't come back, I went out lookin'."

"An argument about what?" Whittaker asked.

Minnow waved him off. "Some shit, man. I don't remember. So I drive around, but I don't find her. Thought she might be dere by da pond, you know, gettin' it on wit dat piece of shit."

"Were they there?"

"Nah, man. But if you got dat CCTV, you already know dat, right?"

"Continue," Whittaker urged. "What did you do when you arrived at the pond and they weren't there?"

"I lit up, man," Minnow said, as though it was the standard course of action in such situations.

"For 26 minutes?"

He shrugged his shoulders and grinned, revealing a mouthful of poor dentistry. "If dat's how long you say I dere. Hell if I know. I got some prime weed, man."

Whittaker sat back and let out a long breath.

"So where was Belle all this time?" I asked. They'd apparently patched things up as we found him at her place.

"She home when I got dere."

"And the guy she left with?"

Minnow shrugged his shoulders. "Dunno, but she lifted sixty bucks off da fool."

I laughed, and both men looked at me.

"She goes missing for hours with a strange bloke and shows up with an extra sixty bucks?" I scoffed. "I bet she told you she stole it."

"What da fuck you sayin'?"

"I'm saying I hoped she cleaned her teeth before you two made up."

Minnow stared at me with his mouth hanging open. I could only imagine how the slow-turning gears were grinding their way to the realisation he may have been lied to. Whittaker subtly held up a hand behind the table so only I could see his gesture. I was done for the moment anyway, so I didn't mind.

"Let's take a break for a few minutes so Mr Bakewell can gather his thoughts," Whittaker said, and rose from his chair.

I followed him out of the room and prepared myself to make an apology I didn't mean if he scolded me again. But he didn't. He closed the door to the interview room and laughed quietly to himself, trying to hide his amusement from me. I pretended not to notice.

"I think we should have a word with the girlfriend," Whittaker said once he'd composed himself.

Belle, whose real name was Annalyn Corbin, had not improved her disposition from the first time we'd met. She'd been handcuffed to the interview room table after scratching one constable and biting another. When we sat down, she bashed her hands on the desk, rattling her restraints and snarling at us. I couldn't tell if the rage was her natural temperament, drug induced, or she'd been bitten by a rabid agouti.

Whittaker waited until she settled down. "I'd like to ask you some questions about Monday night."

"I'd like to wrap dese chains around dat bitch's throat," she spat, glaring at me. I gave her a wink.

Whittaker patiently waited while Belle wore herself out screaming obscenities and yanking on her restraints. I noticed her accent wasn't local. Jamaican was my best guess, and when I finally deciphered one of her tattoos to read 'Kingston Girl', I decided I was right.

Whittaker tried again. "Where were you Monday evening, Miss Corbin?"

She stared beyond us at the wall and said nothing.

"Where did the sixty dollars come from?" I asked.

That got her attention. "What dat son-of-a-bitch sayin'? I earn dat money. He didn't complain none at da time."

"Let's put the prostitution issue aside for the moment…" Whittaker began, but she cut him off.

"Prostitution! I ain't no whore! He appreciate my time and gimme dat cash."

"By definition…" Whittaker began, but stopped himself. "Putting that aside for the moment. Where did you and this man go Monday evening?"

"Just drive around."

"Did you stop anywhere?"

Belle curled her lip. "I dunno. We was partyin', right?"

"When did you get home?"

She shook her head. "I dunno, man. Maybe two. Maybe three."

"Did you go by Jackson's Pond at any time?"

I watched her body tense. The detective must have noticed too, as he quickly continued.

"What time were you there?"

"I didn't say we were," she responded, but there was no conviction in her voice.

"You were on the quarry side," I said, following a hunch.

She tensed again. I knew I hadn't seen another vehicle on the CCTV, so they had to be at another spot. The trail around the quarry could be accessed from the West Bay Road through the housing estate. I was guessing they were there.

"Did you know Minnow was parked a few hundred metres away?"

"I dere before he were," Belle snapped back. "I never see him."

So much for having no idea of the time.

"Did you see anyone else?" Whittaker asked.

"Nah. But I was busy, ya know?"

"Did you get out of the car at any time?"

"Nah," Belle replied, "I made da man smile, den I took a nap."

"And what did your friend do?"

"He ain't no friend," she snapped back. "And I don't know. I just said I was sleepin'."

"For how long?"

She shrugged her shoulders. "Shit, how I s'posed to know? Ten, maybe twenty minutes."

"What did you do when you woke up?"

"We left and he drop me home."

"So you arrived by the quarry at some time around 2:00am, had sexual relations, both fell asleep for a while, then left," Whittaker summarised.

Belle nodded, then shrugged her shoulders. "Don't know what he did."

Whittaker and I glanced at each other.

"You don't know what he did when?"

"When I sleepin'. He woke my arse up when he gets back in da car."

"So this fella could have been gone the whole time you were sleeping?"

"S'pose."

"What's this guy's name?" Whittaker asked.

Belle's head whipped up and glared at the detective. "You say he complainin' about da money. Now you say you don't know who he is?"

"I never said he complained about anything," Whittaker corrected. "We just asked where the money had come from. Who is he?"

Belle tried to throw her arms in the air, but of course they were tethered to the desk. She winced as the cuffs bit into her wrists. "I don't know his name. Some old white guy. He was hanging around

Kellys. Minnow started givin' me shit and dis dude offered me cash for hangin' out wit him."

"He didn't say his name?" Whittaker asked.

"He said, but I didn't care. Jerome, or someting like dat."

"Jeremy?" Whittaker and I said together.

"Yeah, dat's it."

17

FALLING BETWEEN THE CRACKS

Friday 12:30pm

Detective Whittaker absent-mindedly stirred his coffee while he looked out of the break room window. I sat at the table and ate a sandwich Jacob had brought me from Foster's supermarket.

"I can't believe Andrews could be involved," Whittaker said quietly.

I finished chewing a mouthful of grilled mahi-mahi. "Takes some balls to be the one reporting the body of the woman you just beat to death."

The detective turned and finally stopped stirring. "Her story puts him near the scene around the time of the murder, but otherwise, it doesn't make any sense."

"If he planned the murder, why would he take someone along with him?" I said, picking up his train of thought. "If he didn't plan it, why would he walk away from a perfectly murderable woman to kill a stranger?" I was about to take another bite, but stopped. "Plus, where's the baby?"

Whittaker shook his head. "I don't know, but our witness's

statement places him at the scene with time to commit the crime, so we must proceed."

"She could be lying," I pointed out.

"And confess to having sex for money with the man?"

"Disney Girl seems a little confused over the law when it comes to that."

But he was right, it didn't add up. "What if our victim stumbled across Belle giving Andrews a good time, and he went after her to make sure she didn't tell?"

Whittaker sipped his coffee and thought for a moment. "Wouldn't Belle have seen her too?"

I looked at my boss with a slight grin.

"Right, she was busy at the time," he said, catching my hint. "Well, I'll contact Jeremy and ask him to come by the station," he continued with a sigh. "But let's keep our two lovebirds in custody for now. By their own admission, they were both in the vicinity around the time of the murder. They're still suspects."

In my mind, Belle was more likely a killer over Minnow. He was all show and no go, but she had a mean streak. Maybe she was using Andrews as cover.

"If only we knew who the victim was, maybe we could tie her to one of them," I thought out loud.

"Beyond the clinic and the caller who hung up, we're no closer to finding her identity," Whittaker said as he looked up Andrews's number on his mobile. "It's amazing that no one has come forward saying they recognise her. She must have arrived here recently."

"Immigration couldn't find any matching record," I reminded him.

"Recently, and illegally," he countered.

"Or, she's from one of the poorer neighbourhoods. Many don't have TVs."

A thought occurred to me and I jumped up, startling Whittaker, who was waiting for Andrews to answer the phone. "Schools!"

The detective's brow furrowed.

"We need to show the picture around all the schools," I

explained. "I bet she attended a school at some point in her life. A teacher might recognise her."

"Hello, Jeremy," Whittaker said into his mobile. "I was wondering if you have a few minutes to drop by West Bay station? I had a few loose ends you might be able to help me with." He covered his mobile with his hand while he listened to the response, and whispered to me. "Good idea. You and Jacobs start on West Bay schools. Email the picture to the others. Include Little and The Brac."

I asked Clara, the constable at the front desk, to contact the other schools. She pretended to be mad I'd assigned her work, but secretly she enjoyed having something important to do. As we left the station, she was already calling schools and telling them to check their email and get back to her as soon as possible.

Jacob and I went by Sir John A. Cumber Primary School, which is located near Hell. *Where did you go to school? In Hell!* It made me chuckle inside every time I thought about it. We showed the artist's sketch to the office staff, but no one recognised her. It was a stretch to think that anyone would recall her from primary school. We had a better chance with high schools.

Whittaker texted me and told me Jeremy Andrews was coming by at 3:00pm, so we asked the staff to show all the teachers the picture, and left. The school was also a short distance from the maternity clinic, and I wondered if the doctor was there. Having made the leap and agreed to a date, which I subsequently skipped, I now felt torn about the whole situation. The man had the kindest eyes, and I couldn't picture him bludgeoning a woman to death, but the missing file was too convenient.

I stopped by the One Stop Mini Market and bought a coffee-flavoured energy drink. This one was salted caramel. My ulterior motive was the hope I'd spot Puffin Girl again, but she was nowhere to be seen.

When we arrived back at the station, Andrews was already in the reception area, and I nodded a greeting. He was dressed similarly to the first time we'd met, looking like a man who cared about presenting a smart but casual appearance. I was disappointed Luca wasn't with him.

He smiled at Jacob and me. "Constables."

Whittaker opened the door, and I was glad I wasn't stuck trying to figure out what to say to the man.

"Hello Jeremy, thanks for coming in. Step this way, please."

Andrews followed Whittaker's direction, and I was about to follow when Clara called me.

"Hey dere, Miss Skinny-Britches."

I let the door swing closed behind the two men and walked over to the desk. Clara grinned at me.

"I gotcha someting on dat dead girl."

Clara wanted me to beg for the info like a dog at the dinner table. I stared at her, and she stared back at me.

"What have you come up wit, Miss Clara?" Jacob intervened. "I knew you'd find someting useful."

She looked away from me and beamed at Jacob. "Dat's right, Tibbetts, I should be detective by now, don't you know it?"

"Dat's da truth," Jacob bantered.

"She from da Brac, it seem," Clara finally revealed. "Dey recognise her from Layman E. Scott High School. Said she look like dis girl who attended for a few years den stopped, never came back to school."

"How old would she be now?" I asked.

Clara looked at the notes she'd made. "Dey last see her 'bout five years back, so nineteen."

"They didn't report a girl disappearing at age fourteen?"

"Said dey talked to da mudda, and she says da girl run off. Claimed she told police."

"Whittaker had someone check missing persons for her age range, and nothing came up."

"It sound like da kid weren't in school much before dat. I guess da mudda have problems wit drugs and such."

"What da girl's name?" Jacob asked.

"Kendra, Kendra Rankin. Mudda called Sherice Rankin. No fadda listed."

"Can you see what you can find on the mother?" I asked, and turned to leave.

"Not so fast dere," Clara said, stopping me in my tracks. "Already done dis ting." She said, giving me her best look of disapproval. "Mudda dead. Bin gone two years. Hit by a lorry right 'ere on Grand."

"No wonder nobody saying dey know dis girl," Jacob said solemnly. "Nobody do."

"She was pregnant," I pointed out. "Someone knew her intimately."

Clara crossed herself. I wasn't really sure why. Maybe she did think the missing child was the result of the second immaculate conception.

"Thanks, Clara," I said. "Could you see if a dentist on The Brac has any records of her?"

Clara grunted something in my direction as I left.

I used my swipe card and pushed through the door towards the interview rooms. Behind me, I heard Jacob telling Clara what a wonderful job she'd done. I grinned. She'd done well, but while she still insisted on calling me Skinny-Britches, I wasn't about to blow smoke up her arse.

I opened the door to the interview room and beckoned Whittaker when he turned around. It looked like they'd just sat down, both with steaming cups of coffee before them. He excused himself and joined me in the hall.

"We might have an ID on our victim, sir. Kendra Rankin, nineteen-year-old from The Brac. No one has seen her in the past five years. Mother died over here a couple of years ago."

"Our search didn't show any missing person who would match," he responded.

"Sounds like the mother never reported it, but told the school she had. The girl just fell between the cracks. Clara's looking for dental records now."

Whittaker sighed. "Good. Maybe we can make some progress if we have a name." He paused with his hand on the doorknob. "You can sit in. We haven't started." He looked me in the eye. "Let me handle this one. He deserves some professional courtesy until we have proof of any involvement."

"Yes, sir," I replied, deciding not to point out that paying for blowjobs was, in fact, a crime on the island.

Jeremy Andrews was not an idiot. I could tell by the look of concern under his amiable facade that he knew something was up. I was sure he'd been on the other side of the table too many times not to understand the situation.

Whittaker hit record on the machine. "Present in the room are myself, Detective Whittaker, Constable Sommer, and Jeremy Andrews, who has agreed to help us with our inquiries by answering a few questions. Jeremy, you're not under arrest and may terminate this interview at any time, or request the presence of a solicitor."

"I understand," Jeremy responded, knowing he had to verbalise his acknowledgement.

"Great, and thank you again for coming in," Whittaker began. "Prior to discovering the body in Jackson's Pond on Tuesday morning, had you ever seen the young lady before?"

"The only time I've seen her face at all is the artist's impression from the news," he replied. "As you know, she was face down in the water."

"So the first and only time you saw her in person was that morning?"

"That's correct."

Whittaker took his time. "When was the last time you were in that area prior to Tuesday morning when you were walking your dog and discovered the body?"

"The day before. I walk Luca several times every day."

"Can you give me a ballpark time?"

Andrews appeared remarkably relaxed, but tension around his crow's feet betrayed his calm demeanour.

"Where's this going, Roy?"

Whittaker let out a long breath. "Were you in the area the night before, Jeremy?"

"I live right there, so I'm always in the area," he replied with a smile.

Whittaker lifted his chin and looked at the former policeman sternly. "You know what I'm asking."

Andrews nodded. "I figured this would come out at some point," he said, his expression not changing much, except he'd lost any hint of amusement. "My wife left me before I moved here, Roy, you know that. We'd been married thirty-five years. I don't have the patience or inclination to go out dating or finding a relationship. I'm old, but I'm not *that* old yet. Every once in a while, I still have the need to scratch an itch, if you get my meaning."

"Why didn't you tell me this on Tuesday?" Whittaker challenged.

"Because it has nothing to do with the murder, and frankly, it's embarrassing."

"If you were in my shoes, would you consider someone in close proximity to the scene at the exact time of the murder irrelevant?"

Andrews shook his head and looked away. "You're right, of course. I apologise, Roy."

"Do you recall her name?" Whittaker asked.

Still looking down, Andrews replied, "Belle. She said her name was Belle."

"Had you met with her before?"

He shook his head. "No. I was at Kellys. I've found company there in the past. It was really late, and I was about to leave when I passed her on the way to my car. She seemed upset, so I enquired whether she was alright. She asked if I'd drive her home."

"Where does she live?" Whittaker interrupted.

"A run-down looking place on Town Hall Road."

I figured at this stage he had nothing to lose by telling us all this, and Whittaker was carefully pulling the events of the evening from him, leading up to the critical question.

"Did you go inside?"

"No, we sat in the car and talked for a while. She seemed reluctant to leave. Finally she asked if I'd like… to be pleasured."

I noticed Andrews's cheeks actually flushed a little.

"How much did she charge?"

"Roy, I'd really rather not get the young lady in trouble. Can we say she took pity on an old man?"

"These are details that are key to the events of the evening, Jeremy. I'm not saying charges won't be pressed, but it's not guaranteed they will. The murder investigation takes precedence over a prostitution charge."

"Of course," Andrews said. "Sixty dollars. I paid her sixty dollars."

"Okay, and where did the exchange of services take place?"

"She said we needed to go somewhere quiet, so I suggested the spot behind where I live. I didn't want to go anywhere she suggested, in case it was a trap of some sort. We parked off Ernest Jackson Drive, where it meets the trail around the quarry."

"What time were you there?"

"I honestly couldn't tell you the exact time, Roy. It wasn't a concern in the moment. It was around two or three in the morning."

"So, you parked and engaged in sexual relations. Then what?"

"I think we'd both had a bit too much to drink at Kellys. To be honest, I fell asleep and she must have too. I woke up and stepped out to urinate, and when I got back in the car, she was waking up."

"And you never saw or heard anything from Jackson's Pond, just a few hundred yards away?"

Andrews held both hands up. "I swear, Roy, I would have told you if I'd witnessed anything."

"How long did you step out of the car for?"

"However long it took for me to walk to the water's edge and relieve myself. A minute. Two at the most."

"If we returned to the spot, could you show us where you parked and where you urinated?"

Andrews bit his lip and considered the question. "I could take you to where we parked, within a few yards or so, but if you're thinking of finding a trace of where I relieved myself, I'm not sure you'll be in luck. I peed in the water for one, and it's rained several times since Monday night."

"Humour me," Whittaker replied, and stood.

Nudging him with my elbow as I stood up, he looked at me. I frowned, and he frowned back, not understanding what I wanted. I held up my forefinger and thumb a centimetre apart. He realised I was covertly requesting permission to ask a question, and he nodded his assent. I turned to Andrews, who was also standing, staring at the pair of us. So much for the covert part.

"Are you positive Belle stayed in the car?"

Jeremy leaned on the back of his chair and thought for a moment. "I assumed so, but I can't swear to it. She'd been wearing a little crop top thing over a glittery silver sleeveless shirt, but when I woke up, she'd taken the crop top off. She may have put it somewhere, but all she had with her was a small purse no bigger than a wallet. I didn't find it anywhere in the car."

I nodded to Whittaker, and he led us from the interview room. We had a solid case for booking two people on prostitution charges, and Andrews was certainly driving over the alcohol limit, but we were back to three suspects in the murder. Belle's and Andrews's statements each left the possibility that the other had time to commit the crime, and there was still Minnow to account for.

I tapped Whittaker's arm, and he paused, asking Andrews to wait for us in the reception area.

"The cars," I started, and the detective finished my thought.

"Exactly. No way any of them committed the crime and didn't leave evidence in the vehicles."

18

STUPID CLOTHING

Friday 4:00pm

We drove to the neighbourhood where Andrews lived, then down a short marl road towards the flooded quarry. One of Rasha's SOCO team had come from George Town to make a forensic examination of Jeremy Andrews's car, so he'd ridden with us. He'd volunteered his car without a warrant.

Whittaker parked well before reaching the water and we all got out of the SUV. Andrews pointed ahead, a few metres short of the edge.

"Right about there, Roy. That's where I parked."

Whittaker carefully walked along the left-hand edge of the trail, and I took the right. The surface was well enough used that most of the dust and gravel was pushed to either side, revealing well-worn dirty grey limestone. With the showers we'd had over the past few days, any tracks were long gone.

"Where do you think you relieved yourself?" Whittaker asked and waved Andrews over.

The former detective re-enacted his movements from the driver's side of the car to the edge of the quarry. "Hard to be sure, I'm afraid. It was dark, and I'd had a few, but around this point."

Whittaker took several pictures with his mobile, but looking at the ground, we all knew any trace evidence was long gone.

"I'll go for a walk," I said, and he nodded.

Before we'd left the station, Whittaker and I had discussed timing and measuring the walk to the location of the murder. I hadn't made it ten metres when something at the water's edge caught my eye. It was pale blue. I stopped the exercise app on my mobile.

"Sir!" I called out. "Could you grab an evidence bag?"

Whittaker went to his SUV and retrieved a clear plastic evidence bag and two pairs of nitrile gloves. I took pictures of the item and location while I waited.

"What colour…" Whittaker began shouting to Andrews, but the man had followed him and was also looking at what we'd found.

"That's it," Andrews said. "That's the top I told you about."

I wrestled my sweaty hands into the gloves and picked my way down the rocky bank to the water. Retrieving the garment, I held it up with both hands to examine it. Half of it was soaking wet, and water dripped from the heavy knit material. It was a stupid piece of clothing. Why wear a heavy knit cardigan which only comes just below your chest? In the Caribbean. I guess this was why she was dating Minnow and his sleeveless hoodie.

Shaking more of the water out, I noticed a dark stain on the front by the three large buttons. A brown stain, like dried blood. I quickly folded the top and placed it inside the evidence bag, walked up the bank and handed it to Whittaker.

"Thank you," he said, taking the bag, but I kept hold of it for a moment longer and caught his eye. He subtly nodded, and I was confident he'd understood there was something more to be discussed about the garment.

Restarting the timer on my mobile, I continued my walk, trying to keep the steady pace of someone moving with purpose. All we had was Belle's and Jeremy's versions of their timing, which were unreliable at best, but seemed consistent at twenty minutes or so. I glanced at my pace and realised I was measuring in metric. Whittaker would want imperial, so I went to the menu and switched. I was averaging 16.5-minute miles.

Making the turn at the south corner of the quarry pond, I briefly headed towards the dike between the two bodies of water, then turned when the path opened up to the right. One more turn and I was on the narrow trail between the trees where Kendra, if that was indeed her name, had lost her teeth. I kept going around the next bend and stopped the timer at the spot we believed the original attack took place.

The distance was 0.68 miles. It had taken me eleven minutes and seventeen seconds. From this point, the killer would have attacked his victim, followed her while she staggered down the trail, smashed her again, then carried or dragged her to the water and dumped her body. Then swept the trail. If I simply walked back to the car from this point without doing any of that, the overall time would be twenty-two and a half minutes. Minnow would have to have covered a similar distance, and he had less than 26 minutes, as that was the time between him driving in past the camera and leaving.

It all seemed improbable. Belle had blood on the top we'd just found, but she ended up at the quarry by Andrews's choice, not hers. We'd know whose blood by tomorrow. Jeremy was in great shape for his age, but he didn't strike me as a runner, and surely Belle would have said if he returned in a ball of sweat. Not to mention whoever killed Kendra had to have had blood on their clothes. More than I saw on the crop top. We were waiting for forensics results from Minnow's car, but I was getting the feeling it wouldn't show any of Kendra's blood or DNA. I wasn't sure about Andrews's car, although he'd happily allowed us to examine it, so he either had confidence in his cleaning, or there was nothing to clean.

If I continued down the trail, it turned 90 degrees around the corner of the small pond, then headed towards West Bay Road where Jacob and I had stopped the day before. I took a screenshot of the first recording, and reset the app. Out of curiosity, I hit 'start', and continued walking the trail. Turning the corner, the surrounding trees closed in, almost forming a tunnel. The bright afternoon sun made speckled highlights on the marl, overgrown in many parts by weeds. A weird patchwork of light and shadow, seemingly alive as the branches swayed in the breeze.

On my left, I passed a log which had fallen across the path and been sawn and moved out of the way at some point. I reached the screen of trees hiding the road in less than three minutes and stopped the timer. Pushing through the foliage, I swatted at the little biting bastards that tried to feast on my Nordic flesh. Looking back and forth along the road, I wondered about CCTV footage from the condo buildings along the beach side of West Bay Road. Someone else had been assigned the task, so I made a mental note to follow up.

Kendra could have arrived at the trails to Jackson's Pond from either direction, on foot or by vehicle. If she had come from the maternity clinic, West Bay Road would be a more direct route. I texted Whittaker, telling him I was by the road and starting back, then pressed the button on my app, and shoved my way through the shrubs and trees.

The mosquitoes must have phoned their friends, as all I could hear was the high-pitched buzz of their little wings as they dive bombed past my ears. I was glad no one was around to see me windmilling my arms like a lunatic. I reached the fallen log I'd seen before and stopped, dropping my hands to my sides. Something, or someone, had trodden down the weeds and grass in front of the log. Not flattened, but I had the impression someone had sat there recently, or maybe stood and looked into the woods. Could this be where the killer had thrown the weapon?

I stepped closer and peered into the dense mass of trees. It was hard to make out any individual trunk or branch; they all became lost in a tangle of foliage. As I stepped back, I looked down, and there amongst the thin grass was a button. I pulled one of the nitrile gloves from my pocket and picked it up. A small piece of thread hung from the two tiny holes in the plastic. Wrapping it in the glove, I shoved it in my pocket and took several pictures of the log with my mobile.

It was doubtful the button had anything to do with our case, but it was worth looking into. I'd forgotten to stop the app, so I waited until I was back at the spot of the attack, and reset it to start again. I then walked to the water where the body had been found, stopped the timer, took a screenshot, and started it again for the walk back to the car.

Whittaker and Andrews were sitting in the SUV, escaping the heat. I wondered how their conversation was going. The two men had obviously been on friendly terms, and I had the impression it extended beyond professional respect. It had to be incredibly awkward for my boss.

I couldn't imagine Andrews brutally slaying a woman, but there again, maybe he was the baby's father. Removing her teeth was certainly a deliberate and calculated act that a former detective might think about. Could she have been one of Andrews's former girls he'd hired for company? Got pregnant and tried to blackmail him or have him support them both?

Without a proven connection to anyone or anywhere, it was difficult to establish a reason Kendra was killed, but it had to be something to do with her baby. If we had indeed made an ID, perhaps we could finally start piecing her story together.

Climbing in the back seat, I was surprised to find the two men chatting amiably about the rising home prices on the island.

"Get what you need?" Whittaker asked.

"Yes, sir," I replied, putting my seat belt on.

I decided I'd wait to mention the button until we were back at the station. I looked between the front seats and noticed the digital clock on the centre console.

"*Faen*," I muttered, and Whittaker frowned. He was looking behind us as he reversed out of the gravel lane.

"Sorry," I added, although I doubted the civilian in the car spoke Norwegian. It was ten past five, and I was going to be late picking up Hallie.

19

INVISIBLE WOMAN

Friday 5:45pm

I pulled up outside the Boddens' house in West Bay where Hallie was waiting in the shade of a sea grape tree in the front garden. I had texted her to let her know I was delayed, but I'd managed to quickly change at the station and make it to the house by 5:45pm.

She walked up to the Jeep and stopped, holding her hands out. "This outfit okay?"

She was wearing black capris, a well-worn dark green State Radio T-shirt I guessed she'd been given by AJ, and a tatty dark blue Tottenham Hotspurs baseball cap. That would have come from Reg or AJ as well. In her hand was a grey hoodie. Hallie was five feet six inches tall, slender and pretty, with the most amazing golden amber eyes. She was a head-turner, but knew how to evaporate into the scenery when needed. Years of living on the streets in George Town had taught her the art.

"Perfect. Let's go."

She hopped in and I wasted no time zipping through the back roads of West Bay, heading for Foster's supermarket. I figured

Hallie would grab the first bus going south, while I waited to see if Puffin Girl got off at the stop. Once Hallie reached George Town, she'd text me and I'd get on the next available bus. We'd keep lapping the route on West Bay Road to George Town and back until we either spotted her or gave up for the night.

We sat in Foster's car park waiting for one of the minibuses to come by and chatted about Hallie's college. We didn't have long to wait, and she waved at the driver to stop, crossed the road to the little bus shelter, and our plan was underway. I'd given Hallie the best description I could of Puffin Girl, but I figured she'd spot her by her movements more than looks.

Now I had to sit and wait, one of my least favourite things to do. The service used a bunch of the little Toyota HiAce vans varying from ten to fifteen passenger seats, depending on the vintage. They were supposed to be by every four or five minutes. It was the Islands, so the schedule was heavily dependent on traffic, weather, and the mood of the driver. It was the tail end of rush hour on Friday evening, so I expected the timing to be erratic.

The usual afternoon clouds had rolled over the island, making the sunshine patchy, and a particularly grey one began sprinkling rain. I hopped out of the CJ-7 and took shelter under a tree. Steam rose from the tarmac as the raindrops hit the road, sending the humidity from damned sweaty to dripping wet.

I'd chosen a floral summer dress, bundled my hair into a bun and covered it with a beige bucket hat, hoping to look like a tourist. The dress was now clinging to my body and my hat was getting soaked with a combination of sweat and water dripping through the tree. I was glad when Hallie texted, saying she'd reached the bus terminal in George Town. It had taken over thirty minutes.

Trotting across the street, I hid under the bus shelter and boarded the next bus. I sat in the second row of seats, recently vacated by someone getting off at Foster's. The driver had the air conditioning cranked up, which made my damp clothes instantly feel like an ice bath. Now I knew why Hallie had brought a hoodie along. I watched out of the window as we headed south, keeping an eye on both sides of the road. The buses would drop people off and pick them up anywhere along the route, so my guess was the young girl would avoid the busy stops, especially after being spotted by me the other day.

Hallie and I texted back and forth about places we saw crowds of people, and our buses passed each other by the Watercolours condo building on Seven Mile Beach. The long stretch of West Bay Road behind the famous beach had light foot traffic. Most people used shuttles, buses, or hire cars to reach the shops and restaurants from their condo or hotel. I expected Puffin Girl to work the crowds by the waterfront in George Town if indeed she was picking pockets and snagging easy grabs from the stores.

The street lights were on and room lights were steadily replacing the daylight as the sun set with another spectacular display of colour on the horizon. I caught glimpses of the show between the buildings as we approached George Town. The bus had stopped six or seven times, but I wasn't expecting Puffin Girl to be heading south. She'd be returning home from town if my presumption was correct.

I texted Hallie and asked her to get off the bus at Foster's and wait in the Jeep, where she could watch the stop, and more importantly, monitor both directions. Each leg was taking far longer than I'd anticipated and I was beginning to think we should have stayed put in two locations. My heart leapt when a younger girl with her hair wrapped in a headscarf boarded by the Esso station opposite the cemetery just north of town. But her mother soon followed her onto the bus, and I realised the girl was too young anyway.

It was truly dark by the time we neared West Bay and seeing the Silver Sands condos reminded me about the CCTV footage. It was on my list for the morning, along with checking on the statements from the tenants in the subsidised housing apartments. I was becoming convinced Kendra had arrived from the west.

My mobile buzzed, and I read the text: 'I think I see her'.

The bus was pulling to a stop, but we were still at least half a kilometre from Foster's. An older lady took her time getting out, pausing to thank the driver and ask about some relative who was in hospital, or died, or some shit I didn't have time for right now. I slipped past her and took off running.

Trying not to trip over on the ruts and gravel at the edge of the road, I called Hallie as texting was out of the question.

"Where is she?" I panted.

"Are you running?" she asked.

"*Ja*, the stupid bus kept stopping. Where is she?"

"She got off the bus before it reached Foster's. She was walking in the shadows down the east side of the road, but… I've lost her."

"Look carefully, she's probably hiding where she can see the car park, making sure there's no one watching." I was starting to breathe heavily.

"Yup, I think I see someone behind a tree. I caught a quick look in the headlights of a car. What should I do?"

Approaching the corner of the Sundial condos, I slowed up to a walk. Next was Foster's car park, and I didn't want to draw attention to myself. Not too many people wear summer dresses for their evening jog. More cars came by in both directions and I scanned the trees on the other side of the road. Finally, I caught a glimpse of a pair of brown-skinned legs behind a large mastic tree.

"Okay, I see her. I think she's waiting for the next bus to arrive, making sure no one is paying attention to the stop. She has to walk past the shelter to turn on Willie Farrington Drive."

I looked over my shoulder and saw the bus I'd been on approaching.

"Quick, walk along the pavement until you're opposite Willie Farrington, then cross the road."

"She'll see me for sure," Hallie replied, but I could hear she was already moving.

"I'm hoping she does," I explained.

There was a gap in the traffic, and I watched Hallie start across West Bay Road. At the same time, I did the same, staying well south of the tree we believed she was hiding behind. If my plan worked, Puffin Girl would be too distracted by Hallie to notice me. I quickly ducked behind some shrubs at the side of a driveway.

"Now what?" Hallie asked. "I can't see her from here."

"Unless she knows a way through the homes behind her, she only has three choices," I replied. "Move to the bus shelter. She may think you're waiting for the next bus and walk your way. Or, if she's still suspicious, she'll move my way."

"Okay, but if I was her, I'd stay where I am," Hallie said.

I thought about that for a moment. She was probably right. Puffin Girl was well concealed and probably not in a hurry. If she thinks we're a threat, she'd force us to make the first move.

"You're right, let's both close in. If you speak to her first, try to reassure her we just want to talk."

"Okay," Hallie whispered.

There was no pavement on this side of the road, just a rough edge where tarmac met the underlying limestone covered in dirt and stones. To my right was now a white picket fence and a screen of small trees hiding a house from the road. Ahead, I could see Hallie approaching, silhouetted by the headlights of a car, but the legs I'd spotted by the mastic tree were gone.

"*Dritt*," I muttered. "Where did she go?"

"Maybe she hopped the fence," Hallie offered.

I stepped behind the large old tree trunk. There was just enough room next to the fence for someone to hide between the two. It was definitely where I'd seen the girl. I thought back to the other times I'd seen her. She had an amazing ability to vanish into thin air. Maybe she was the Invisible Woman, I chuckled to myself.

I was about to call it a night when Hallie nudged me. When I looked her way, she flicked her eyes up. I opened the light app on my mobile and held it above my head as I looked up. A white tennis-shoed foot pulled up and away from the beam, but I could still see dark blue amongst the green foliage.

"How are you doing up there?" I asked.

"What d'you want?" came an angry young voice.

"Buy you something to eat and talk a bit."

"Don't need nuttin'. Best you leave me be. My papa'll be mad you pesterin' his girl."

"Is that so? Where do you live with your papa?"

"Ain't none o' your business."

"What if I told you I'm a policewoman, so maybe it is my business?"

"I know who you are. Why you botherin' me?"

"Because I'm worried about you."

"I'm fine," she snapped. "Now, see, don't have to worry no more."

"Yeah, but I'm curious too, and that's not going away until we talk a bit."

"We talked a bit now, so you can go."

"I'll make you a deal," I offered. "You let me and my friend here buy you something to eat, we'll chat a bit, then I promise you can go on your way."

"Why I gonna believe you?"

"Because I'm a police constable and we're not allowed to lie."

I heard a scoff. "Don't mean nuttin'"

"You best come down," Hallie said. "Otherwise you'll be stuck up that tree until you drop off to sleep and fall down. Believe me, she'll wait you out and I'll have to stand here with her. I got better places to be."

"Who are you?" the girl asked, and I heard her shifting in the tree to get a better look at Hallie. "I seen you before."

"I was living like you a few years back. I worked downtown," Hallie replied.

"Why you hangin' wit da cop?"

"She saved my arse."

There was more rustling from above. "Get dat light offa me."

I closed the app on my mobile.

"You swear I get to go after we talk?"

"You have my word," I said.

"Not you," the girl replied. "I want her to swear."

"I swear," Hallie said. "And you can trust Nora. She does what she says."

"We'll see," Puffin Girl grumbled as she dropped to the ground.

She was shorter than both of us, and her frizzy mass of hair was tied back in a ponytail.

"What's your name?" I asked.

"Jazzy."

"Really?" I said, remembering the names I'd found in the missing persons. "Are you Jasmine Holder?"

She looked at me, searching my face as though my trustworthiness and intentions were hidden in my features. "How d'you know?"

"I told you. I've been worried about you."

20

INDOOR PLUMBING

Friday 8:00pm

My Jeep wasn't the best vehicle for conversation, which usually suited me fine. Hallie sat up front and Jazzy rode in the back on the small bench seat. It took some persuading by Hallie to get the young girl into the vehicle at all. She was convinced we were driving her to jail or foster care. Once we were under way, she seemed to enjoy the wind in her hair, but couldn't hear a word we said.

It was Friday night, so they expected me at the Fox and Hare pub where my island family gathered and Reg Moore's wife, Pearl, played on the little stage. The bustling pub was worse than the Jeep for conversation, but I figured I could show my face, order some food, then we'd sit outside. I pulled into the busy car park and managed to find an open space in the corner. There was a big rut in the dirt which had kept cars from using the spot, but the oversized tyres on my lifted CJ-7 rolled through the divot without any trouble.

We hopped out, and I noticed Jazzy kept herself several paces from me. I figured she was ready to bolt if she felt vulnerable or trapped. Curiosity and hunger were my main allies in keeping her with us.

"I like da car," she said, following Hallie and me across the car park.

"Thanks, my boyfriend did all the work on it."

"Where's your boyfriend?"

"He's dead."

It wasn't my intention, but my answer halted the conversation. Maybe I needed to lead in with 'he's not very well'.

From the outside, the pub was a plain-looking stucco building. A traditional English public house sign hanging over the front doors was the only clue to what greeted customers inside. To the right of the doors was a wooden bench, often used by the smokers, or anyone needing fresh air. Which they didn't get if a smoker was already there.

"I'll get us food if you want to wait out here?" I said, nodding to the bench.

"Can I look inside?" Jazzy asked.

"Of course. It's gonna be noisy in there, though."

Undeterred, the two girls followed me inside, where Pearl's booming voice greeted us with a background buzz of conversation and laughter from the crowd. My guess was Jazzy had never been inside a place like this before. But there wasn't much else like the Fox and Hare on the island except Fidel Murphy's Irish Pub & Restaurant along Seven Mile Beach. But they didn't have Pearl Moore playing every other Friday night.

Jazzy was wide eyed. I suddenly had a thought as we pushed through the busy crowd and turned to say something to her, but Hallie was already whispering in her ear. Jazzy rolled her eyes, but nodded. Old habits die hard and this was pickpocket heaven, but I pressed on, confident Hallie had told the teenager to keep her hands to herself.

AJ stood up as we arrived at the long table Reg always

commandeered near the stage. She gave me a hug, and then Hallie. Jazzy looked at her suspiciously, so AJ extended a hand.

"I'm AJ."

"This is Jazzy," I said, not offering any further information.

They shook hands, which Jazzy seemed uncomfortable doing. Her eyes appeared to look down at the floor, but I could tell they were everywhere, assessing threats and escape routes. I nodded a greeting to Reg, then AJ's boyfriend, Jackson. Down at the end of the table, Thomas - Hallie's cousin, who worked for AJ - waved to us. He was sitting next to his girlfriend.

"Hallie, what do you want to eat?" I asked.

"Fish tacos, but I can get them."

I shook my head. "Hang out with AJ, I'll order, then we'll sit outside and eat." I picked a menu up from the table and handed it to Jazzy. "Bring it with you. Choose what you want."

I made a pathway through the people towards the bar, and lured by the prospect of a real meal, Jazzy followed me. I found an opening and waved to the bartender, Frank. After finishing with the customers he was serving, he moved our way.

"Two orders of fish tacos, two white wines, and what do you want?" I asked, turning to Jazzy. She was studying the laminated menu intensely. For a moment, my heart sank as I wondered if the kid could read. Maybe I'd just put her in a ridiculously embarrassing situation. She pointed to the fish and chips, and I breathed again.

"To drink?"

"Coke."

Frank nodded and repeated the order back to me. I nodded.

"I'll get the drinks, and hand this in to the kitchen. Be right back," he said.

I had questions for Jazzy, but the noisy bar wasn't the place to ask them, so I waited. She seemed fine looking around and taking in the sights and sounds. When our drinks came, we joined the others at the table, and Hallie must have briefed everyone, as no one inundated her with questions. Ten minutes later, the food arrived, served in baskets we could easily carry, so we moved outside.

Jazzy didn't waste time tucking into her dinner. She ate like someone who wasn't sure where the next meal would come from. I left her alone and enjoyed my tacos, occasionally conversing with Hallie about nothing in particular. Hallie liked to talk more than I did, but she was one of the few people I didn't mind prattling on.

Jazzy finished her dinner, and I noticed there wasn't a scrap left in the basket. How she crammed all that food into her petite frame, I had no idea. She looked at me.

"Okay. Ask."

"Why were you in foster care?"

I hadn't researched beyond the basic missing persons files for her and the Ebanks girl, so I didn't have any background information. I figured I'd start with the basics.

"'Cos I didn't have no family."

"What happened to your parents?"

"Just Mama. She had problems, so dey took me away."

"Where is she now?"

Jazzy shrugged her shoulders. "Said she had family in America. She left, so guess dat's where she went."

I glanced at Hallie, who was listening intently. Her own mother had run them into poverty and then killed herself with drugs. She could relate.

"How long were you in foster care?"

"A while. Maybe six months or so."

"Why did you leave them?"

"They no good for me."

"Why?"

She shrugged her shoulders again and looked anywhere but at me.

"Hit you, touched you weird, what? I'm a policewoman. I can do something about that."

Jazzy looked at me now. "Ain't nuttin' to be done. I left and dat's fine."

There was obviously so much more to her situation with the foster family, and despite my blood starting to boil at the idea they had messed with the kid, I let it go for now. I needed to establish a better relationship with the girl before she'd share anything more about it.

"Where do you stay now?"

She glared at me. "I ain't tellin'."

I felt like I'd asked a stupid question. Why should she tell me? For the first time since I began tracking down the young girl, I wondered what it was exactly I hoped to accomplish. I'd been hell-bound in helping her, but how? Put her back in the system? Apart from missing out on a proper education, and indoor plumbing, she was managing just fine on her own. There were plenty of kids with roofs over their heads doing far worse than Jazzy.

But of course, all of that was temporary. At some point, she would need a doctor, a dentist, or she'd be caught stealing and arrested. I couldn't expect her to see the bigger picture, so somehow I needed to show her a better alternative. To do that, I had to think of a better alternative. Hallie had been fortunate in the fact that she had distant family on the island willing to help.

"Was your mother born and raised here?"

"Best I know."

"Was Holder her surname or your father's?"

"Didn't have no fadda."

Now didn't seem like the best time to explain that everyone had a father. Or perhaps the immaculate conception was as common as iguana shit in the Cayman Islands. I doubted that to be the case.

"Do you remember anyone else around when you were really young?"

Jazzy shook her head. "We lived in back of dese houses. Mama s'posed to clean for dem and such, but dey always mad at her."

"This was down the East End?"

She nodded.

"Remember the names of those people?"

"One lady I call Aunt, but Mama say she not really my aunt."

"What did your mother call her?"

"Bad words most da time."

Hallie and I both laughed.

"Gloria. She call her Gloria when dey not yellin' at each other."

Maybe that would give me a place to start if I could find this woman named Gloria.

"Do you remember where these houses are? If we drove down to the East End, could you find them?"

Jazzy's eyes got bigger. "I don't wanna go back dere."

"You wouldn't have to see anyone. Just show me where."

"What for?"

Yeah, what for? I asked myself. "Maybe I can trace some family you don't know about. I need somewhere to start. This Gloria woman might have useful information."

"Why?" she said suspiciously.

The girl was a long way from seeing a bigger picture, and family hadn't been kind to her in the past. I couldn't blame her for being reluctant.

Hallie stood up. "I need to use the loo. I'll take our baskets in."

Jazzy handed her empty basket to Hallie and I did the same.

"I need a pee too," Jazzy said, and the two girls walked inside the pub.

I was glad of a break for a few minutes. It irritated me when I wasn't prepared. Usually I had a plan, even if it was a lousy one. I wanted to talk to Hallie about the situation. When she'd been living on the street, she had a tiny shelter she lived in with running water, at least. It was the promise of something better which lured her away. It turned out to be a lie and nearly got her killed, but it finally led to the Boddens taking her in. I hoped she had some insights into Jazzy's world which might help me sort out a plan.

Sipping my wine, I chewed over different options. I wondered if it was possible to screen foster families before they'd even met the kid. I was sure child services would want to handle every step of the process, and my role would come to an end. That would be fine if I could trust them, and more importantly, Jazzy did. Fat chance of that, based on what she'd been through.

The door to the pub opened, and Hallie walked out. Alone.

"She take off?" I asked.

"I'm really sorry," Hallie replied. "I came out of the stall and she'd vanished."

"That's okay. I have a lot to figure out before we speak to her again. And I'll need your help."

21

SECOND BREAKFAST

Saturday 5:00am

I'd slept soundly for five hours, but had woken up at 4:30am, and my nemesis had insisted I think about all the things I wouldn't be able to fit into the day ahead. I was good at prioritising my tasks, but when the sheer number of items on my plate accumulated, I felt an urgency and building pressure. Almost a fear of not being able to keep up. I think I hid it all quite well, so people didn't notice I was stressed, but it made me more impatient. That's probably why no one noticed, as they thought I was an arse in the first place.

Darkness still covered the island. It would be another hour or more before sunrise. I made coffee and ate a banana for breakfast. My soul needed a dive on the reef, but that would delay my day too long. Officially, I wasn't on duty over the weekend, but that didn't matter with a murder investigation going on. At least it didn't matter to me. Jacob had a family, which came with obligations, so no one expected him to work overtime, but I knew Whittaker would want me in the office.

Besides, I needed to stay busy. I'd never been any good at sitting still. Occasionally, I sat on my porch and watched the sunset, but not for long, or very often. I felt adrift if I didn't have something to do. It was also the perfect hunting ground for my nemesis. A year on, and I could finally think about Ridley and see him as a happy, laughing, loving man. But if I lazed around and let my mind have free rein, his bloody corpse would quickly reappear. Maybe in another year I would be able to spend an hour relaxing, without paying a price.

It was too early for Edvard to show himself. It was hot and balmy outside, but my ectothermic buddy needed sunshine to warm his blood for the day ahead. Maybe I'd be home in daylight to see if he was still around. If things went really well with Edvard, maybe I'd get a goldfish and see if it survived my karma.

Setting a pebble in the front door jamb, I used the torch app on my mobile to guide me through the woods and the gap in the fence to the road. I wiped the dampness from the seats and warmed the Jeep up for a few minutes. I was anxious to be under way, but Ridley had drilled into me the importance of warming the oil and all that shit, so I waited until the water temperature gauge moved to the first mark. Sometimes I could see him sitting next to me, tapping on the gauge and reminding me.

The station was a ghost town. The clerk at the front desk was playing a game on her mobile and barely looked up when I walked in. She grunted a greeting of some sort, and I grunted something back. Putting my coffee mug on the desk, I woke up one of the computers they made available to all of us and logged in. I wanted to look up all I could find about Jazzy, but that needed to wait. Priorities.

Finding the folder for the murder case, I started by reading the constable's reports from canvassing West Bay Road. Unsurprisingly, no one had seen or heard anything in the early hours of Tuesday morning. I moved on to the CCTV. There were only two video files. One from the Sea Breeze condo building to the north, and one from a private home to the south.

I opened the file from the condos. The camera was mounted on the building, aimed through the car park to the road. Trees lined each side of the entranceway, making the view of West Bay Road a narrow slot where headlights whizzed by. It was unusable for identifying a car, but offered a timestamp for traffic on the road.

The second file was from a camera mounted above and behind an ornate wrought-iron gate between tall walls. It was high resolution, had good quality night vision, and a wide enough angle to see both lanes of the road. I fast-forwarded until headlights went by, then rewound and played at regular speed. I couldn't make out anyone inside the vehicles, or their exact colour because of the green tint of the night vision, but the type of car was identifiable.

I found 1:00am on the time code and began my search. In a spiral notepad, I wrote down the type of vehicle, colour shade, time of day, and direction of travel. When I reached 4:00am, I had a list of 27 vehicles. Using a mapping program, I ran directions from what I could see from the satellite view was an enormous mansion to the Sea Breeze condos. It was only 400 metres, so would take 22 seconds at 40mph.

Back to the first CCTV recording, I added or subtracted 22 seconds from the timestamp and matched the vehicles passing the camera at Sea Breeze. As both systems were fed over the internet to a security company for recording, I had a high degree of confidence the times would be accurately in sync.

Twenty-four of the vehicles passed by both cameras in less than 30 seconds. Unless someone jumped from a car which barely came to a stop, there was no way any of these were involved in the murder, although I kept my notes on each one in case we could track them down as potential eye witnesses. Two cars never continued past the second camera. A pale SUV heading south, and a dark saloon car going north. The third, a small white or silver car heading south, stopped somewhere between the two cameras from 2:20am until 3:51am, then returned north.

I could only presume these weren't reported as no one had gone through this footage yet, or it was disregarded as the registration plates and drivers weren't visible. In my mind, with so little evidence to work from, this could be a promising lead with more effort.

I leaned back in the chair and stretched, yawning and rubbing my sore neck. My posture was shit when I sat at a computer for too long. Taking my coffee cup, I stood and was surprised to see a few other people milling about. I looked at my watch. It was 7:50am. I hurried to the break room and refilled my travel mug. I thought I could get a lot more done before the shift change at 8:00am, but the time had flown by.

Dialling Whittaker's number, I sipped the hot coffee and made my way back to the desk I'd been using.

"Good morning, Constable Sommer," he greeted me, sounding formal in case I had him on speakerphone. I didn't.

"Hey. I pulled three cars we should investigate from the West Bay Road CCTV."

"Where are you?"

"West Bay station."

"How long have you been there?"

"A few hours," I replied impatiently. I didn't want a pat on the back. We had a murderer to find. He must have got the point, as he moved on.

"Do you have registration plates?"

"No, the footage is pretty shit, but I think two are residents. We should do a door-to-door to verify. The third spends over an hour somewhere between the two cameras and leaves the way they came."

"Can you come to Central?"

"*Ja.*"

"I'll set a briefing for 9:00am. Bring what you have."

We ended the call, and I gathered up my notes. I checked my watch. It was 7:58am. I had plenty of time to grab another breakfast on the way. It already felt like I'd been up for ages.

22

SMALL APPENDAGES

Saturday 9:00am

I had expected a larger gathering, but Whittaker held the briefing in his office. There was a guy from TSU, our Technical Support Unit who handled mobile traces, computers, and anything else electronic, Rasha, our lead SOCO, and the Central Station Sergeant. He was a stern, grumpy bloke called Hadley. He greeted me with his usual look of condescending disdain. I smiled and said hi to Rasha and the TSU guy, ignoring Sergeant *Drittsekk*. I thought the TSU guy's name was Don, but I wasn't sure.

Whittaker stood behind his desk, Rasha and Don sat in chairs to the side of the desk, and Hadley sat on the opposite side. I stayed standing, leaning against the door jamb. It meant I could look down at Hadley, which I knew would bother him.

"Let's get started," Whittaker began. "We have several items to go through. Rasha, please update us on your findings."

Rasha had a file on her lap, which she glanced at before speaking. "We're finishing up with Andrews's car this morning, but so far there's no trace of blood or anything suspicious. There is evidence of the activity he has admitted to," she said, with a smirk, "and we have hair, which is definitely not his. We'll know by the end of the day if it matches the young lady who accompanied him."

"Could it be from the victim?" I asked before she moved on.

"It's possible, but unlikely. There's no trace of blood, dirt, or any other contaminant I would expect."

"Unless she was in the car before she was murdered," I pointed out.

"True," Rasha conceded. "The other car," she continued, with a quick reference to her notes, "belonging to Rashid Bakewell, is a Petri dish of forensic evidence, mostly drug related. No trace of the victim's blood, but there's enough hair in that car to weave a wig. We'll have DNA results later today."

"The garment?" Whittaker asked.

"We were a bit lucky with the top," Rasha replied. "Where you found it was probably where it had been thrown. It had been rained on, but hadn't been completely submerged in the pond, which preserved evidence for us. Mr Andrews's semen was present, and the blood was Miss Corbin's. Again, we found no trace of the victim."

"Where did Corbin's blood come from then?" Hadley asked.

"We found a small trace of cocaine in the blood. It's possible she gave herself a nose bleed after snorting cocaine."

"That would explain her not mentioning the nose bleed or throwing the top away," Whittaker said.

"And lying about not getting out of the car," I added.

"Did you find evidence of cocaine in either car?" Whittaker asked.

A few days ago, the detective had a friend he could lean on for his experience in law enforcement. Now Andrews was guilty of paying a prostitute, and based on the answer to Whittaker's question, he may be involved with drugs.

"No, we didn't. Not even in Bakewell's car."

I could see the relief in Whittaker's eyes.

Rasha held up another page from her file and looked at me. "The button. Good find. By itself, we can't tell what garment it came from, but it could be matched to the other buttons if we had the piece of clothing it came from. At least as being from the same manufacturer. But there was a small strand of hair caught in the thread still attached to the button itself."

I found myself leaning forward as though the answers would come quicker if I were closer to the woman.

"On the strand of hair, there wasn't any blood, but there was a stain which we've identified as breast milk. We ran DNA on the hair as a priority, and it does match our victim."

Whittaker and I exchanged a brief look.

"Don, can you project the satellite view of the crime scene area onto the monitor?" the detective asked.

Apparently I was right. His name was Don. Whittaker tipped the blinds, darkening the room so we could see the large display monitor on a sideboard behind where Hadley was sitting. The sergeant moved his chair out of the way and stood, blocking my view. I stepped farther into the room to see the map showing Jackson's Pond. Don zoomed out and scrolled until both the pond and West Bay Road were visible. The crime scene, body's location, and the spot where both cars had been parked were marked on the map already.

"Constable Sommer, where did you find the button?" Whittaker asked.

I walked across the room, stood in front of Hadley, and pointed to the spot on the map. The canopy of trees obscured the pathway, but it was visible at either end and I knew it ran straight between the two. Don marked a circle on the map where I had indicated the button's location.

"So far, our focus has been on the vehicles we know were in the vicinity," Whittaker said, pointing to the two locations on the map. "But based on the time we believe both parties had at the scene, it's becoming more unlikely any of them could have made it here..." he tapped the map on the monitor where the attack took place. "...and back in the available time. The button is the first evidence we have of our victim, who we now believe to be Kendra Rankin, arriving from the West Bay Road side." He paused and nodded to me. "Constable, could you tell us what you discovered this morning?"

I hated addressing a group. I'd heard once if you imagined they were all naked it made it less uncomfortable. That's a bunch of *dritt*. I didn't want to see anyone in this room naked, and the idea was yucky. Whittaker would be like seeing an uncle without any clothes on, one step worse than seeing your father *free willy*. I was confident Hadley had a small dick, so it would be fun to laugh at him, but Don was a computer nerd who was allergic to a gym or exercise. Rasha was a nice-looking, shapely woman, so she would just remind me I was lacking in the chest department.

I realised everyone was looking at me.

"We have CCTV from two locations on West Bay Road," I said, finding the obnoxiously large house and pointing to it. "At the entrance to this residence, and from the Sea Breeze building." I indicated the second location on the screen. "Sea Breeze is a shi…" I just caught myself. "Lousy camera view, but gives us a timestamp of passing vehicles. The other camera is better quality and helps us identify the make, or at least type of vehicle."

I took a few breaths. This is why I hated talking to a group, there were always too many words involved and I had to think about how I was delivering those words. It would be much easier to say, 'Sarge, your guys fucked up and didn't do what I spent hours on this morning, and now we have three cars we need to investigate.'

"I've narrowed our interest down to three vehicles, two of which enter the area and don't leave during the time we're interested in. One enters, stops for over an hour somewhere between the cameras, then leaves again."

Hadley shrugged his shoulders. "That's great, but you can't pull a reg plate or ID anyone from those cameras."

No question in my mind. He had a little dick.

"That's true, so it requires a bit more work," I said, giving him a blank stare. "If we pull the CCTV from Foster's where the car park lights stay on at night, we might be able to get a plate. As for the other two vehicles, we need to canvas all the condos and see which cars match the type and shade, then see who was coming home early Monday morning."

Hadley shook his head. "That'll use up a lot of resource, and half the people in those condos will be flying home today or tomorrow."

I couldn't help myself. "I agree. Would have been much better to do this earlier in the week when the CCTV was first examined."

The sergeant's whole body tensed, but Whittaker quickly took over.

"Okay, we have a lot more to work from than we had yesterday. Don, can you take over the CCTV footage? Get Nora's notes and start looking at other cameras in West Bay and see if you can track down a registration number." He turned to Rasha. "Anything else from your group?"

"Just one thing," she replied and looked at me again. "The victim had a lot of dirt, marl, and other debris in her wounds, hair, and various parts of her body. Between her toes there was quite a bit, along with the wounds on the soles of her feet, supporting the theory she'd walked some distance. A small amount of marl from between her toes and under her toenails was dark with signs of the filamentous algae which makes the limestone at Hell look black."

A thought fell into my head. The poor girl came from Hell, then went through Hell. I didn't verbalise my morbid humour.

"I didn't see anyone walking past either camera, but unless she'd been lit by passing headlights, the Sea Breeze camera wouldn't show someone on the far side of the road," I said.

"I'll take another look and see what footage we have from farther north," Don added.

"Great," Whittaker said, with an air of finality. "Let's get to work. Constable, wait for me downstairs, please. Sergeant Hadley, I'll take another minute of your time. Thank you, everyone."

The three of us filed out, and Whittaker closed his office door behind us. I lingered at the end of the hallway for a few moments and looked back. Hadley was becoming animated, and then I heard Whittaker raise his voice. He never shouted at anyone.

Great, I thought, he's giving Hadley a bollocking over his men missing the CCTV footage evidence. Probably for missing the crop top in the water, too. This would not help my tenuous relationship with the Sarge, but screw him and his pin dick. They should do their jobs right the first time.

23

A TASER IN THE CROTCH

Saturday 10:00am

I followed Detective Whittaker north towards West Bay. The tourist traffic was heavy along Seven Mile Beach and I had to pay attention as half of them were thoroughly confused by driving on the left-hand side. It was common to find someone stationary in the middle turn lane, disorientated and panicked after pulling out of a business or restaurant. Horns blazed and people waved, but that was almost always the other tourists. Locals only tooted their horns to say thank you.

I needed to sit down and study a map. If Kendra had walked all the way from the maternity clinic in West Bay, she would have passed a camera somewhere. Also, there wasn't much traffic on the road at two o'clock in the morning, but enough for one of the drivers to have noticed a barefooted woman wandering about. The black marl between her toes didn't guarantee she'd walked around near Hell, but it certainly opened up the possibility. The clinic kept cropping up in the investigation.

We parked outside Silver Sands and walked across West Bay Road. I showed Whittaker the trail on the other side of the trees.

"Maybe she left the maternity clinic, was picked up, driven here, and then led to where she was attacked," I proposed. "That would explain the lack of eyewitnesses seeing her walking, and we have a car coming from that direction that spends over an hour somewhere nearby."

I swatted at mosquitoes while Whittaker thought it over. Apparently, my blood was far more sought after in the insect world, as he was unbothered by the little *jævler*.

"We can plot different routes from the clinic to here," he mused. "See what cameras we have along the way." He looked at the motel building nearby. "They don't have cameras, I assume?"

"Only in the lobby, I believe."

"Our constables were able to talk with a few residents the other day," he said, walking towards the front entrance. "Maybe one or two more are home now."

I followed the detective and looked around the covered front entry for signs of cameras. I didn't see any. Whittaker held the door open for me and we walked inside. The reception area looked just like a motel from the movies, without the rack of tourist brochures. A long counter split the room, separating a small office in the back from the customer area in front. A door to our left led farther into the building, and through the glass window in the door, I could see a long hallway with rooms to each side.

A Caucasian man in his thirties appeared from the office. He had thinning hair, dressed casually in shorts and a T-shirt, and smiled pleasantly as he leaned on the counter.

"How can I help?" he asked in a northern English accent.

We both showed the man our badges.

"I'm Detective Whittaker, and this is Constable Sommer."

The man looked me over. "The outfit's a giveaway," he said with a smirk.

"We're investigating an incident which happened near here in the early hours of Tuesday morning."

"Aye, some of your lot were round here the other day."

"Is someone here twenty-four hours a day?" Whittaker asked.

"Of course. Someone's always home," the man answered.

"I meant, is the front desk manned twenty-four hours a day?" Whittaker clarified, remaining more patient than I felt.

"No, eight in the morning, till eight at night."

"Is that your only CCTV?" Whittaker asked, pointing to a camera mounted over the office door.

The man turned and looked at the camera. "Aye, and that don't work half the time."

"Would you mind if we spoke with some of your residents?"

"Don't know who's home, but knock yourselves out," the man replied, gesturing towards the door to the rooms.

I looked around the counter for the usual business card holder, but didn't see one. "Are you the manager?" I asked.

"Aye, me and the missus."

"Do you live here?"

"Aye. Number one," he replied. "First on the left."

"Name?" I asked.

"We don't name the rooms, just a number."

I couldn't tell whether he was being deliberately difficult, or if he was really that stupid. I gave him a look which indicated the latter.

"Oh, *my* name," he said, laughing. "Rog, Rog Hargraves."

"And your wife?" I asked. I wanted to add, 'or does she have a number', but I restrained myself in front of the detective.

"Sheila. She's in our gaff."

"Did you or your wife hear anything out of the ordinary on Monday night or Tuesday morning?" Whittaker asked.

"Your blokes already asked us, but no, sound asleep, the pair of us."

"Thank you," Whittaker said, and opened the door to the hallway.

I followed, after giving Rog another condescending look. It had little effect as my eyes were the last place he was looking.

Whittaker knocked on the first door, and we waited.

"I'm coming, I'm coming," came an annoyed voice from inside. "What da bloody hell you want? Where your key at?"

The door opened and a dark-skinned woman crammed into bright red leggings and a frilly pale blue blouse with a plunging V-neck stood before us. Her expression immediately shifted from annoyed to surprised.

"Where Rog at?"

"Good morning, Mrs Hargraves. I'm Detective Whittaker, and this is Constable Sommer. We were hoping to ask you a couple of questions."

We both showed her our badges.

"I already talk wit you," she said dismissively.

"We appreciate your patience, ma'am. We're doing a follow-up to see if anything may have come to mind in regards to Monday night."

"I told da udders I sleepin'. Don't reckon I all o' sudden decide I not sleepin' just 'cos you come round again."

"Thank you, Mrs Hargraves," Whittaker said politely, stepping back. "Have a good day."

The door closed, and we moved on to the next apartment. I wondered if the Hargraveses got to stay in the building because the owner paid them so poorly that they were considered low-income. Neither one struck me as the type to turn away or be embarrassed by taking government handouts.

Whittaker knocked on the door across the hall. When no one answered and we didn't hear any movement inside, we moved on to number 3 and knocked again. I could hear a television playing. After a few moments, the show muted, and the door opened as far as the safety chain would allow.

"Hello?" came a young woman's voice.

Whittaker introduced us, and we held our badges in front of the opening. The woman said nothing.

"Did the constables talk to you the other day, miss?"

"No. About what?"

"Would you mind unlatching the door so we can talk?" Whittaker asked.

There was a long pause, before she pushed the door to and unhooked the chain. She opened the door wider but not all the way.

She was a pretty woman with perfect light brown skin and hair in long braids. Nearly as tall as me, she was slender and early twenties, if I had to guess. Her brow was tight with concern.

"Were you here on Monday night, miss..?"

She nodded, but didn't offer her name.

"Did you happen to see or hear anything unusual in the middle of the night or early hours of Tuesday morning?"

She shook her head, and I wondered if she understood English or was just incredibly shy.

"You slept through the night?" Whittaker persisted.

She nodded.

"Alone, or does someone stay with you?"

She frowned. "Alone."

"Do you work here?" I asked.

She shook her head.

"Where do you work?"

"I'm a student."

"What university?"

"Online. If that's all, I need to get back to a class?"

"You were watching TV," I pointed out.

She rocked about on her feet like she needed to pee. "I have it on as background noise."

"What's your name, miss?" Whittaker asked. "So we can cross you off our list and not bother you again."

"Marcella."

"Surname?"

"Wallace."

She hurriedly closed the door, and we moved on. She was not what I was expecting from low-income housing. The next two apartments had nobody home as we zigzagged from side to side down the hallway. Knocking on number 6, I was surprised when the door opened right away. A young man dressed in gym gear greeted us.

"Hey. I was just headin' out. Wassup?"

The guy had a square jaw and the lean face of someone in great shape. He was sculpted, but not overly beefed up. The kind of frame which clothes hung perfectly from, and the normal people hoped they'd look like if they bought the same outfit. Their mirrors at home usually reflected their disappointment. Whittaker introduced us.

"Did the constables talk to you on Tuesday, sir?"

"No, I heard they by here, but I was out."

"I'm glad we caught you, then. Were you here Monday night?"

"Monday?" he said, and thought for a moment. "No, man, I stayed at a friend's place Monday night."

"All night? When did you return?"

"Yeah, all night. I came back after breakfast."

"May I ask where your friend lives?"

The man laughed. "She staying at da Kimpton, man."

"I see, and she could vouch for your whereabouts that night?"

He laughed again. "She remember I dere, believe me."

"Your friend's name and room number?"

"What's dis all about, man?" he asked, losing the smile on his face. "What ya askin' me all dis for?"

"Routine questions, sir. Helps us rule out folks as we proceed."

The man didn't look convinced. "Her name's Raquel, or Rachel… someting like dat. I don't remember da room number, but it were fifth floor."

I wondered if this lady stumbled into her good time in a bar, or ordered him via the internet.

"And your name, sir?" Whittaker asked.

"Anton Jeffries. Can I roll now, man?"

"What do you drive?" I asked before Whittaker could respond.

He gave me his best smile, which I'm sure melted many ladies. "No car, sister. I roll on two wheels."

"Thanks for your help, Mr Jeffries," Whittaker said.

The man closed his door and walked away, giving me a wink before he did so. He didn't realise I wasn't one of his easily meltable women. He was more likely to get a Taser in the crotch from me.

The next room had what I'd been expecting. The woman was probably in her forties, but looked older. Dressed in a shabby cotton dress, she looked tired and unhappy. The constables had already talked to her, she'd been asleep, and didn't know anything. I jotted down her name below the other two and we moved on.

"How does a student and a gigolo get subsidised housing?" I asked before we knocked on the next door.

Whittaker shook his head. "I was wondering the same thing. Figured I might stop by again by when this case is over and dig a little deeper."

Whittaker's mobile rang, and he answered the call. I waited, ready to knock on the next door.

He listened for a moment. "Good work, Don. Text me the address and email me any details you have."

Ending the call, he looked at me. "Let's go. Don pulled a reg plate for the car you picked out of the CCTV."

24

RAT'S ARSE AND A MOUSE WHEEL

Saturday 11:00am

Detective Whittaker was one of the most even-keeled people I'd ever known. That's saying something coming from a Norwegian. Our nation is renowned for our stoic, unemotional manner, narrowly topped by the Finns in our reputation for being dispassionate. He had to be under enormous pressure to close this case quickly, but he rarely let it show to those around him.

I'd learnt that most mainstream criminal cases, especially involving murder, are either solved very quickly or drag on for a long time, with the odds of solving them dropping with every passing week. The reason was simple. Often the thief or murderer commits the crime without any intelligent planning, which means they leave a trail to follow. The guilty party is usually connected to the victim in some way. The spouse is always the first suspect in the murder of a female.

This one had all the markings of a case which would take forever to solve. Whether by planning, quick thinking, or dumb luck, the killer had left no trace we'd been able to find so far. So it wasn't surprising that my unflappable mentor was energetically drumming his fingers on the steering wheel as he drove us into West Bay. This could be the lead which broke the case.

As he was driving, he'd handed me his mobile with the email open from Don. The address was a newer condo complex on Town Hall Road, and as we made our way there, I read out the other information.

"Andrew Bentham, 24 years old, from Canada. The car registered to him is a silver 2017 Hyundai Accent hatchback. He's here on a work permit. Works for a real estate development company…" I read through a bunch of uninteresting text to myself before getting to something worth talking about. "Looks like his father is a partner in the firm. They are mainly working on projects in the Bahamas, but they have one development here along South Church Street."

"Any prior record in our database?"

"One parking ticket, paid on time. He's been here for a year and a half."

"What's his job title at the firm?"

I laughed. "Project coordinator."

Whittaker smiled. "That could mean he coordinates coffee for the important people, or he oversees the entire operation."

We pulled into the condos, which comprised five buildings with four units in each one. Two downstairs and two up. They were nice, clean-looking rabbit hutches, but a far cry from the ritzy units on the water.

"I think he makes the coffee," I said as we got out.

We found the right block and knocked on the door of unit 3B, a ground-level condo on the left side of the middle building. Some kind of thumping death metal was playing inside. I looked around the car park for the silver Hyundai and saw it several spots away from his building. He had parked it nose in but I could see the rear bumper had damage on the left corner.

"There's the car," I said to Whittaker, who turned to look.

The door opened and a young man who looked like he'd just

got out of bed peered outside. How anyone could sleep with the racket playing on his stereo, I had no idea.

"Andrew Bentham?" I asked.

"Yeah," he mumbled, scratching his messy hair.

We showed our badges and introduced ourselves.

"Mind turning that shit down so we can talk?" I said and immediately regretted opening my mouth.

Whittaker didn't flinch, and the scrawny guy in the boxer shorts and wrinkled T-shirt left the door open and went inside to turn down his stereo.

"Sorry," I said quietly as we stepped inside.

"I know English is your second language, but you really need to get a grasp on the severity of some of our words," Whittaker whispered back to me.

That's good, I thought, he doesn't realise I'm well aware of the swear words in my vocabulary. I needed to limit my swearing to Norwegian, so no one knew what I was calling them. I did when I was really wound up, but leaned on my arsenal of English foul language under normal conditions.

The living room reeked of cigarette smoke, and empty beer cans were scattered across the coffee table. The blinds were closed and a single floor lamp put out less light than the open door. I found a wall switch and turned on the ceiling light. Bentham stood by the entertainment centre and looked at us.

"Am I correct in saying you own a silver 2017 Hyundai Accent, Mr Bentham?" Whittaker began in a pleasant tone.

"Uh-huh."

"Perfect, and that's the car you use every day?"

"Uh-huh."

"By any chance, have you been out late at night in your car, Mr Bentham, in the past two weeks?"

I loved watching the detective work. He had such a warm, easygoing manner that he lulled people into feeling comfortable while he grilled them for information.

The pride of Canada was now contemplating the question and,

no doubt, figuring out the lies he would spew. He flicked his head to swing the hair from his eyes. He had oily-looking straight hair, which he wore long enough that it came down over his eyes when he dipped his head, requiring a head toss to throw the dark mop back in place. I'm sure he thought it made him look cool and interesting. It made me want to kneel on his chest and buzz it all off with a blunt set of trimmers.

"I guess a few nights," were the words he finally graced us with.

"Perhaps you could tell me which nights?"

"What's this all about? Why the interest in my car?"

I wanted to tell him the interest was actually in him. The car was simply the way we'd found him.

"Which nights, Mr Bentham?"

"Shit, I don't know. Friday nights, usually. Sometimes Saturday."

"Were you out last night?"

"Yeah, for a while."

"How late?"

"Ten, maybe eleven. Then a few friends came back here, and we hung out."

"So, eleven at the latest?"

The hungover mouse was turning the wheel awfully slowly in Bentham's head, but I could see he was all consumed with what he may or may not have done last night. Which we didn't care a rat's arse about. Whittaker was brilliant.

"Yeah."

The detective turned as though he was done and ready to leave.

"Oh, one more thing," he said, pausing and turning back to a relieved-looking Bentham. "Were you out and about earlier in the week? Say Monday night?"

The Canadian's face dropped, and his stupid hair flopped over his face. He wiped it back with his hand, sparing us the 'look at me' head toss.

"Why? What's this about?"

His voice was beginning to sound panicked, and any relief had vanished from his face.

"Between the times of 2:20am and 3:51am on Tuesday morning," Whittaker pressed on.

"I'm done answering your questions. You can leave now."

"That's not really how this works here in the Cayman Islands, Mr Bentham. If you refuse to answer our questions here, we arrest you on suspicion and you accompany us to the station."

"No, you're not arresting me. I haven't done anything wrong. I'm calling my lawyer. You can deal with him now."

"Yes, but you see, it's not your lawyer we're arresting," Whittaker said calmly, nodding to me. "So you may certainly call him when we reach the station, but as of this moment, you're under arrest, sir."

"Hold your hands in front of you," I ordered, but I could tell Bentham was getting ready to melt down and do something stupid. "Hold your hands out front, or you'll be handcuffed with your hands behind you. The ride in the car is really uncomfortable with your hands behind you."

He held his hands away from me and began stepping backwards.

"Don't make this harder than it needs to be, Mr Bentham," Whittaker warned him, but the mouse must have been on a break, as nothing we said appeared to be processed in Bentham's addled brain.

He turned to bolt, but tripped over a big box next to the entertainment centre, which I guessed was a subwoofer speaker. He flailed his arms and had just about caught his balance when I shoved him in the shoulder, sending him crashing face first to the ground. I dropped my knee into the base of his back and cuffed both hands before he could catch his breath.

"I warned you, *drittsekk*," I said, remembering to slip into my native tongue.

. . .

Rather than drive him straight to the station, Whittaker made another brilliant play. While Bentham sat on his living room sofa with his front door open, two police cars showed up with red and blue lights turning the car park into a carnival show. Whittaker spent the time on his mobile organising warrants to search the house and the car. The SOCO van arrived fifteen minutes later, and a tow truck to haul the Hyundai away once initial forensics had been taken.

A terrified young man had a front-row seat to his life being turned into a shitstorm. He looked ready to cry when a constable finally led him to the back seat of his patrol car.

"We'll follow them to the station," Whittaker told me, after he finished on his phone. "Maybe he'll start talking before his lawyer shuts him up."

"He's worried about us, but I bet it's his father he's terrified of," I said, watching the patrol car leave the car park.

"I dare say you're right," Whittaker replied, looking at the mess in the apartment.

I was glad it wasn't me searching the house. "Unless something's gone pear shaped that didn't come up in the background check, his family is loaded, yet he's driving a crummy little car and living in a relatively cheap flat by Cayman standards. Doesn't look like Daddy's letting the kid have the keys to the castle."

"Where do you learn all these English idioms and phrases?" Whittaker asked with a slight grin.

I shrugged my shoulders. "Same place I learn my swear words. AJ and Reg are full of them."

25

FLIPPER FOR LUNCH

Saturday noon

They took Andrew Bentham to Central in George Town instead of the much smaller West Bay station. I figured it was all part of Whittaker's ploy to scare the shit out of the bloke. By the time we arrived, he was in an interview room and had been released from the handcuffs. He sat at the table in the middle of the stark room, looking sorry for himself.

"He's guilty as hell of something," I said, standing next to Whittaker, looking through the one-way glass.

"Most people are who sit in that chair," he replied. "It's whether he's guilty of brutally killing Kendra Rankin that we're interested in."

"His flight instinct seemed a lot stronger than his fight when we arrested him," I pointed out.

"True, but you were facing him. Kendra was struck from behind. It's possible she never knew who did it."

"He fits the profile of a chickenshit."

"Is that your professional diagnosis?" Whittaker asked in a stern tone.

"No, sir. That's my personal opinion of men who bash women over the head from behind."

"In that case, I agree," he said in a softer voice. "But let's keep our professional police hats on when we go in there."

"Yes, sir," I promised, and hoped I could live up to it.

"I'm not saying anything until my lawyer gets here," Bentham snapped, the moment we walked into the room.

I looked at Whittaker for permission, and he nodded.

"That's not true," I said as we took our seats.

"I'm not saying a damn word to you," he reiterated at a higher volume.

"You continue to lie," I responded calmly.

"I haven't lied!" he barked.

"We'll see, but you're off to a bad start."

He glared at me and the mouse appeared to be back on the wheel, albeit with little enthusiasm. The cogs and gears in his mind still hadn't realised every word he'd spoken contradicted his initial statement.

Whittaker started the interview recording and officially introduced everyone at the table before commencing. "The best way to walk out that door and put this behind you is to tell us what happened on Monday night and Tuesday morning, Mr Bentham. If there's an innocent explanation for your movements that we can verify, then you'll be free to go."

"Since when it is illegal to drive around at night?" he spat back.

"It isn't, and I hope it never will be," Whittaker replied. "But beating young women to death is, and always will be."

Bentham's mouth fell open. "That's what this is about? The woman I saw on the news? I have no idea who she is! I had nothing to do with her!"

"Are you saying you've never met Kendra Rankin?"

"I don't know anyone by that name!"

"Then explain why you were in the same area on West Bay Road at the time she was murdered," Whittaker fired back.

"What?" Bentham mumbled, looking thoroughly confused.

"Times, Constable Sommer?" Whittaker prompted me.

"You drove south on West Bay Road at 2:20am, remained in the vicinity of the murder for an hour and a half, then returned north at 3:51am."

Bentham let out a long breath. "Lawyer."

"That's how you plan to clear yourself and show us you're not guilty?" Whittaker responded. "You have every right to have your lawyer present, but a simple explanation of the missing ninety minutes could have you walking out the door and getting on with your life."

Bentham shook his head. "I didn't kill anyone."

"We could empty the jails and everyone would be innocent of their crimes if we just took your word for it. You need to give us an explanation we can verify."

He stared at the table. "I'm done talking. I want my lawyer."

Whittaker stood up. "If you're as innocent as you say, then a killer is loose on our island, and you're forcing us to pursue you as our primary suspect. I don't take obstruction of justice lightly, Mr Bentham."

The man continued staring at the table, remaining silent.

We walked around to the observation room and looked at Bentham through the one-way window. He had his head resting in his arms on the table.

"For that idiot to leave no trace at the scene, it would have to be dumb luck," I said.

"The spontaneous nature of the attack, and the clumsy teeth bashing and dumping of the body fits," Whittaker replied.

He was right. I could see Bentham in a drunken panic, clubbing Kendra after a disagreement of some description. But why? Was he seeing her? Whose baby was it? And where the hell was the kid? Certainly wasn't at Bentham's flat.

"Do we know for sure she was Kendra Rankin?" I asked.

Whittaker nodded. "The teacher on Brac recalled she had fallen in the playground and had stitches in her right arm. Rasha found a matching scar. It's not perfect proof, but it might be all we get."

I wasn't sure what we could do now. We'd get preliminary reports from the apartment and car search, but until the lawyer showed up, we were done talking to Chickenshit.

"Let's have a bite to eat while we can," Whittaker said, walking out the door.

"I have research I need to do," I replied, following.

"About this case?"

"No, it's a cold case."

"Trying to solve it?"

Thinking for a moment, I realised I hadn't considered that since I'd verified Jazzy's identification. "I've already solved it," I replied.

Whittaker stopped in the hallway. "What case? Anything to do with the young girl from the other day?"

Shit, why didn't I just say I wasn't hungry? "I have one more piece to put in place, then I'll bring everything to you, sir."

He hesitated, clearly not satisfied with my answer. But after a few beats, he nodded. "Okay. Want me to bring you something back?"

I was starving again despite having two breakfasts. I dug in my pocket for the money I'd shoved in there this morning. "Yes, please."

He waved a hand at me. "I got it. What would you like?"

"Where are you going?"

"I hadn't decided."

I looked at him blankly.

"I'll find something I think you'll like," he said with a grin, and left.

• • •

I sat down at the computer and brought up the case file for Jasmine Holder. The East End police had interviewed the foster family several times, kids and teachers at her school, and a woman named Gloria Middleton. Beyond a couple of reported sightings by members of the public, Jazzy had disappeared. A trick she'd perfected over the past three years. The report stated the police could find no evidence of foul play, but never came up with an explanation. The case remained open, although nothing had been added to the file in several years.

Noting the address of both the foster family, and the woman named Gloria, who Jazzy had mentioned, I began looking into her mother, Delores Holder. She had spent more than her fair share of time in trouble by the length of her rap sheet. Drug possession, shoplifting, and two charges for driving under the influence. The Department of Children and Family Services declared Delores unfit in January 2019 after her second DUI, which also resulted in her fourth possession charge. She spent six months in jail, then left the Cayman Islands on a flight to Miami shortly after. Delores was the primary suspect in a grocery store robbery, but had left before they could interview her. She paid cash for her ticket at the airport.

The authorities had placed Jazzy in a permanent foster home by then. I scanned for more information on the family who took her in. Jack and Rosalyn Barton. UK passports with permanent residency in the Cayman Islands. He was some kind of civil servant, which explained how they gained residency status. No children of their own, but fostered several. All girls. There was one other girl with them when Jazzy ran away.

I sat back and absorbed the new information. I quickly concluded it didn't help me much at all. Maybe there was some-thing dodgy with the Bartons, but all I had was a young runaway's say-so. Maybe she didn't like them telling her to be in bed by nine o'clock. I didn't want to start a big fuss if they were genuinely nice people doing the world a favour by fostering kids. Of course, if there was substance to her claim, something had to be done about it.

The report mentioned nothing about other family members on the island, which was strange as Delores held a Cayman Islands passport - which was actually a British passport issued to British Overseas Territories Citizens. I decided Gloria might be able to help me with the family question, and at some point, I needed to contact DCFS. I couldn't really walk into their office and start with, 'In theory if I came across a thirteen-year-old who'd run away from foster care...' Which meant I'd be grassing on Jazzy to the authorities, and the wheels of the system would be forced into motion.

At some point that had to happen, as she couldn't live on the streets until she was eighteen, and some schooling wouldn't be a bad idea. Not that she'd agree with any of that. I heard someone behind me and swivelled around in the chair.

"I got you a tuna sandwich," Whittaker announced, handing me a package. "They promised me they only use dolphin-safe tuna."

"You know that's a bunch of bullshit, right?"

"I trust them at Treats – lovely people," Whittaker said defensively.

"I love Treats, it's the dolphin-safe claims on the tins that's bullshit."

"Really?"

"They pay to have the logo on the tins, but no one ever checks to see what they're catching. It would be impossible. So they catch tuna, dolphins, and whatever else they drag up, print the logo like they're all concerned about Flipper, and carry on making a fortune. It's a scam."

Whittaker frowned. "I didn't know. Can you eat that?"

I unwrapped the paper and revealed the sandwich. "Ja, not eating it now would be a waste."

"Figure it out?" Whittaker asked.

"Huh?" I mumbled with a mouthful of sandwich.

"The cold case. You said you'd solved it."

I took my time chewing, buying time to come up with a way to stall a little longer. I couldn't lie to the man.

"She's a girl who went missing three years ago. I found her."

His eyes lit up. "That's wonderful." Then he frowned. "Wait, is she okay, or are you saying you found a body?"

"She's okay."

"Who is she?"

"Puffin Girl," I replied.

It was his turn to give me a blank 'Are you kidding?' look.

"I need a bit longer to sort things out with her, sir."

"You said 'girl'. How old is she?"

"Thirteen."

"Nora, Children and Family Services need to take care of that. Have you told them?"

I shook my head. "If they picked her up right now, she'd just run away again. I need a bit of time to win her confidence. She has to believe we can help her."

"This is what that department does, Nora. They know what they're doing with these things."

"From their perspective," I said. "Not from her experience."

He thought about my comment for a moment, then sighed. "Fine. It sounds like you have a promising lead. Make sure you keep me informed of your progress. But I do expect a result within a week."

I grinned. *"Takk."*

26

A FISTFUL OF MARL

Saturday 1:00pm

Whittaker left me to finish my sandwich while he went to his office to respond to his mounting number of voicemails, emails and whatever else accumulated while he was out of the office. Bentham's lawyer wasn't arriving for another hour or two. His day on the golf course, or boat, or with family had likely been turned upside-down, but I was sure he'd bill a trillion dollars an hour for his trouble, so I couldn't find any sympathy for him. Plus, he represented Chickenshit.

I know someone has to, and everyone has a right to be defended, but I don't know how people do it. How could you do your best to find a loophole in the law or the police's procedure to get a rapist off the hook? Win the case and shake hands with someone who murdered, raped, or sold drugs to kids, and let them thank you for doing a great job. Go home to your wife and kids, knowing you worked the system to send a piece of shit back out on the streets. Your own daughter could be his next victim.

My job was to find the *drittsekker* and hand them over to the court system. In the past, I'd been guilty of forgetting my role ended there. Of course, some dipshit lawyer hadn't set free a rapist or murderer I'd caught, but that day would probably come. I doubt I'd handle the situation very well.

Whittaker appeared in the doorway and pulled me from my wandering thoughts.

"Let's go," he said.

I followed him down the hallway. He seemed on a mission.

"Are we going back to finish talking to the people at the apartments?"

He held the door to the lobby open for me. "No. We're going to the West Bay Maternity Clinic. Bee called. She's found more files missing."

"So she's a shitty office manager, after all?"

Whittaker hurried across the reception area, pausing only to hold the front door open for me.

"All the missing files have one thing in common," he said, as we strode across the car park to his SUV. "All the women came in once and never came back."

Twenty minutes later, Bee waved us into her office behind the counter. She seemed flushed, although it was hard to tell with her dark skin, but she was certainly agitated.

"Sit down and I show you what I talkin' about," she said without preamble.

She pushed and shoved her computer monitor around until it was at one end of her desk where we could all see it.

"Dis da log o' all da files been produced."

"I thought you didn't keep electronic records," I pointed out.

"I keep all da files demselves in folders, da log and udder stuff I use da computer for," she replied indignantly. "I ain't in da dark ages, you know."

She moved the cursor around on the screen. "See here? Dis is da sequential numbered log for da records. Name go here, den date o' birth. When da patient come in, if she new, she get da next number in da log. I can sort all dis by log number, first name, surname, and dates."

"Okay," Whittaker said. "And you mentioned you've discovered other missing files?"

"Yes, yes, I gettin' to dat part," Bee rolled her chair away from the desk and pointed to a large grey filing cabinet. "Dat's where all da files kept. Dey in number order, which make dem also in order o' date of first visit." She stood and opened one of the long drawers. "Dis whole business about a file gone missin' got me so I ain't sleepin', so dis mornin' I came in early and start goin' through all dese," Bee explained, indicating the rows of hanging files.

Whittaker and I stood, moving closer to see. I expected to see folders with all the coloured tabs I'd seen in doctor's offices before. But these were simple manilla folders with a neatly handwritten number on the tab. The tabs were staggered perfectly, making each number easier to see. Some files were a lot thicker than others.

"I didn't find no more files missin', but I found eight wit nuttin' in dere," Bee said. "We never have a file wit nuttin' in dere. If someone go through dat door out dere," she continued, indicating the door into the clinic itself, "dey gets a file wit a number and at least a form wit da details."

"What if they don't give a name?" I asked.

"Don't matter. Dey refuse to give da name, we make a file and put 'unknown' by da name, den what dey here for."

"So the log would show the name from the missing file," I said, wondering why she hadn't mentioned this before.

"No name given," Bee replied, giving me a stern look. "I checked dat da udder day."

"So, regardless of how long they're here, every patient will have at least one slip of paper in their file." Whittaker confirmed.

"Yes, sir," Bee agreed. "Dis mornin', I check every file by da number, and da one I said still missin', but I found eight more got nuttin' in dere."

Whittaker nodded. "And how do you know they were patients who only came by once?"

"'Cos we don't have dat many patients, so I remember most. I bin here since we open," Bee said, peering over her glasses at us. "And den da files," she added, pulling one from the drawer. "Da one wit more pages start to go flat at da bottom, and if da girl come in a few times, dis file start gettin' pretty tick. None of da empty ones like dat."

That was hardly scientific evidence, but I followed her logic.

"So, from your log, you have the name and the date they came in, but we don't know why they came in?" I asked.

"Dey come in 'cos dey pregnant, dat much I know," Bee said, with a hint of a grin.

I smiled back. I was starting to like Bee.

"Who has access to these files, Mrs Ebanks?" Whittaker asked.

"Everyone dat work here. Can't keep da door locked in case dey need a file when I ain't here."

Whittaker and I exchanged a glance. That meant every employee, and in theory, every person who stepped through the door. Anyone could walk around the counter and enter the office the same way we had.

"Let's start with the list of names, Mrs Ebanks, and phone numbers for those patients if you have them."

"Everyone just call me Bee, Detective. I'm fine you doin' da same. Names I got. Phone numbers, dey be on da missing pages."

She tapped on her keyboard and the printer on a sideboard behind us came to life. Whittaker took the page once it spat out from the rollers and looked at the names.

"Thank you, Bee," he said, glancing up. "Who else is working today?"

"Sarika is back dere, and one of our part-time girls, but I tink she went for lunch."

"Could we talk to Miss Kumari?" he asked. "Probably better to do that out here rather than disturb your patients. Could we borrow your office for a few minutes?"

Bee looked a little put out at the prospect of being booted from her own office, and she left to find the Indian nurse, still pouting.

"Did anything more come up about Kumari?" I asked. "She was the only one with any kind of record, right?"

Whittaker nodded, still studying the list of names. "It didn't seem like too much to get excited about," he replied without looking up. "By all indications, she did the wrong thing for the right reasons."

"I get that," I mumbled.

Whittaker looked up and raised an eyebrow.

"Here you go," Bee said, showing Nurse Kumari into the office. "I'll wait out here, I s'pose."

I smiled at Bee and pushed the door closed.

"Hello Miss Kumari, we're sorry to intrude on your day, but we have new information which generates new questions," Whittaker explained.

"Okay, I'll help if I can, but I only have a few minutes. I'm the only one here right now."

"We'll be brief," Whittaker assured her. "Who has access to the medical files in this cabinet?" he asked, pointing to the large grey file drawers.

"We all do."

"How often do you have cause to access the files?"

"Me in particular, or any of the nurses?" she asked in way of reply.

She'd been relaxed when we'd started, but had already tensed. Of course, part of that was a natural reaction to the police firing questions at you, but she was quick to become defensive.

"The situation would be the same for all of you, I presume?" Whittaker responded.

"That's correct. We ask Bee if she's here, or we get the file ourselves if she's not."

"What about a new patient when Bee isn't here?" I asked before Whittaker could speak again.

Kumari looked at me as though I was a child interrupting their parents. "We start a file, put the paperwork we generate in it, and leave it on Bee's desk for her to catalogue and put away."

"And how do you find an existing patient's file when they come in?" I asked.

"We ask Bee."

"When she's not here."

"We search for the name in the log file. It's a shared document on our server."

"How many computers are there in the building capable of accessing the server?"

She shrugged her shoulders. "I don't know. I've never counted them. There's one in each of the examination rooms; that's two. Two more at the rolling nurses' stations. I think Doctor Kirkconnell has a laptop so he can remotely access from home. And Bee's, of course."

"Another at the counter upfront," I pointed out.

"Yes," she agreed. "So seven, but maybe there are others I'm forgetting."

"Anyone besides the doctor have remote access?"

She shook her head. "That's a question for Bee, but I know none of the nurses do."

I glanced at the detective, indicating I was done, and he gave me a subtle nod in return.

"Have you noticed anyone spending an unusual amount of time in Bee's office while she's not here?"

Kumari shook her head. "No, but there's only one person here overnight, so I've no idea what they do."

Whittaker smiled. "Thank you for your time. I know you need to get back to your patients, Miss Kumari. If you think of anything that may be of interest to us, please call."

"This is all about one mislaid file?" she asked, pausing with her hand on the doorknob.

"It's become more than just one missing file, I'm afraid," Whittaker replied.

The nurse acknowledged with a frown, then left the office.

"May I come back in my office now?" Bee said from the front counter.

"Please do," Whittaker smiled. "Thank you for all your help, Bee. We'll be in touch."

The woman beetled back in, still looking disgruntled about her eviction. We walked outside and didn't speak until the front door closed behind us.

"We need a warrant for their computers," I said.

"I was wondering about that," Whittaker replied. "You think we can see who looked at the log file?"

"That'll depend on their login procedures, but Don should be able to see which computer accessed the patient log file. We can match that to who was working at the time."

Whittaker took out his mobile before we reached the SUV.

"Sir?"

He looked up.

"That's the marl trail I was talking about," I said, pointing to the driveway next to the clinic.

He thought for a moment before responding. "You'll find evidence bags in the glove box. Grab a fistful of the gravel. Get the small stuff from the edge. It was tiny pebbles between her toes."

27

WARM TRICKLES DOWN THE TROUSER LEG

Saturday 2:30pm

Pulling out of the car park, Whittaker received a call telling him Bentham's lawyer had arrived. This time, he took the bypass to expedite the trip. By the time we reached Central, the detective had a warrant organised for the clinic's computers, and Don from TSU was on his way to West Bay with a pair of constables. At the station, I dropped my bag of gravel off with Rasha, who looked at me with a frown.

"What am I supposed to do with this, young lady?"

"Match it to the marl between her toes," I replied.

"It's not as easy as that," she said with a grin.

If she said it wasn't easy, I believed her; partly because I trusted Rasha, and partly because I had no idea what was possible and what wasn't.

"Okay," I said, and left it for her to figure out.

Whittaker was waiting for me in the hallway, so we walked straight to the interview room. Someone had given him several pages of information, and I saw by the heading they were preliminary reports from Bentham's apartment and car.

Andrew Bentham looked slightly fresher than he had earlier. I'm sure his hangover was wearing off, but his lawyer's presence seemed to add a coat of armour. In his tiny mind.

"Blake Weinstein," the man said boldly as we entered the room. He spoke with an American accent. New York, I thought, but I wasn't great at placing American accents.

He was shorter than me, soft looking like the heaviest thing he ever picked up was his briefcase, and he was losing his hair, which he denied by combing what he had in weird directions and using product to hold it in place.

"I'd like to see what actual evidence you have of my client's wrongdoing in relationship to the murder case. It's preposterous to think he had anything to do with whatever happened to this woman."

We sat at the table, and Whittaker started the recording.

"I'm Detective Whittaker. Also present is…"

"Constable Sommer," I said on cue.

Whittaker held his hand out towards the lawyer.

"Blake Weinstein, representation for Mr Andrew Bentham," he said, with the wind already knocked out of his sails. You'd think the guy would know how these things started.

Whittaker looked at the Canadian.

"Andrew Bentham," the suspect muttered.

Whittaker continued before the lawyer could chime in. "Mr Bentham, now your lawyer is present, are you willing to explain your movements on Monday night, and the early hours of Tuesday morning?"

Bentham looked at Weinstein and the lawyer leapt into action, albeit a little less enthusiastically than before. "As I said, I'd like to see what actual evidence you have tying my client to your case."

"We have CCTV of Mr Bentham in close proximity to the murder site during the time frame in which the crime took place.

As yet, he's been unwilling to provide us with a reason," Whittaker replied.

"Can you see my client in the vehicle?" Weinstein asked.

"We have the registration plate."

"I see. So you can identify the vehicle, but not the driver."

"Your client already admitted to driving his vehicle that night."

"He was confused about the timing."

"You're telling us it was not Mr Bentham driving his own car that night?"

"I'm saying there's no evidence to prove he was."

Whittaker sat back in his chair. "We have your client's mobile phone, and shortly we'll have his call log and cell tower pings showing his location."

I wondered if Weinstein knew there were only a few towers around, and triangulating an exact location was really inaccurate on an oddly shaped island.

"He left his phone in his car," came the lawyer's reply.

I guess he didn't know, or he was happy to stack up the lies. Of course, he would say he wasn't lying. He was providing an alternative sequence of events that we couldn't disprove.

"Okay," Whittaker said, as though he was admitting defeat. "We'll proceed with the drug charges and go from there."

"What drug charges?" Weinstein snapped, spinning from Whittaker to his client. Bentham stared into the table and wouldn't look up.

The detective pulled the papers from a file he'd tucked them inside. "Let's see here. We found traces of marijuana in your client's car…"

"That doesn't prove my client was in possession," the lawyer quickly retorted.

"That's true," Whittaker responded. "Perhaps the mystery driver from Monday night also broke into your client's apartment and left a bag of ganja there, too?"

Weinstein sighed. After a few moments of silence, he said, "I need a few minutes to confer with Mr Bentham."

"Of course," Whittaker responded, rising from his seat. "Oh, and you might also want to discuss the pornography we found. It appears the unreported intruder also dropped off a few unsavoury magazines. They're considered pornography in the Cayman Islands."

The lawyer's shoulders dropped.

"Interview paused at 2:56pm," Whittaker said, then hit a button on the recorder.

The detective walked towards the door, but I stayed behind a moment.

"Are you related to the film guy Weinstein?" I asked quietly across the table. "You know, the rapist bloke?"

The lawyer glared at me, so I shrugged my shoulders and turned to join Whittaker.

"Are you?" I heard Bentham ask as we left the room.

"Do you like him for the murder?" Whittaker asked once we were down the hallway, with the door closed behind us.

"We're nowhere on motive," I replied. "Without the baby, we can't check paternity."

"But does he strike you as capable?"

I shook my head. "His reaction when I approached him at his flat was to back up and run. I still think someone capable of bashing Kendra to death would be more aggressive."

"I think you're more intimidating than Kendra. She was a small woman."

I didn't mind being called intimidating. I'd been a victim in my past and didn't plan on being one again.

"And remember, the killer struck from behind," Whittaker added.

He had a point. It doesn't take too much bravery to whack someone who doesn't know you're there. Just a lot of rage. Or evil.

"I still don't see this guy clubbing her in the face. If he went berserk and lashed out, I could see him beating her several times initially, but what the killer did next required thought, and then a second round of violence."

Whittaker nodded. "Perhaps. But maybe he panicked. She was walking away from him; he lashed out, then realised he'd killed her and starting covering his tracks."

"Hard to know what someone is truly capable of doing," I replied. "Most of us never know what our own limits are unless we're pushed or provoked. Judging another person's potential is impossible."

"True. Which is why we need evidence."

The door to the interview room opened, and Weinstein stuck his head out. "Detective?"

We walked down the hallway and entered the room where the lawyer was returning to his seat. Whittaker restarted the recording as we sat down, repeated who was present, and gave the time of day.

"I want to make it clear that my client had no part in whatever happened to the girl. If he helps you out by explaining why he was in the vicinity, we expect you to take his cooperation into consideration and these other minor offences will go away."

Whittaker leaned forward. "So, to be clear. Your client is willing to impede our investigation, unless we ignore multiple charges against him for which we have damning evidence. Is that correct?"

Weinstein waved his hands around. "Come on, Detective, that's being ridiculously harsh. All we're saying is Andrew is offering to help you as much as he can, and that deserves some leniency."

"No, what you're saying is you and your client don't care one bit about a murdered Caymanian citizen, or the fact that a killer is still at large; if indeed your client isn't the murderer. Regardless, all he cares about is himself."

"That's not true," the lawyer retorted.

"Then why didn't you come forward when we asked for witnesses days ago, Mr Bentham?" Whittaker challenged, pointing a finger at the young man. "Right now, you're our number one suspect in a murder case. If I were you, I'd worry less about the drug charges and more about coming up with a verifiable reason for being on West Bay Road in the early hours of Tuesday morning."

Whittaker impressed me once again. The detective knew how to turn up the heat when he needed to.

"Okay, let's just all calm down," Weinstein said, straightening his tie and patting his client on the arm. Bentham hadn't moved a muscle and still stared at the table. The only thing coming out of him might have been a warm trickle down the leg of his trousers.

Whittaker returned his attention to the lawyer. "Here in the islands, we expect those graced with work permits to adhere to our laws and respect our people, the same as everyone else. Now, what happened on Monday night?"

Weinstein had to nudge his client to get him to lift his head. "Go ahead, explain what happened."

Bentham looked like a man offered a chance to utter his last words before the noose was slung around his neck. I suspected the greater fear was of his father more than the law. He licked his dry lips and struggled to find the words to begin a statement that would likely, at a minimum, have his work permit revoked.

"Monday night I didn't have any plans, you know?" he began reluctantly. "So I grabbed takeout when I left the office in George Town and went home. A buddy calls me around ten and says a few friends are getting together. I was watching a movie, so I said maybe, but didn't feel like doing anything."

I was ready to lean over the table and punch this idiot in the nose. I didn't give a shit about his 'who called who' crap. But Whittaker was patiently letting him ramble, so I kept my mouth shut.

"Later, he called from a bar and they were all having a good time, so I thought maybe I'd join them after all."

"What time was this?" Whittaker asked.

Bentham shrugged his shoulders. "I was watching one of them late night chat shows, so after eleven."

"Which show?" I asked.

"The one with the English guy, James something."

I didn't own a television and had no idea what shows were on or who was on them, but I made a note to check the broadcast schedule. I nodded to Chickenshit, and he continued.

"I changed to go out, then I get a text telling me they were going to a girl's place, and he'd send me the address once they got there. Then we had a bunch of texts back and forth for a while, and I gave up and went to bed."

"And what time was that?" Whittaker asked.

Bentham shook his head. "Late, but I don't remember for sure. It was well after midnight."

The detective indicated for the man to continue.

"Yeah, so I was asleep, and probably should have turned my phone off, but I didn't, so a call wakes me up around one something. It's my buddy again, and he's at this girl's house. Sounds like they're having a big party and he's telling me I gotta come over."

"Did he say where this party was?" Whittaker asked.

I held my breath for a moment. I was sure he was going to say one of the places on West Bay Road.

"London House condos," Bentham replied.

I was right; West Bay Road. But south of the house with the better quality security camera.

"Okay," Whittaker urged, "and you left your apartment at what time?"

"I remember looking at my watch and thinking the next day at work was gonna suck. It was a few minutes after 2:00am."

"What happened then?"

"I drove down West Bay Road, and I guess I nodded off. Next thing I knew, I was facing the wrong way with my bumper up against a pole."

"Where exactly on West Bay Road was this?" Whittaker asked.

"I've no clue, man. I was kinda freaked out, so I pulled across to the other side of the road and parked."

"You don't remember which buildings you parked beside?"

"It was the middle of the night and there aren't any street lights along there. I remember trees, and lights behind them, but that's about it."

"So, what did you do next?"

"I tipped my seat back and went to sleep."

"Did you see anyone else?"

"Not that I recall, but I was…" Bentham caught himself. "Tired."

Whittaker tapped the table with his finger. "You were drunk and/or stoned. Everyone at this table knows that, Mr Bentham, and there's nothing the law can do about it because we didn't test you at the time. So let's stick with the whole truth."

Bentham let a long sigh escape. "I may have been a little buzzed."

"My client has cooperated as promised, Detective, so it's time to let him go home," Weinstein interjected.

Whittaker shook his head. "Not even close. Maybe we can verify the car incident from tyre tracks and lining up damage to the bumper with a telegraph pole, but there's still over an hour unaccounted for."

"He's told you, he was in his car by the side of West Bay Road."

"And I was having drinks with Elvis Presley," Whittaker scoffed. "Both are going to be hard to prove, aren't they?"

"That's true, Detective," Weinstein retorted, "but if you had one stitch of evidence involving my client in the actual crime, this would be a very different conversation. So unless you can prove Mr Bentham was involved, which you can't because he wasn't, then I believe we're done here."

Whittaker stood up. "You're right, we're done here."

"Thank you," Weinstein said, looking very pleased with himself as he also stood.

I rose from my seat, and Whittaker gave me a nod.

"Mr Bentham, I'm arresting you for possession of illegal narcotics and pornography," I began, enjoying the stunned look on Bentham's face as I read him his rights.

28

MISTER NICE GUY

Saturday 4:30pm

I ran a tape measure up the telegraph pole from the dirt to the fresh marks in the wood. Before we'd left the station, I'd done the same to the rear bumper of Bentham's Hyundai, which was impounded by our forensics team in the yard out back of the station. The dimensions were within a few inches of each other. The bumper had also contained wood splinters imbedded in the plastic.

"Tyre tracks have been washed away," Whittaker noted aloud. "I can see marks, but not clearly enough for tread comparison. All we can do is get a track width."

I walked a few steps over to where the detective stood. He held one end of the tape while we estimated a perpendicular path from one tyre track to the other, and measured from centre to centre. A quick internet search revealed it matched the Hyundai.

Beyond the pole to the south were the apartments we'd visited that morning and I wondered if anyone had heard tyres screeching in the night. Of course, it looked like all the skidding had been done in the dirt and gravel, so there probably wasn't much noise.

Based on the limited damage, he couldn't have been going very fast by the time he hit the pole, so the thud wouldn't have been loud either.

"Okay, so we know Bentham told us the truth about spinning out his car," Whittaker pondered, staring down West Bay Road. "And I can see where he dropped two wheels off the tarmac, which caused him to lose control."

"I think the drink, drugs, and falling asleep *caused* the loss of control," I mentioned. "The tyre marks indicate *where*."

"Good point," Whittaker replied. "Seems like most of the island was stoned on Monday night." He shook his head and looked at me. "Did I miss something? Was it a full moon Monday night?"

"We are talking to suspects in a murder," I replied. "Not the best citizens the island has to offer."

Whittaker nodded, but his mind was already on his next thought. "He hits the pole, then drives across the road and parks."

I led the detective along the verge, looking for more marks that might show where the car rejoined the road.

"Here," I said, spotting two scrape marks on the edge of the tarmac. "These don't line up with the other tracks. I think he bottomed out driving out of the dirt."

We both looked back and forth between the pole and the scrapes, sighting a line to the west side of the road. Waiting for a break in traffic, we crossed and agreed on the approximate location he likely would have parked. The northbound side of the road had a narrow parking lane, then a pavement, so again, no tracks.

We were standing close to the entrance to Silver Sands Condominiums. On either side of the entryway, palm trees lined the property. If only they had a security camera, we might have got a shot of the parked car.

"If we believe him, he parked here and went to sleep," Whittaker said, with his hands on his hips.

"Or, he got out of his car and followed Kendra Rankin towards Jackson's Pond and killed her," I responded. "With no motivation we can fathom, or personal knowledge of the victim we can find."

"Hmm," Whittaker replied thoughtfully. "Doesn't add up, does it?"

His mobile rang, which was fine, as I figured it was what they called a rhetorical question in English. Phrased as a question, but didn't require an answer. Seemed pointless to me. If you know the other person already knows the answer, why say anything? Maybe it helped the detective think through the scenarios, but I hoped I'd never bother anyone with rhetorical questions.

After a brief conversation, which I couldn't hear as I walked farther down the road looking for any clues Chickenshit might have tossed from his car, Whittaker called me back.

"Let's go. That was Don. He's still working on the clinic's computers, but he's found several people besides Bee accessed the patient file number log this week. One of them being Doctor Kirk-connell."

I jogged along the pavement to Whittaker's SUV parked to the south.

"Is that unusual?" I asked, sliding into the passenger seat. "He does run the place."

"First time was 5:30am Tuesday morning, and the second was Thursday evening," Whittaker replied while starting his SUV and pulling away.

"That's the morning of the murder, and the evening after we went to the clinic for a second time," I processed out loud. "Where is he?"

"Don said he showed up at the clinic rather upset we hadn't informed him of the warrant. Bee called him and told him."

"He'll be more upset when we ask him to explain his logins."

We were greeted by a different man from the easy-going, dreamy-eyed doctor I'd met a few days ago. Conroy Kirkconnell was not a happy chappy.

"I've cooperated every step of the way, Detective. Why didn't you call and ask me to access our server? We have patient files on there you shouldn't be looking at, but I would have given you whatever else you needed."

"I appreciate that, Doctor, but this way you're protected from suspicion of covering anything up between the time we warn you and subsequently arrive. It's really for you and your staff's protection," Whittaker explained.

"Clearly we're under suspicion already, or you wouldn't be looking at our server," he replied accurately.

"Is there somewhere we can speak privately?" Whittaker asked.

"Bee's office, but your people have taken that over. I don't want the patients upset by any of this, so I'd rather not go inside our ward."

"Let's step outside, shall we?"

Kirkconnell reluctantly followed Whittaker out of the front door and I trailed them both. The doctor had avoided eye contact with me since we'd arrived, which bothered me. I wanted to see the look in his eyes now that we'd turned up the heat. I thought he was Mister Nice Guy the other day, but now I was kicking myself that I'd been suckered by his charm.

"Who has access to the server, Doctor?" Whittaker began once we were outside and standing in the shade close to the building.

"Everyone who works here," Kirkconnell replied. "We store everything on our server – test results, patient information, you name it. We also host our email system there."

"I thought Bee insisted on keeping hard copy records?" I asked.

He finally looked at me, and I tried to read his face. Clearly he was upset, but his eyes showed far more. Despite his anger at the situation, I saw something else in those caramel-coloured windows into the man's true self. It took me a moment, but then I realised what I was seeing. Hurt. Then it was me who had to look away.

"Bee prints everything for her files. I know that's frowned upon these days, and I don't like it either, but she runs a tight ship for me. I'd be lost without her."

Grunting a response, I let Whittaker take over again. I needed to get my head straight. The evidence was building against the doctor, more so than a mislaid file, and I was still in danger of being swayed by his disarming personality. Which wasn't like me at all.

"Why would your patient file number log be accessed by members of your staff?" Whittaker asked.

"Mostly to pull the correct file of a visiting patient. If Bee is in the office, she handles that, but when she's not, one of the staff looks up the file number and pulls it from the office," Kirkconnell replied.

"Any other reasons?" Whittaker pressed.

The doctor thought for a moment. "Verifying a new patient is, in fact, a new patient. We make sure we're not starting a file for someone we already have one for. We can search by name or date of birth." He pondered a moment longer, and the detective gave him time to think. "If we receive a request for patient information, that would be another instance. We'd start by looking up the log."

"Which of those scenarios applied when you accessed the patient file number log early Tuesday morning, Doctor?" Whittaker asked.

Kirkconnell looked stunned. This guy had a team of mice spinning wheels in his intelligent brain, but I guessed they'd all been caught off guard.

"Am I a suspect in your case?" he asked.

Whittaker answered his question with a statement. "Doctor, you accessed the log remotely at 5:30am Tuesday morning, which happened to be a few hours after Kendra Rankin's murder. A young woman who'd been through your doors some months prior, and whose file mysteriously vanished by the time we came by the next day."

"Fuck me," Kirkconnell muttered.

I didn't take the doctor for a man who swore often, but this was a point in time that would forever be etched in his memory, regardless of where things went from here. We all have those moments in our pasts which make our stomachs tighten when that paralysing recollection finds its way into our thoughts. For me, I had too many. A sailboat boom striking a teacher in the head. Being beaten and abused at the Fellowship of Lions resort. And of course, the moment I tried to hide the most. The vision that refused to become blurred or filtered in any way with time. I could still clearly see, as though it were yesterday, Ridley moving his body in front of mine, so the bullet meant for me hit him instead.

I swallowed the lump in my throat and realised Whittaker was speaking again.

"…Thursday evening at 8:55pm, you remotely accessed the log again, and on Friday morning, eight more files were missing."

Kirkconnell stood before us in stunned silence. His eyes danced around the car park and the road beyond, searching for answers. I was sure they weren't out there. After all, we were in Hell.

"Tuesday, I was up early…"

"How early?" Whittaker interjected.

"A little after five," Kirkconnell replied tentatively, still fumbling his way through the situation.

He was either shocked he'd been caught and was scrambling for viable reasons, or he was genuinely baffled and trying to recall his actions. If someone asked me to come up with exactly what I was doing at a certain time five days ago, I'm sure it would require some thought.

"I go to the gym most mornings before work, so I get up early."

"Did you go to the gym Tuesday morning?"

"Yes, in Camana Bay."

"They use swipe cards, correct?"

Kirkconnell nodded. "Yes, they should have a record of what time, but it was around six or just after."

"What did you do between five and six?"

The doctor looked squarely at Whittaker, regaining his composure. "I prepared for the day by reviewing charts for the patients I was due to see. I noticed on my calendar there was a patient I didn't have the chart for, so I looked it up in the log. That way, I could grab it first thing. I'm usually at the clinic before Bee starts at eight."

I scribbled notes down as he talked. We would be able to view Bee's calendar and see the doctor's patient schedule.

"What about Thursday night?" Whittaker continued.

"The same. I had pulled several files, but I noticed one patient had been added after I'd left the clinic."

"How come you prepared in the morning on Tuesday, but in the evening on Thursday?"

Kirkconnell shook his head with an incredulous look. "I was meeting someone for breakfast after the gym on Friday morning, so I prepared the night before."

"Who did you meet?"

The doctor looked at me as he replied. "My sister."

If he thought there was still a chance of a date at this stage, he had to be nuts. "We'll need a contact number," I said sharply.

The door to the clinic opened, and Don stepped outside. "Detective?"

Whittaker turned to Kirkconnell. "That'll be all for now, Doctor."

We waited a few moments while Kirkconnell went back inside.

"What do you have, Don?"

"Matching times the log file was accessed against employee shifts, the majority are by nurse Kumari. She worked nights earlier this week, so that's not surprising."

"On her own?" I asked.

"Correct. They schedule two nurses during the day and one overnight. The nurses work four twelve-hour shifts a week. Mrs Ebanks works regular eight-hour days, five days a week."

"We saw Kumari here earlier today," I said, wondering what she was doing there if she worked nights.

Don looked at his notes. "She worked nights last Friday through Monday, then started day shifts Wednesday."

"What about the bloke we spoke with the other day?" I asked. "The Englishman."

"Ian Belfrey worked the day shift Sunday through Wednesday this week. We can see one time the log file was accessed during his shifts and that was Monday evening at 6:35pm. Before the murder happened."

"Do they have any CCTV?" I asked.

"Not recorded," Don replied. "There's one camera in the lobby which can be viewed live on any computer."

"The doctor and nurse Kumari knew each other in the UK, didn't they?" I asked, turning to Whittaker.

"They did. He defended her when I asked about her leaving the hospital in England after being accused of stealing," he confirmed.

"Speak with her again?" I asked.

Whittaker thought for a moment before replying. "I think it's time we invited the doctor and his nurse to the station for a longer chat."

29

———

PIZZA SECURITY

Saturday 6:00pm

Whittaker drove south along the back of Seven Mile Beach, the hotels and condos to our right, and small retail parks and restaurants on our left. I was getting hungry again.

"Perhaps we should pick up food before we get to the station," Whittaker said, as though he read my mind. Or heard my stomach rumbling.

"Anything but Burger King," I replied, looking at the gorgeous autumn-coloured sky to the west.

"No argument from me," Whittaker replied. "I was thinking of a pizza from Le Vele."

My mouth began to water at the thought. Le Vele was an Italian restaurant on the water and served fabulous pasta, but even better oven-fired pizzas. They were reasonably priced considering the food quality and location, but not an everyday eatery on a constable's salary. Putting that thought aside, I called them right away and ordered food to go.

Ten minutes later, Whittaker pulled into the restaurant's narrow car park and found an open space. It was early for many diners, and most patrons were soaking up the sunset with a drink on the deck above us. The police radio crackled and Whittaker turned up the volume.

"…outside Rackam's. Do we have anyone in the vicinity? Over." The familiar voice of one of the dispatch ladies from Central came over the radio.

Whittaker keyed the mic. "Whittaker here, can you repeat? I'm close by. Over."

"A couple say dey been robbed, sir. Outside Rackam's. Over."

"I'll go," I said, and quickly got out of the SUV before he could protest.

Something gave me an uneasy feeling about the call, and I wanted to be the one to find out what was going on. I ran the 300 metres and picked a man and a woman out of the crowd, standing on the pavement looking bewildered.

"Did you report a robbery?" I said, catching my breath.

"Yes, yes, we did. It's my husband's wallet," the lady said, trying and failing to keep herself calm.

She was probably in her early thirties, English by her accent, plain but not unpleasant looking. Her husband may have been a couple of years older. They must have recently arrived on the island, as their pale British skin had a warm red glow to it.

"Are you sure you didn't leave it on your table?" I asked.

"We thought the same thing, so we went back in, but it wasn't there," the husband explained. "Then I realised. As we'd been leaving the restaurant here, a young girl bumped into me. She apologised, but she never looked back and kept going. I'm pretty sure she nicked my wallet."

"Could you describe her?" I asked, knowing I didn't need a description.

"She disappeared into the crowd on the pavement. I barely caught a glimpse of her," he replied.

"Does this happen a lot here?" the wife asked. "We were told the island was safe."

"The Cayman Islands are very safe, ma'am. But these things happen from time to time." I turned back to her husband. "You saw her from behind. How tall? Hair colour? What was she wearing?"

"Bugger. I didn't think anything of it until I realised she'd pinched my wallet. She was shorter than my wife. Dark hair." He thought for a moment. "I think it was tied back, and she may have been wearing a hat of some sort. Shit, I don't know. I really paid little attention at the time."

"I'll open an official police report and we'll see what we can do," I said. "I need your names, a contact number, where you're staying, and when you're leaving."

"We're only here over the weekend for a meeting," the wife said disconsolately as I handed her my notebook. "Is there any chance you'll get it back?"

"Doubtful," I replied. "What was in your wallet, sir?"

"The usual. Driver's licence, credit cards, and some of our cash."

"How much cash?" I asked. "And don't lie."

They both frowned at me before the man replied, "Around two hundred dollars. We left the hotel with three hundred and bought dinner, so whatever was left."

"You're not giving us much hope," the woman complained.

I shrugged my shoulders. "I can tell you I'll find your wallet in the next hour and everything will still be in it, if that makes you feel better? But that's not what will happen."

"You won't even try?" the man challenged.

"I'll try, and I'll alert the other constables to keep an eye out. But you just described the majority of female teenagers on the island, sir. I would cancel your credit cards right away."

They grumbled some more and filled out their details before I made my way back to Le Vele. As I walked, I wondered who flies from England to the Caribbean for a weekend. Maybe it was business as they said they had a meeting, but even if they burned reward miles for the second ticket, it seemed like a lousy use of the points.

I reached the SUV as Whittaker was coming down the steps from the restaurant with two pizza boxes in hand. We got in the car and the smell assaulted me, making me drool and my stomach growl.

But I would have to wait. Firstly, I figured Whittaker didn't want us eating pizza in his nice SUV, and secondly, I don't like pizza when it's steaming hot. The cheese is all runny and the toppings tend to slide off in one lump that ends up slapping you on the chin and making a mess on your shirt. Well, I've seen that happen to other people, but it's never actually happened to me. And that's because I prefer to wait until it's warm instead of piping hot. It's also because I eat pizza with a knife and fork, which I've noticed for some reason baffles Americans.

By the time we reached the station just a few minutes away, I'd given Whittaker a brief summation of the wallet theft, and told him I'd join him once I'd filed the report. What I really wanted was a few minutes alone to think. I was torn. Part of me felt I should run to the bus station and try to catch Jazzy, who I was certain was the pickpocket. Another part of me was anxious to pin down the good doctor and his nurse to see what they were hiding. And I had to admit, there was also a pull towards slumping into a chair in the break room and munching on my Pearadise pizza topped with mozzarella, pears, gorgonzola, walnuts and honey.

Heading out the front door, I paused in the car park. It was getting dark and felt cooler without the sun beating down, although I knew the air temperature probably hadn't changed. I was being crazy. The odds of catching Jazzy were about the same as the couple ever getting their cash back. She wouldn't board the bus at the main depot in town. Instead, she'd jump on at a smaller stop. I'd have to ride the bus and see if she got on the one I took. The odds were terrible.

Taking out my mobile, I looked through my recent calls. Finding the person I was looking for, I hit the *call back* option. After several rings, my call was answered, and my explanation didn't take long.

Turning around, I walked back inside the building and began

filling out an incident report. Kirkconnell, Kumari, and my pizza were all guaranteed to be where I knew they'd be, unlike Jazzy. Well, the first two anyway. Apparently police officers didn't consider it stealing to nick food left unattended. I filled out the computer form as quickly as I could.

With a scrumptious slice in my tummy and the rest shoved in the fridge with Whittaker's name written on it, I joined him in the interview room. I figured his ownership reduced the odds of my food getting stolen. Now I just had to worry about the detective absent-mindedly walking off with my box.

He was just beginning to question nurse Sarika Kumari, who looked more annoyed than worried. Whittaker announced my presence to the recording, and I sat down.

"You work alone in the clinic on the night shift?" Whittaker asked.

"We all do. We rotate weeks of days and nights, so everyone pitches in."

"Is the front door locked during this time?"

"We lock the front door at 8:00pm and unlock at 8:00am. There's a buzzer if anyone arrives while it's locked."

"That's when the shifts change?"

"Yes."

"Is there an alarm?"

"Yes, but it's almost never set, as someone is always there."

"When is it set?"

"At night if we don't have any patients."

"You had overnight patients all this week?"

"Two."

"Who has keys to the front door?"

"Everyone."

"Did anyone come by this week during your shifts?"

The nurse took a moment to reply. "Saturday or Sunday I had a patient buzz the front door. But I don't recall any others."

"Who was the patient?"

"Her name's Matilda. It's her first child, and she's really nervous."

Whittaker briefly looked at his notes. "Can you recall which night this was, and the time?"

"I could see by pulling her file. I noted the visit."

"You don't recall? Could it have been Monday?"

Kumari sighed. "Maybe. Actually I think it was. I was off the following night, so it must have been Monday."

"Time?"

"That I do remember as it was right after Ian left from day shift. Would have been a few minutes past eight."

"Okay, any other night-time visitors?" Whittaker persisted.

She shook her head. "None that I recall."

I was dying to ask a question, but I held back, knowing Whittaker was taking his time pursuing the path he was on.

"Monday night was quiet after that?"

"As best I remember."

"Then why did you access the patient file number log twice that night?"

There it was, the question Whittaker had spent the past ten minutes building up to. Kumari looked stunned, and she stared at the detective's file folder as though he kept a monster tucked inside, ready to be unleashed.

"I don't recall."

"Let me see if I can help you," Whittaker said, opening the folder. The monster appeared in the form of two time stamps. "11:26pm on Monday night, and again at 3:24am on Tuesday morning."

The nurse shook her head. "I don't remember anything about that," she mumbled.

I noticed her hands were leaving a sweaty residue on the table as she fidgeted about.

"Kendra Rankin was murdered sometime around 2:00am Tuesday morning, Miss Kumari, and coincidentally, her patient file went missing. Was that the file you were looking up?"

"No! I wasn't looking up any files that night," she said, her hands becoming animated. "It was a quiet night. I caught up on paperwork, helped one of the patients to the bathroom a few times, and that was about it."

"Then how do you explain the patient file number log being accessed from computers inside the building at those times?"

"I swear…" she began, then abruptly stopped. "Wait, I did look up a file number! When I was cleaning up some paperwork, I wanted to cross-reference a family member. They're sisters, so I wanted to make a notation in both files. The younger girl had been in that day as a new patient. She'd told me her sister had given birth in the clinic last year."

"What time was this?"

"It would have been the eleven something one you mentioned," she said, relief flooding through her words.

"Which computer did you use?"

"The nurse station I always use. It's the one with the newer keyboard. The other one sticks on a few of the letters. Ian spilt coffee on it months ago and we haven't replaced it yet."

Kumari was finally relaxing. She swept her black hair behind her ears and sat up straighter.

"What about the other login?" Whittaker asked, and her shoulders immediately slumped.

"I have no idea about that. Are you certain it was from the clinic?"

"Absolutely."

Kumari shook her head. "Then I don't know. It wasn't me."

"You were the only one there," Whittaker pointed out.

She looked deflated and defeated. "I don't know. I swear."

The faint drone of cool air being blown through the ducting was the only sound for a few moments, so I took my opportunity to speak.

"You said there's a buzzer at the front door, correct?"

The nurse looked up at me, her brow furrowed. "Yes."

"And that's a button?"

"Yes."

"Does the door make a noise when it opens?"

"What do you mean?"

"Does the door buzz, ring, or alert you in any way that someone has entered?"

"Oh, no."

"But there's CCTV in the lobby, correct?"

"Yes."

"Is there a monitor dedicated to the camera?"

"There's one above the door to the lobby, but it's hard to see from down the hall."

"Do you ever look at it?"

"We can bring it up from the computers, so I usually do that if Bee steps outside and asks us to keep an eye out."

"Or between the time she leaves and the door's locked."

"Yes."

"What about after the door's locked?"

"The camera's still working, but anybody arriving has to use the buzzer."

"So you don't have the camera up on your monitor?"

"There's no point, and the screens aren't that big, so it's just in the way."

I sat back and after a few beats, Whittaker said he was pausing the interview and hit stop on the recorder. We got up and left the room.

"You spoon-fed her a way out," Whittaker said, but not unkindly.

"She's a smart woman," I responded. "If she was guilty of being involved somehow, she'd have a better plan going into this interview. We've been asking questions for days. She had plenty of time to come up with a good lie."

"You just gave her one, and she didn't take it."

"The other access was from Bee's computer, wasn't it?" I asked.

Whittaker shook his head. "No. The one on the counter."

I shrugged my shoulders. "Same difference."

"Using Kumari's login?"

"Correct."

"We're looking for someone else with a key who could have Kumari's password," I said.

I started walking down the hall.

"Where are you going?" he asked.

"To get another slice of pizza."

"Good idea. I only ate half of mine."

"How did the interview with the doctor go?"

"Nothing much new," he replied.

"Did you ask about how they met in England?"

"I did," he replied, taking the pizza box I handed him from the fridge.

"They dated, didn't they?"

"For six months, according to Kirkconnell."

I put my pizza box on the table and Whittaker noticed his name written on it. He swung his lid open and looked at me in confusion.

"Security measure," I said, finding a knife and fork in a drawer.

He smiled, and I sat down, cutting off a piece before my arse hit the seat. "I'd say six months is long enough to know your girl-friend's favourite password," I said before tucking into my dinner.

30

ALWAYS BOIL THE WATER

Saturday 7:30pm

Whittaker allowed Kirkconnell and Kumari to go home. We stood in the lobby, about to leave ourselves. It had been a long day.

"We're still nowhere," I said, feeling the pressure on the detective's behalf.

"We're making headway," he replied, and I looked at him as though he was mad.

"Often we must rule out all other possibilities until there's only one left. Then it's our job to find proof."

"Are we ruling out Minnow, Andrews, and Belle?" I asked.

"Unless we find new evidence, I think they're unlikely to be our killer, although they're all guilty of other charges. The timing doesn't seem to fit."

"What about Bentham?"

Whittaker pondered a moment before replying. "He has the timing, but again, unless we find evidence we missed from the murder scene or a connection between them, then it doesn't seem likely."

"Which leaves us Kirkconnell and his nurse."

Whittaker nodded. "We can't place either at the scene, but he claims he was home alone, and she was at the clinic. The only actual piece of evidence pointing towards them is the missing files, which could simply be poor housekeeping."

"We could find the nearest CCTV to the clinic and see if she left during the night," I suggested.

"I think that's worth doing for two reasons," Whittaker replied. "It might well prove she didn't leave…"

"And it might show who entered the clinic and grabbed the file," I said, finishing his thought.

"Exactly. I'll ruin Don's Sunday and ask him to look in the morning."

"I'll do it," I volunteered.

He gave me a fatherly look of concern. "Are you okay working again tomorrow? You've had a busy week. You've done your part and more."

"You'll be in, right?"

He nodded. "Until we solve this case, or it becomes a long-term thorn in our sides. But that comes with my job."

"We're still no closer. I'll be in."

"Okay," he relented. "Then let's get some rest and hit it with fresh eyes in the morning."

The wind rushing all around me felt wonderful in the balmy heat of the Caribbean evening. The thought of a shower was desperately inviting, but it would have to wait. I realised Whittaker had derailed my afternoon routine and I'd skipped my energy drink booster, which I now blamed for my lack of zeal. It was tempting to stop and grab a can, but then I'd never get to sleep when I finally reached the shack.

Hallie was waiting for me in the Foster's car park, and she hopped in the Jeep.

"Hey. Thanks," I greeted her, and she smiled.

"No problem, but I can't be long. I still have a paper to finish tonight."

"Drive or walk?" I asked before moving.

"Take Willie Farrington. I'll show you where to stop."

As I pulled out of Foster's and took the road opposite the car park, Hallie explained how she'd waited for Jazzy as we'd done before, and carefully followed her. There weren't many people who could do that without being seen, but I'd figured if anyone could, it was Hallie.

"Park behind that building," she said, and I followed her instruction.

The building was newer and looked like a small government or utilities office. As I parked, I noticed a CUC sign with their turtle logo. It was a substation for the island's power company. Security floodlights on the corners of the building cast a soft yellow light over the tarmac, and we hopped out of the Jeep. I reached in the back and grabbed my rucksack. Pulling out a change of clothes, I stripped down to my underwear and began putting on black leggings and a dark blue T-shirt.

"Nora!" Hallie hissed at me mid costume change.

"What? I have underwear on. Besides, no one's looking."

The area was dead quiet outside of the cicadas and the breeze in the trees. But of course, a car went by and the guy wolf whistled at me out his window.

"See?" she said with a big grin. "Some covert operative you are."

I slipped my trainers back on and gave her a playful shove. "Which way, smartarse?"

Hallie led us down a small side street called Hydesville Close. From the light in the car park, I could already see the short road turned to dirt within a hundred metres. A couple of old cottages were tucked in the trees to our right. One had a light on inside, but the other was dark. We moved beyond the homes where the dirt road made a hard left and then curved right before opening up into a wider area.

Once we were away from all the buildings, the stars provided meagre light, and I strained to make out the terrain. I'd brought a torch with me, but knew it would be like sounding an alarm to use it. Hallie didn't seem to have any problems seeing and walked confidently towards the trees on the left. We dodged around bits of junk and discarded car parts along the way.

Nestled in the trees, I saw a faint glow around the edges of what appeared to be a window. I couldn't tell if it was part of a shed or a house, as everything around it was pitch black. Hallie pointed into the woods, indicating we'd found Jazzy's home. She crouched down and waited for me to come alongside.

"What do you want to do?" she whispered.

"I want to go around the back, but I can't see my hands in front of my face," I replied. "We'll do it the easy way and knock. Hope she doesn't bolt."

"She'll have a second exit," Hallie said.

"I know, but we can't cover both sides without making too much noise. I'll just knock and tell her it's us."

Hallie nodded, and I was about to move forward when a voice came from behind us.

"You already make a racket."

We both spun around and saw a small form silhouetted in the clearing.

"Damn," Hallie mumbled.

I laughed as I stood up straight. "No way you heard us."

"What you want?" Jazzy asked, sounding just as annoyed as when we found her in the tree.

"Can we go inside and talk?" I asked, already being bitten by all kinds of flying insects from hell.

"May's well. I gotta move now anyhow."

"We're not going to tell anyone," I said as she passed us and walked into the darkness. I heard her scoff.

I followed Hallie, who seemed to have the same built-in night vision as Jazzy. The structure was no bigger than a small bedroom, perhaps three metres square. The walls were concrete block and looking up once we were inside, I could see the roof was tin. I couldn't believe the incredible tiny home she'd put together. A single light fixture hung from the ceiling with an old yellowed shade. Along one side, a wooden plank on more blocks formed a counter. Opposite, a neatly made single bed was elevated on similar blocks with storage bins underneath. I assumed the floor was a concrete slab, but it was mostly hidden by a grey carpet, curled slightly at the edges.

"Where do you get power from?" Hallie asked, staring around the place in awe.

"House over back," Jazzy replied, pointing farther down the dirt trail.

"They let you use theirs?"

Jazzy looked at her like she was nuts. "Shock myself good gettin' dat run, but figured it out."

"This is impressive, Jazzy," I said, noticing a two-burner portable electric cooktop on the counter. "What was this place?"

Jazzy shrugged her shoulders. "Dunno. Found it all run down. Fixed da roof and bin addin' stuff till now." She sat down on the edge of her bed. "So what you want?"

I couldn't tell where her second exit was hidden, but I made sure I was between her and the door. "I need you to give me back the wallet you stole in town earlier this evening."

She glared at me. "What you talkin' about?"

Now I looked at her like she was crazy. "They got a good look at you and filed a report," I half lied. "If I give them their wallet back, I can make the report go away. I'll claim someone handed it in."

"Don't got no wallet," she said, shaking her head.

"Jazzy. I told you I'd try to help, but I can't if you bullshit me. If I don't make that report go away, your description will be in the morning briefing for the next two weeks. Every constable from George Town to Barkers will be looking for you."

She stared at the carpeted floor and sighed. "I bin just fine witout you."

"I can see you've done more than fine," I told her. "But you can only nick people's stuff for so long before your luck runs out, and it's about to run out."

"Since you came by it has!" she snapped.

"Don't be stupid, girl," Hallie jabbed back, slipping deeper into her local dialect. "You lucky Nora come by. They bust you den you go in da juvie system, and that sucks big time. Let her help you now."

Jazzy looked up. "Why you tink it was me?"

"I told you, they saw you," I said, holding to the exaggerated truth.

She smirked and shook her head. "Now who bullshittin'?"

"They got a good enough look, Jazzy. How do you think I knew to tell Hallie to follow you off the bus?"

She switched her glare to Hallie. "So you da one who screw me?"

"We're not screwing you," I reiterated. "Believe me. When we leave here, we promise not to tell a soul about your digs. But you can't show your face anywhere for weeks, maybe a month. You got enough food and water to last you?"

Jazzy continued looking at us both defiantly, but I could tell she was thinking over the situation. While I gave her time to consider the options, I looked around the little room again. I wondered what she did for a bathroom. I noticed a plastic pipe coming down through the roof into a 30-gallon clear plastic drum sitting up high on a stack of blocks. It was three quarters full of water with a tap just above the bottom to dispense the liquid.

"You built your own cistern?" I asked.

Her brow creased. "I do what?"

I pointed at the tank. "You built a cistern."

"I dunno what you sayin', but I put dat tank dere to catch da rain. Got a funnel up top wit a mesh to keep out da leaves. I boil what I drink. Learnt dat real fast."

On a shelf she'd made below the counter, I saw a stack of books. Several were how-to construction guides. Others were novels mixed in with books about a plethora of subjects. She must pick up whatever she stumbled across and kept what interested her. I half expected a secret lift down to the underground bat cave below.

Jazzy reached under her bed and dragged a bin out just far enough to squeeze her hand inside. That was okay; it was better I didn't see what else she had in there. I took the wallet she handed me and flipped it open. I recognised the driver's licence as the man I'd met earlier, James Layton. The credit cards were still there, and surprisingly, so was the cash. I counted the money. There were two hundred and ten Caymanian dollars.

Shoved in with the money was a business card. It was from Lloyds Bank with Layton's name on it. Apparently, he was a graphic design manager. I noticed a handwritten web address on the back of the card. It was a long string of letters and numbers which looked more like a server address. The extension was dot onion, which I'd never heard of, although new extensions seemed to be popping up all the time. Below it was written 'LaYt0n%8825391', which I guessed to be a password. I slid the card back into the wallet.

"Gonna leave me be now?" Jazzy asked.

I handed her the cash and slipped the wallet into the inside pocket of my leggings. "No. I'm not done helping you." I turned and opened the patchwork wooden door. It looked like the original had rotted away at the bottom and been broken around the lock. Jazzy had used scrap wood to make it whole again.

"You swear you not tellin' about my place?" she asked, looking at me suspiciously.

"I swear," I assured her.

Before I walked out, I noticed a sprig of leaves hanging from a piece of fishing twine beside the door. Once outside, I led Hallie through the bigger shrubs around the outside of several larger pieces of junk.

"You noticed her alarm too," Hallie chuckled.

"I like that kid," I said as we walked down the dirt road.

31

KINKY IGUANA

Sunday 7:00am

Standing under my outdoor shower, I let the cool, fresh water wash the salt from my skin. At first light I'd given up staring at the ceiling and swum out to the reef. Spending thirty minutes with no one except a million sea creatures had helped prepare me to face another challenging day.

The ceiling hadn't surrendered any new answers or epiphanies, but the serenity of the early morning reef had given order to my scattered thoughts. The investigation was still struggling to get out of first gear, but Whittaker was right, we'd eliminated several suspects. If nurse Sarika Kumari was to be believed, we were looking for the person who sneaked back into the clinic early Tuesday morning.

Turning off the tap, I grabbed my towel and began drying my hair. I was keen to begin the monotonous process of going through available CCTV near the clinic. I wrapped the towel around my body and stepped from one little paver to the next, keeping my feet out of the dirt. Before reaching the deck, I noticed somebody watching me.

"Good morning, Edvard," I greeted the blue iguana.

He tipped his head to one side like some dogs do when they listen to a person speaking. I always wondered what was going through their minds. *Why doesn't she just bark so I'd know what she was saying? Intelligent beings, my arse.* I doubt that's what it was, but it's always fun to project human thoughts onto animals' actions.

"Are you a kinky iguana?" I asked the lizard. "Been checking me out while I shower?"

He's probably wondering what happened to all my tough scaly skin and spiky bits. *Big, ugly looking thing with all that smooth, soft flesh.* I'd decided to address Edvard in English, as despite his Norwegian name, it seemed unlikely he knew the language.

"Gotta go," I told him, and continued into the shack.

Twenty minutes later, I was heading south on West Bay Road, with a stop to make on the way to Central station. I'd woken James and Gillian Layton up when I'd called their hotel room while waiting for the Jeep to warm up. They were surprised and happy to hear I'd recovered their wallet. I was eager to hand it over and get to work.

The couple were staying at the Sunshine Suites Resort, which was a nice hotel set back on the inland side of the road behind Seven Mile Beach. It didn't have ocean views, but was a 300-metre walk from the sand at half the price. I parked and walked through the lobby, out the back of the hotel, and past the pool to Sunshine Grill at the back of the property.

Their restaurant was island-renowned for their Sunday brunch, and the smells coming from the kitchen as I opened the door made me realise how hungry I was. Working every day had kept me from the grocery store and I hadn't had breakfast.

The couple were sitting at a table near the entrance, sipping coffee and looking like they'd just got out of bed. Which I knew they had.

James stood and extended a hand. "Thank you for bringing it by. Would you like some coffee?"

Once I'd shaken his hand, he sat back down, expecting me to join them.

I dropped the wallet on the table. "Somebody handed it in last night. Said they found it on the ground outside Rackam's."

"Really? Do you think the pickpocket threw it away that quickly?" he said, looking at the contents.

"No. I think you dropped it."

James shook his head in disbelief. "Did the person say where exactly? I just don't see how I could have done that."

"They left it at the station's front desk and said they'd found it at Rackam's," I continued the lie. "Didn't leave a name or any details."

"The money's gone," he said, holding the wallet open so I could see the empty section. He quickly realised it wasn't completely empty and awkwardly removed the business card, shoving it in his shirt pocket.

"Maybe the person handing it in took themselves a reward, or someone walking by had already lifted the cash."

"Please, sit down," his wife, Gillian urged. "We really appreciate you bringing it by."

"Yes, yes. I'm sorry," James added, getting to his feet again. "I'm being awfully rude. Please join us for coffee at least."

I looked at my watch. It was 7:35am. Whittaker would be at the station around eight. I succumbed to my hunger and took a seat.

Gillian waved to a waiter. "Order whatever you want, Miss Sommer. The least we can do is buy you breakfast. We already ordered."

"Coffee and an omelette. Whatever you have with veggies. Cheddar cheese. No meat. Nothing else with it."

The waiter was dying to ask me what this, that and the other options I wanted, but he realised I'd answered all the questions he was about to ask. Nodding, he left to put the order in. I turned back to the couple, and it dawned on me I'd locked myself into conversation with two strangers for at least fifteen minutes. I wished I'd ordered a bagel to go.

"I assume you're not originally from the Cayman Islands," Gillian said.

It was a statement despite her using inflection as though she was asking a question. Normally I wouldn't respond, but I was stuck here for a bit, so I played along.

"Norway."

"Oh really?" she responded. "Quite a difference, I'd imagine. Not much snow here." She chuckled at her own joke. James was still trying to figure out how he'd dropped his wallet outside Rackam's and wasn't paying attention. His wife continued, undeterred. "What brought you here?"

I wanted to say a sailboat, but I stopped myself. "I was travelling the Caribbean and liked the island, so I stayed." Skipping all the parts about human trafficking, escorts, and boyfriends being gunned down seemed appropriate.

"Why did you come all this way for a weekend?" I asked, just to steer the conversation away from me. And because it seemed odd. I understood the private jet crowd burning tens of thousands of dollars in fuel to lie around on Seven Mile Beach and enjoy a few evenings of fine dining, but this couple didn't strike me as multi-millionaires. Middle class, doing well for themselves, judging by the watches and her wedding ring, but the big spenders didn't stay at the Sunshine Suites.

Gillian looked at her husband, who was still miles away, deep in thought. "We had a meeting, so just a short trip this time," she replied.

"Leaving tomorrow?" I asked.

"This afternoon," she said. "We fly through Miami."

That flight was at four or five o'clock, if I remembered correctly.

"What do you do?" I asked, doing maths inside my head, trying to figure out how many more questions I'd have to ask before my food arrived.

"We both work for Lloyds Bank at their head office in London. That's how we met."

I recalled the business card from James's wallet. "I didn't know Lloyds Bank was in the Cayman Islands," I said to keep the conversation going. There were over a hundred banks on the island, which was known around the world as a stable financial centre. Most had a small office in George Town simply to meet the physical address requirements to do business here. The Cayman Islands' reputation as *the* place to hide money was a stigma which lingered from the past. Banks were now required to report account information upon request from most nations.

"They don't," Gillian replied. "We're here on a personal matter."

"No kids?" I asked.

"Not yet," she replied and looked at her husband again. "But soon, we hope."

She made it sound like they'd flown all the way over just to shag. Maybe he needed a tropical environment to perform at his best. Or she'd organised a substitute on the island to get the job done. My musings made me smile inside, and I realised I was staring at James. He chose that moment to become aware of the other two people at the table. We looked at each other awkwardly.

To my relief, the waiter arrived with their food, but neither one of them touched their plates.

"Oh please, don't wait on me," I said, when I sensed they were being typically British.

"Are you sure? We don't mind waiting," Gillian said.

"I insist," I replied. I wanted them to eat, so they'd observe another piece of etiquette; not talking with their mouths full.

The couple reluctantly obliged, and I busied myself sipping coffee. My piping hot omelette arrived soon after, and I furiously blew on each bite so I could start eating right away. Gillian had ordered toast and jam, so she finished sooner than I would have liked.

"Why did you choose the police force?" she asked.

"They offered me a good opportunity," I replied between bites, avoiding the longer and more truthful answer once again.

"You said the island is safe, so what crimes keep you busy?"

"Drunk tourists," I replied, and she laughed. Apparently, she thought I was kidding.

"We saw something about a murder inquiry on the news last night. That's awful," Gillian continued.

I nodded.

"Does that happen often here?"

I shook my head. I was shovelling omelette down my throat in an attempt to be chewing at all times, but she was determined to continue chatting.

"Are you working on the murder case?"

I nodded. "But I can't discuss details," I broke down and said, hoping to end that line of questioning.

"Of course, of course."

"Do you get many pickpockets in town?" James asked, appearing back in the conversation as he'd finished his yogurt and fruit. Apparently, he still hadn't come to terms with the idea he'd dropped his wallet.

"Not often," I replied. "We try to watch for it. Our bosses consider it bad for business."

"Stealing from tourists?" he asked.

"It's our main industry," I replied. "Tourism, not stealing," I quickly clarified.

"And banking," Gillian added.

I nodded.

"But you're not here for banking business," I said, still slightly curious why they'd come all this way for a couple of days.

"No," Gillian replied, and looked at her husband. They both seemed to fidget nervously.

"Have you been here before?" I asked, finishing the last bite of my breakfast.

"A couple of times," she replied.

"We love it here," James added. "We've always found the people friendly and welcoming."

"It doesn't suck," I said, sliding my chair back. "I have to go to work. Thank you for breakfast."

They both stood. "I appreciate you taking the time to return my wallet," James said, and shook my hand.

I nodded and left the restaurant. I hoped they'd let the wallet incident go and enjoy the rest of their trip. My lies to keep Jazzy out of trouble could easily come back to bite me. Fortunately, I only had eight hours to worry about it.

32

BABIES IN GYM BAGS

Sunday 8:10am

When I reached Central station, I noticed Whittaker's SUV was already in the car park. I hurried inside and found an open computer terminal. That wasn't difficult as it was Sunday. I closed out the Laytons' case file, noting the wallet had been recovered and appeared to have been dropped, not stolen.

"Good morning, Constable," Whittaker said, appearing in the doorway.

"Sir," I replied. "I was about to start looking at CCTV."

"Good. Thank you," he said, taking a step inside the room. "Don is coming in too. I figured we needed all hands on deck."

I clicked with the mouse, navigating through the database in search of the right cameras. Finding a map showing the locations, I zoomed in on Hell Road. Hearing a foot shuffle, I realised the detective was still in the room.

I looked over my shoulder. "Did you need something else, sir?"

Whittaker stroked his goatee. "How does a baby go missing?"

Swivelling the chair around, I looked at him curiously. "Sir?"

He pulled another chair from a desk and sat down a few metres from me. "We've solely focused on Kendra and whoever killed her. Apart from checking with all the medical facilities, we haven't approached the case from the other side. How does a baby vanish?"

"About as easy as throwing away a gym bag," I replied.

He frowned. "Physically, yes, but babies get noticed a lot more than gym bags. Assuming the birth went fine, and the baby's alive, somewhere on the island is a newborn who's in the care of someone other than its mother."

I nodded. "True. Which brings us back to a crime of passion. The baby's with the father?"

"Although I tend to agree with that thought," Whittaker countered, "the actions of the killer do not fit the usual pattern of violence from a partner."

Which had been my argument. "Someone stealing babies?" I offered.

He frowned even more. "That's a horrible thought. But a possibility none the less."

We both sat in silence for a few moments.

"I was thinking," I said, switching subjects as he seemed to be finished, "we should run by the low-income apartments today. More people might be home as it's Sunday."

Whittaker stood. "Agreed. Let me know if you find anything on CCTV. I'll have a look through the reports from the licensed midwives. I was told there was nothing pertinent, but it won't hurt to look again." He started towards the door. "When Don gets here, hand the CCTV project over to him. We'll visit the apartments."

"Okay," I replied, returning to the computer screen. I didn't mind passing this job over to someone else. It was tedious work, and Don appeared to be thorough.

The closest camera we had immediate access to was at the three-way junction down the road from the clinic by the school. There was another camera in the opposite direction, where Hell Road met Watercourse, but it was out of action. It was always out of action. Every time the city workers repaired it, someone cut the wires or ripped it down the very next day. They'd given up. Jacob and I pulled an overnight vigil a few months back to catch the culprit, but no one showed up. The next night when we weren't there, the wires were cut again.

Having a timestamp to work from helped, and with little traffic in the early hours of the morning, I quickly narrowed it down to three cars. One came from Town Hall Road and turned left on Hell at 3:12am. The camera never picked up the registration plate, but I could see it was a dark blue two-door hatchback with one person visible. They appeared to be male, but I couldn't be sure.

Shortly after, at 3:21am, a second vehicle approached from Reverend Blackman and continued straight down Hell Road. It was a red minivan and I could read the reg plate. Looking it up in the system, it was a 2019 Renault Espace registered to a couple who lived off North West Point Road. I found a phone number and called.

"Hello? This is Peter," a man answered with an English accent.

"This is Constable Sommer from the RCIPS. Do you own a Renault Espace minivan, Mr Whittle?"

"You're from the police? What's happened?" the man's voice rose in panic. "Is it my wife?"

"I'm not calling about an accident," I reassured him. "Do you own a red minivan?"

"Bloody hell, you scared the living daylights out of me. Yes, yes, we have a Renault minivan. My wife drives it."

"Was your wife driving it at 3:00am on Tuesday?"

The line went quiet.

"Sir?"

"I don't know," he said tentatively. "I was in New York for work. But I have no idea why she'd be driving anywhere at that time of night."

"Is your wife with you?"

"No, she's out with the children. They were going snorkelling while I finished a work project."

"What's her mobile number?"

He gave me the number, which I noted. "Where were they going?"

"She said Cemetery Beach. I was planning on joining them shortly."

"If she hasn't spoken to me by the time you see her, please make sure she calls me right away." I gave him my mobile number, which he repeated back to me.

"What's this regarding?" he asked.

"I'll try the number you gave me. It's very important I speak with her as soon as possible. Thank you, sir."

I hung up and paused a moment before trying her number. I had a bad feeling about this. It was unlikely the woman was involved in our case, but it sounded like she had some explaining to do with her husband. I tried the number. It rang and rang. I guessed he'd beaten me to it and was now trying to find out who she was playing around with while he was in America.

The third car in the time window I'd searched came from Hell Road and turned right on Town Hall. No reg plate on the front, but if the timestamp was accurate, it was driving away from the direction of the clinic at 3:24am. That meant they would have needed to log into the computer, leave the building, and drive down the road, all within the same minute. It was a black BMW with a male driving and a female in the passenger seat.

I ran through the footage in fast-forward for the following two hours, looking for the dark blue hatchback. It didn't return the way it had come. We needed a camera in the opposite direction. It startled me when my mobile rang.

"Constable Sommer."

"Are you the one who called my husband about the damn minivan?" a woman with a polished English accent barked into the phone.

"Is this Mrs Whittle?"

"Too right it's Mrs bloody Whittle. What the fuck are you doing telling my husband I'm out driving around in the middle of the bloody night? Have you any idea of the trouble you've started?"

I took a deep breath and heard Whittaker's reprimand echoing in my head. "Mrs Whittle, your vehicle was seen on Hell Road at 3:12am on Tuesday morning. Were you driving?"

"What bloody business is this of yours?"

"We're investigating an incident which took place around that time on Hell Road. Please answer the question, or I'll drive over and drag your arse off the beach in front of half the island, and you can answer my questions at the station. I don't have time for your bullshit."

Fy faen. I guess I hadn't heard Whittaker's voice as loudly as I'd first thought. To be fair, I really didn't think I should be blamed when people provoked me.

I heard movement behind me and swung around, praying Whittaker hadn't heard me. Don stood in the doorway, grinning.

"What fucking incident?" the woman yelled.

"I can't disclose details of an ongoing investigation, ma'am. Were you driving your vehicle or not?"

"Who says I was?"

"You're on CCTV, and seeing as your husband was in New York, it was either you or one of your kids."

"Fuck."

Her swearing sounded funny in her posh accent, but I managed not to chuckle. "I don't care who you're shagging, I just need to confirm it was you in your minivan and where you were going."

"Fuck."

"We've established that part of the story, ma'am. Now can you verify it was you behind the wheel?"

"Fuck," she muttered again. "Apparently you already know it was me."

"Where were you going at 3:12am?"

"Home."

"Did you see any other vehicles along Hell Road at that time?"

"How the fuck would I remember that?"

"Because it's odd seeing anyone driving around at that hour."

"I was having enough bloody trouble finding my own way home."

"You were intoxicated?"

The line went quiet.

"I was tired. That's all I meant."

"Thanks for your help, Mrs Whittle. We'll be in touch if we have any more questions. Have a lovely day at the beach."

I hung up to the sound of her swearing like a sailor.

"That sounded fun," Don laughed, sitting in the chair Whittaker had vacated.

"We should find a camera between Hell Road and her house on North West Point Road to verify her story about going home," I said and moved the playback slider until I found the dark blue car. "This guy is of more interest. He doesn't come back through the junction by the school anytime during the following two hours."

"The camera broken at Watercourse?" Don asked.

I nodded. "Can you see what you can find beyond that?"

"Sure."

"Thanks. Whittaker and I have to interview more people at the apartments on West Bay Road," I said, standing up and stretching my legs. "Let me know if her story doesn't jive. She's at Cemetery Beach telling lies to her husband for a while, so I could pick her up."

I grabbed my travel mug and headed for the door, then paused a moment. "Don, what's a dot onion web address?"

He quickly spun around. "You didn't go to one from here, did you?"

"No."

"Dot onion is deep web stuff. Most of it's safe, but some isn't, especially dark web sites. You always want to go through a VPN with safety protocols in place."

"Could you find out more about a site if I had the address?"

"Some take an address and a password."

"I'd have the password too."

He looked reluctant. "I don't know, Nora. Not from our system, it's too risky. I'd have to set something up on an independent connection. It's doable, but it might take time. What do you have?"

I shrugged my shoulders. "Probably nothing, and it's not related to this case, so don't worry about it."

Walking upstairs, I couldn't help wondering why a couple from London, who were only here for a few days on personal business, were playing around on the deep web. It was possible the business card had been in his wallet for ages and nothing to do with the trip, but he sure whipped it out of my view in a hurry.

"Ready?" I asked Whittaker when I reached the open door to his office.

He came around the desk and grabbed his jacket from a coat rack. "Any luck with the CCTV?"

I skipped mentioning the angry lady who was screwing around on her husband and hoped she was another citizen who'd go away quietly. "We have a car with the right timing. Don's trying to get a plate for us."

33

DRIVING MISS SOMMER

Sunday 9:30am

I explained the few details I had about the dark blue hatchback as Whittaker drove north. We soon fell into silence, and I searched using the internet on my mobile for answers to a curiosity I had. Traffic was light, as many locals were in church on a Sunday morning. They gathered with family in backyards, at the beach, or on boats in the afternoon. Grocery shops and every business outside the tourist industry were closed, ensuring their employees could enjoy the Sabbath.

AJ's dive boat would be out on the water, but crewed by Thomas and a Cuban friend, Carlos. Thomas took Saturdays off, and AJ stayed home on Sundays. Thomas insisted on working Sundays as he wasn't a churchgoer and this gave him an excuse he could provide his family. I often spent Sundays with AJ, and as focused as I was on this case, it would be nice not to think about dead people for a day.

We passed under the footbridge for the Ritz-Carlton and a thought occurred to me.

"Pull over please, sir," I said and took out my mobile.

"Everything okay?" Whittaker asked as he slowed to the side of the road.

"*Ja*," I said, realising I wasn't sure how to explain myself. I clicked on the number I'd called this morning and held the mobile to my ear.

"Gillian Layton," she answered tentatively, probably wondering why a local number was calling her.

"Hello, Mrs Layton. This is Constable Sommer."

"Oh, hello. We were just heading out the door. How can I help you?"

"I screwed up and forgot to take a picture of your husband's wallet and the recovered contents," I said, lying about needing any photos. "I'm outside your hotel now if I could take a quick picture before you leave?"

Gillian stammered and mumbled for a few moments. "Could we do this later? We really were just leaving."

"It'll only take a moment, I promise," I insisted. "You'll be saving me from getting in trouble. I'll meet you in the lobby in two minutes."

I hung up before she could argue any more. Whittaker was frowning at me.

"Sunshine Suites please, sir. I'll explain everything afterwards."

He pulled away from the kerb and drove a few hundred metres up West Bay Drive to the small lane on the right leading to Sunshine Suites.

"Should I wait in the car?" he asked.

"Would you mind coming in?" I asked, knowing I was pushing my luck, considering he had no idea what I was up to. I wasn't sure I'd earned back that much trust. "If you could chat with the couple while I take a picture or two. It would be better if they were distracted."

I could tell he was dubious about the plan, but he found a parking spot and got out with me. Gillian was standing under the covered lobby entrance, pacing.

"Here," she said. "Please be quick. We don't want to be late. James is getting the car now."

She handed me the wallet. "This is Mrs Layton, sir. The wallet incident from last night. Gillian, this is Detective Whittaker."

He extended a hand while I stepped inside the lobby through the automatic doors. I heard him asking about her trip as the doors closed behind me.

I rifled through the wallet, pulling out the cash they'd added. The business card was gone. *Faen,* I did all this for nothing, and now I'd have to explain myself to Whittaker. Pulling all the credit cards out, I laid them on a sideboard. I slid the driver's licence from the clear plastic sleeve and tucked behind was the business card. Relief flooded through me. Until I flipped it over to discover it was just that; a business card. No web address handwritten on the back.

I made a production of taking several pictures of the contents with my mobile, before stuffing the cards and licence back in. I checked between each of the bank notes one more time before returning them to the long cash section of the leather wallet. As I did, I noticed a row of vertical stitching inside, which didn't perfectly line up with the outer sleeves. Using my fingernail, I picked at the material just below the top seam and found a small, hidden compartment. Inside was one business card.

The automatic sliding doors opened behind me.

"Are you all done, Constable? We really must leave," Gillian said urgently.

I flipped the card, took a picture and stuffed it into the cash section where I'd originally seen it. There was no time to wriggle it into the secret compartment.

"Thanks. Here you go," I said, handing the wallet back. "Where are you heading?"

Gillian took the wallet and shoved it in her purse. "We have a meeting," she replied and quickly retreated.

I followed her through the doors and stood by Whittaker as she hurriedly bundled herself into their hire car. James gave me a stern look, and I waved with a smile. They drove off without waving back. I snapped a picture of their hire car.

"Care to tell me what that was all about?" Whittaker asked as we walked to his SUV.

I opened photos on my mobile and showed him the picture I'd taken.

"What on earth is that?" he asked, peering at the odd web address.

"I noticed it when I returned their wallet this morning. I should have taken a picture then, but I didn't know what I was looking at. It's a deep web address and login."

We got into the car and out of the heat.

"Deep web, like dark web?" he asked.

"The dark web is just a small part of the deep web," I explained, sounding smarter than I was thanks to Robbie's explanation and my Google search just before I'd come up with the idea to stop at the hotel. "The deep web is everything that doesn't appear on search engines. Information housed on the cloud, online servers, banking and financial information, stuff like that. But also gaming, information sites, and sellers, who don't want their stuff seen by just anyone. Most of it requires not just the web address, but a password to access."

Whittaker drove us back to West Bay Road. "Okay, so what's so interesting about this web address?"

"I have no idea," I replied. "But something struck me as odd about the couple."

"She seemed nice enough," he said, "albeit a bit stressed about whatever meeting they had."

"They flew here from England for the weekend," I continued. "They leave this afternoon. Half of their trip is in an airport or an aeroplane, and they were here for a personal meeting, not business."

Whittaker continued north at a leisurely pace. I could tell he didn't share my suspicion, but he didn't appear mad about my little exploit, either.

"Probably buying a condo," he suggested. "Came over to sign the documents."

I shook my head. "I don't think so. Whatever it is they didn't want to talk about it. All they said was a meeting, but never what or where."

"Okay, so what do you think they're up to?"

"My guess is they're trying to move money around and think they can hide it here."

Whittaker chuckled. "They wouldn't be the first. Have Don check out the web address for you."

"He can't. Well, he can, but it would take too long."

"He's at the office. I thought you saw him?"

"Yeah, but he's not set up for deep web stuff. You have to be careful how you access these sites. Most of them are legit and nothing illegal is going on, but some are not and can crash your whole system."

We reached the detour around the Kimpton Seafire where the old coast road had been dug up and traffic moved to the bypass. Apparently, enough money bought the developer that privilege, much to the dismay of the locals who used to enjoy the drive and easy access to the public beaches.

"So, what can you do with the web address?"

"I have a friend who I think can check it out for me."

I searched my contacts for a number, putting this call through the SUV's hands-free system. It rang three times before being answered.

"Hello Constable Sommer," came a young man's voice. "Are you picking me up for a date to the movies?"

I smiled. "Not today Robbie, I have something even better for you."

"I doubt there's anything better than that," he said, laughing.

"Who's that?" I heard his mother ask in the background.

"My Norwegian police friend," he shouted back, unable to cover the phone.

"If I text you a deep web address and password, can you check it out?" I asked. "I have no idea what's on this site, so you need to tread carefully."

It suddenly dawned on me I could be sending a teenage boy to look at things he shouldn't see. Snuff films, pornography, or someone's bitcoin account.

"Sure. Don't worry, I have safeguards in place," Robbie replied. "Text it to me and I'll take a look."

"Hey Robbie. Better have your mum there, okay? I don't think it's anything she wouldn't want you to see, but I can't be sure."

"Is this something to do with your case?" he asked excitedly.

"Not the case you helped me with. It's something I found suspicious and wanted to check up on. I'm expecting it to be financial, and if it is, just let me know the site, but don't look at the account details, okay?"

"Hey mum," he called out, but I didn't hear a response. "She's back there somewhere wrapping my dad's birthday gift while he's out playing golf. Can I call you back when she's done? It'll only take a minute to access the site."

"Sure, no problem. Call me back."

I ended the call.

"Probably not the best idea using a citizen to investigate IT issues, Nora. How old is this guy?"

Shit. Here comes another reprimand. "He's the kid who helped me with the CCTV across the little pond. He spends all day, every day on his computer."

"That's not healthy for anyone, young or old," Whittaker said with concern more than criticism.

"He's in a wheelchair, sir. So basketball's out of the question."

"Oh boy," he said quietly, and I hoped my smartarse reply had scared him away from his original question.

"So how old did you say he is?"

Fy faen. Ironically, I couldn't get anything past the detective.

"Fifteen."

"Nora," he groaned, and then my mobile rang. I was never so happy to get a phone call in all my life.

"Hey Robbie, that was quick," I said as I accepted the call.

"Your money was on financial, huh?"

"Just a guess," I replied.

"What about your partner?" Robbie asked.

"How do you know I'm with someone?" I said before Whittaker could speak.

"Because you're on hands-free in a car as I can hear the engine and traffic, and you have a Jeep with no top, so you're either in your patrol car with your sleepy partner or in a friend's car."

I laughed. "Bloody hell, we better get you on the force when you turn eighteen."

"Sorry, I'll be going to MIT or Carnegie Mellon by then."

"That'll be their gain and our loss, young man," Whittaker said. "This is Detective Whittaker. I have the privilege of chauffeuring Miss Sommer around town today."

"Pleased to meet you, sir. What was your guess?"

"This is Constable Sommer's investigation, so I'm afraid I haven't had time to form an opinion. Care to enlighten us?"

"It's an adoption service," Robbie replied.

"What?" I blurted.

"An adoption service, you know, for adopting children."

"Where?" I asked.

"Here in Cayman."

"Adoption in the Cayman Islands is strictly handled through the Adoption Board," Whittaker said, his tone becoming serious.

"I don't see any mention of an adoption board. These kids are delivered to wherever the family lives."

Whittaker and I looked at each other.

"Would it be okay if we came by?" Whittaker asked.

"It would make my day," Robbie replied.

34

BABY BUMP

Sunday 10:30am

Detective Roy Whittaker almost never went over the posted speed limit. This was one of the times he made an exception. He glanced at his watch as he sped past the apartments we'd planned to visit.

"It's already ten-thirty. We can't let the day slip away from us," he said. "If there's something to this adoption business, I'll assign it to Detective Weatherford. We need to focus on Kendra Rankin."

"Right on Cemetery," I directed, looking at a map on my mobile. Whittaker made the turn.

I wasn't so ready to pass this off. "The Laytons are probably with whoever runs this adoption site right now. That has to be the meeting they were rushing off to. Can we put a BOLO out for their hire car? Right, then first left."

The detective slowed through the residential neighbourhood, following my directions.

"Let me call the station and have someone check with the hire car companies," he said, taking his mobile from his jacket pocket.

I held up my phone. "No need, here's the reg plate."

He looked over at me and grunted his approval. As Whittaker parked outside the Barkers' house, I called in a BOLO for the Laytons' car on the radio. It was a long shot anyone would see them as the meeting was unlikely to be in a public place, but worth a shot.

We walked up the path to where Mrs Barker stood in the open doorway inviting us inside. I made the introductions, and she led us through the living area. Robbie met us with a broad smile, and I could tell this interaction with people outside his usual bubble was indeed a highlight for him.

"Here's the site," he said, skipping any pleasantries. "The link and the password are to a personalised portal, geared specifically to these people."

"The Laytons," I said, looking over him at the screens.

"Yeah. It looks like they're getting a girl who's not even born yet."

"Can you tell who operates the website?" Whittaker asked.

"No," Robbie replied. "It's hosted on a server somewhere, but they routed the login through a site in Russia, and I can't follow it beyond that."

"There are Russians involved?" Whittaker responded, his concern escalating.

"Probably not," I replied. "It's just bounced through a site there."

"Exactly," Robbie confirmed. "They might even host the site on a server there, but it doesn't mean the people involved are. They could be anywhere in the world."

"Looks like at least some of them are here," Whittaker muttered. "I'd like to start by finding them."

"Our best bet will be the Laytons," I reiterated. "What else is on this site, Robbie? You said they were adopting a baby who isn't born yet?"

He quickly clicked around from the header menu and brought up a page with several pictures of a woman in various stages of pregnancy. In the most recent shot, she looked about ready to burst.

"*Fy faen*!" I blurted.

"Nora!" Whittaker and Robbie said at the same time. Mrs Barker laughed.

"Sorry. But look who that is, sir," I said, pointing to the screen.

Whittaker leaned in closer, and Robbie enlarged the image.

"Is that the student we met yesterday?" Whittaker said, aghast.

"Marcella Wallace," I replied. "And she either had her baby and bounced back into perfect shape really quickly or her baby bump is for show. Is the father on here?"

Robbie clicked and scrolled around, but didn't find anything except a bio on Marcella, which was probably bullshit. Whittaker took out his mobile and walked away, making a call.

"Is there any method of contact on the website?" I asked. "A phone number, email, anything?"

"There's a message form, but it's routed the same way so I can't find the source," Robbie replied, showing me the built-in messenger.

"Scroll back through the message history."

It took a few moments. There was a lot of conversation exchanged, starting over six months ago. I began reading and could tell the early messages were tentative from both sides as they built trust. As time wore on, the Laytons became more relaxed, and several weeks into the process, they appeared to choose a baby. Or more accurately, they chose a mother who was carrying the baby.

Whittaker rejoined us.

"I haven't seen any reference to the cost, but they were asked to make the first deposit shortly after they picked out a baby," I told him. "I'm guessing their personal site on this portal was updated each step of the way. It probably started with a selection of pregnant mothers, and once they chose one, her progress was followed and they created a timeline."

It would take too long to read the whole chat file, so I asked Robbie to scroll ahead to the past few weeks.

"Here," I pointed out. "They're confirming the trip over to meet the mother. According to this, she's due next week."

"Which means wherever this meeting is taking place, Marcella Wallace is going to be there," Whittaker said, looking at his mobile as though he were willing it to ring.

"All the chat is written by someone else, or made to look like it's someone else," Robbie observed.

"If the Laytons began with a choice of mother, it means there were more like Marcella, so I doubt she's behind this," I responded. "But Kendra Rankin may have been one of the mothers."

Whittaker's mobile rang, and he answered it right away. After a series of grunts and yeses, he ended the call by thanking the person on the other end.

"There's no one resident in the Cayman Islands named Marcella Wallace, but there is a Marcella Rodriguez, and guess where her name cropped up?"

"I feel slightly disadvantaged in this quiz," Robbie said with a grin. "I've only just been assigned the case."

"I think this case just became our existing case," I said, before answering Whittaker. "One of the missing files?"

"Exactly. It's looking like the good doctor is behind this after all."

I looked at my watch. It was nearing 11:30am. "The Laytons will be heading to the airport in about three hours. If we don't find them beforehand, we can pick them up there."

Whittaker thought for a moment. "I'll call immigration and make sure they detain them if we don't get to them first."

"We should post someone to watch the apartments in case Marcella returns there too," I suggested.

He nodded. "I'll also see if we can pick up Kirkconnell. Acting Constable Robbie, could you please copy the transcript of the chat and paste it into an email or another document?"

Robbie beamed. "Yes, sir."

He began selecting the text from the most recent part backwards.

"What was that?" I blurted, and he stopped scrolling.

"Sorry, go ahead and finish copying, but we need to look through the chat from a few days ago."

Robbie finished grabbing the selection and copied it into a text file. The words spread across the page instead of being squished in the narrower messenger format, but the transcript still took up six pages. He scrolled to the last page.

"There," I pointed to the screen. "He gave them directions for the meeting."

"Seabreeze Lane off Uncle Bob Road," Whittaker read from the page. "It's a boat. They're meeting on a boat. Seabreeze is a cul-de-sac at the end of a channel from the North Sound. There are a few moorings and a boat ramp the locals use."

"*Dritt,*" I muttered.

"Nora!" Whittaker and Robbie both scolded me again.

"Shit, sorry."

"Saying it again in English doesn't make it okay, Constable," Robbie said, trying not to laugh. "Besides, what's the problem? If you know where they are, just go arrest them."

"Thank you, *Acting* Constable. We don't know where they are. We know where they were. Do you know how many boats are on the North Sound on a Sunday?"

"I don't get out there much," Robbie said, still smiling.

"Don't be a smartarse or I'll unplug your computer."

He smiled even wider.

"I'll send a car to cover the boat ramp," Whittaker said, interrupting our banter. "Let me give you an email address to send that transcript to, Robbie."

I stepped back while Whittaker took care of the email and noticed Robbie's mum beckoned me over to the kitchen.

"Thank you for including him," she said. "This is a thrill for Robbie."

"He's been a big help," I said truthfully. "I would have waited days to get this information from our TSU guy. We're not set up for this. Robbie's an exceptionally smart kid."

"Well, I'm glad he could help you, and I hope you catch whoever's behind this."

"We've made progress this morning," I said and was about to walk away when she placed a hand on my arm.

"Robbie thinks the world of you," she said. "He really looks up to you."

"Then he's looking down, not up. He can find much better people to admire. I shouldn't be one of them," I replied, more tersely than I'd intended.

I was shit at taking compliments. The lady was being really nice, but I never felt like I deserved nice, or anyone's praise. I had crossed lines, hurt the ones I loved, and been unable to save the person who meant the most to me. All the good I could do from now until eternity wouldn't make up for my mistakes.

Mrs Barker looked puzzled and hurt. "I don't know why you're so hard on yourself. Maybe you have good reason, but all I know is the person I've seen with my son. You treat him as an equal, and most people can't find a way to do that. It's difficult to see past the chair and the disabilities, but you see Robbie, the young man. He appreciates that, and I can't thank you enough."

I had no words to respond. I'd been raised in a loving home, but Norwegians aren't known for their effervescence when it comes to compliments. My parents were probably more outwardly supportive than most. They always supported me at swim meets and sailing races, whether or not I did well. Fortunately, I won most of the time, so I didn't face too much disappointment.

But when I was sixteen, I screwed up in the biggest possible way. I fell prey to a teacher at my school, and when he ended our affair to move on to his next young victim, he was involved in an unfortunate sailing accident. Looking back, I should have gone to my parents and the police. But I was an angry teenager, embarrassed, and unsure whether the boom which knocked him into the chilly water was simply unfortunate, or unconsciously deliberate.

I panicked and ran. Well, sailed. Then staged the wreckage of the little sailboat and stowed away on a freighter. That error in judgement set me on a path I've struggled to break free from. Whittaker and AJ saved me. They kept me going when I didn't care to live, and the detective gave me an opportunity for a new life. Yet still, I've struggled to make the right decisions at times.

I felt a lump in my throat as she searched my eyes, trying to figure out what was going on behind my emotionless exterior. Her words were genuine and incredibly generous. Hopefully, I had made the kid's day a little better. He deserved it. For a moment, I felt an overwhelming need to hug the woman.

"*Takk*," I said instead, and walked away.

35

———

MISSING JOHNNY CAKES

Sunday noon

Seabreeze Lane was tarmac, barely wide enough for two cars, and lined on both sides by sea grape trees. A short marl trail branched off to the boat ramp, which sloped into a square-shaped basin sixty metres across. The canal ran from the opposite side and led into the North Sound half a kilometre west. Parked down the trail was the Laytons' hire car.

Whittaker made one slow pass down the lane, turning around in the driveway of a home at the end, and returning to Uncle Bob Road. We saw six boats moored along the edges of the basin with an additional four or five empty spaces. He made a right onto Uncle Bob and parked behind an unmarked police car. A broad-shouldered man in a shirt and tie got out of the car and walked towards us. Whittaker hit the unlock so the man could climb into the back seat of the SUV.

"Good afternoon, Vincent," Whittaker greeted him.

"I'm missing a family cook-out at Smiths to watch nothing

happening here, Roy," he griped in good humour. "My wife's Johnny cakes are the best on the island."

"Maybe she'll save you a couple," Whittaker said, looking over his shoulder.

Weatherford scoffed and glanced at his watch. "Gathering started at 11:30. They'll all be gone by now, every single one of them."

"I expect that's true," Whittaker replied, returning his gaze to the basin through the side window. "Your wife is one mighty fine cook."

They both fell silent for a minute as we all observed the lack of activity in the basin to the background hum of the SUV's engine.

"We should go back to the apartments, sir," I said as a thought came to me.

"We have someone watching the building," Whittaker replied. "I don't want to do anything to raise the alarm until this boat comes back."

A text dinged on his mobile. "Doctor Kirkconnell was at his home. He's been taken to the station," he told us after he'd read the message.

"The Laytons weren't meeting him then," I pointed out.

"Maybe he handles the patients and someone else is behind the website and dealing with the customers," Whittaker replied.

"I can hold down the fort here if you want to question the doctor," Weatherford offered. "I have two uniforms at the public dock by Calypso Grill, watching for boat traffic, and Ben with the Joint Marine Unit on call in the sound. There's plenty of back-up only minutes away."

Whittaker thought for a moment. "All we have is missing files from the clinic. We still don't have anything concrete tying the doctor to the adoptions, or the murder," he finally said. "He doesn't strike me as the type to buckle in an interview when he knows we have nothing."

"The couple who manage the apartments, sir. There's no way they aren't involved in some way. Neither Marcella nor that gigolo bloke in number 6 qualify for low-income housing. That's why I'm saying we should go back there."

Whittaker pondered the idea for a few moments.

"I think all we'll catch here is the Laytons and someone paid to take them wherever they went by boat," I added.

"See, I am missing my wife's Johnny cakes for nothing," Weatherford quipped.

I shook my head. "We still need the Laytons and they can tell us where and who they met with. I bet it's all taking place on a boat or a shoreline location. Either way, the perp won't be there any longer by the time we grab the Laytons."

"What makes you think the perp didn't pick them up here in his own boat and is conducting the meeting while idling around the North Sound?" Whittaker asked.

"Because he's built levels of security into the process every step of the way. I think he waited and watched to see if we followed them. Best place to see that is a nice flat calm stretch of open water. Kendra's murder was the only sloppy thing he's done."

"If the murder is related," Whittaker countered.

"There's evidence she came from the trail next to the apartments. The apartments in which we've found one of the people involved in the illegal adoption scheme. And that person has ties to the clinic. It's all related, sir."

"Agreed," he said.

I knew I was probably one step behind his own conclusions. He was challenging me to see how waterproof his own ideas were.

"Alright. Vincent, we'll leave you to pick up whoever comes back here. Call me as soon as you see them, please."

"Sure, Roy," Weatherford replied, and opened the back door. "But this is costing you a nice lunch next week."

"Sounds like a deal," Whittaker said, and Weatherford closed the door.

Five minutes later, we drove past the apartments and pulled into the car park for Silver Sands Condominiums. A row of trees screened us from the building across the road, but we could still catch a peek between the branches. Two constables waved to us from the patrol car we parked next to. I hoped they'd not been spotted arriving. I guessed we were out of plain clothes detectives and unmarked cars at midday on a Sunday.

"Don't you find it strange that there's only four cars parked at the apartments?" I asked.

"It is Sunday. People do things on the weekends," Whittaker replied. "And if it's low-income housing, many residents would use public transport. They can't afford a car."

"How many apartments do you think there are?" I asked.

"We made it to, what? Number 7 or 8? And we were a third of the way down the hallway. Twenty something?"

There had only been a handful of cars outside the last time we visited, which still seemed odd to me. "Are we going in?" I asked, my hand poised ready to open the door.

"How could Kirkconnell handle patients at the clinic without Bee knowing?" he asked, instead of responding to my question.

"He couldn't," I replied. It was a good question. "But the files are still missing and undoubtedly taken by someone with access. Or they're all lying."

We both sat quietly, chewing it over.

"Bee wouldn't call us about the other files," I said, throwing more confusion on the argument.

"Right, and if they were all in on the adoption scheme, why even mention Kendra's file?" Whittaker said, looking over at me.

"Could be the doc and his girlfriend, nurse Kumari. She sent us chasing after a mystery person who looked at the patient number log the night she was working."

"But she didn't come up with that excuse. You gave it to her," Whittaker commented thoughtfully.

"Or I simply beat her to it."

"Possibly," he agreed. "But where are they getting babies from for adoption? We'd have noticed before now if they were murdering local mothers and snatching newborns. I can't remember another case which matches this from the recent past."

"They said Kendra came by the clinic for an abortion," I said, tapping the dashboard.

"Right."

"What if the clinic is the initial contact point?" I continued. "A single mother comes in seeking an abortion which the clinic can't legally provide. The doctor offers the expectant mother an alternative solution. She has the baby and gives it up for adoption."

Whittaker nodded. "In exchange for money?"

"Of course," I replied, and looked through the leafy branches at the apartment building. "And accommodation during her pregnancy."

Whittaker swung his door open. "There's one way to find out," he said, getting out and motioning for the constables to accompany us.

Crossing West Bay Road a hundred metres from the apartments, we hugged the treeline beyond the verge to hide our approach. Once we reached the car park, we walked briskly along the front of the building to the covered entrance at the south end. Pushing the door open, we found Sheila Hargraves behind the counter, sitting on a stool, playing a game on her mobile. She tucked the phone in her bra and slid off the stool.

"What da hell is dis?" she said, scowling at us. "Damn scare da hell outa me come bargin' in like dat."

I was pretty certain she hadn't recently returned from Sunday morning church. Today she was sporting a low-cut silvery top with plenty of cleavage on display. Her chest, along with most other body parts, jiggled as she moved.

"Where's your husband, ma'am?" Whittaker asked.

"Out," she replied.

"Out where, ma'am?"

She shrugged her shoulders. "Didn't say."

"Please step around from the counter, ma'am," Whittaker said, beckoning her.

"Why for?"

"Because I'm going to ask you to stand out here with the constables while we talk to some of your residents."

She frowned at the detective. "What I done? You can't come in 'ere and start pushin' and shovin' me around."

"Mrs Hargraves, we haven't touched you, but if you'd prefer, we can arrest you on suspicion of aiding and abetting criminal activities. I'll have the constables escort you downtown for questioning there."

"I ain't bettin' on nuttin'," she shouted. "I give dat up long time back."

"Mrs Hargraves," Whittaker said in a firmer tone, and beckoned her again.

She waddled out from behind the counter and didn't disappoint with the rest of her outfit. The sparkly silver top only reached as far as her belly button, revealing a prominent belly. She'd snugly encased her lower half in matching silver leggings, topped off with four-inch heels, which may have tipped her over the five-foot mark.

"Leave your mobile on the counter please," Whittaker said as she came around to the front.

The woman reluctantly slapped the heavily sequinned device on the counter in a show of defiance.

"Keep an eye out for anyone arriving," Whittaker instructed the two constables.

I knew them both from the West Bay station. One was a nice guy, but the other gave me a dirty look as I followed the detective through the door to the rooms.

We went straight to apartment 3 and banged on the door. I listened carefully for sounds inside, but heard none, and our knocks went unanswered. We found the same result at many of the rooms, and the ones who did answer proved to be locals in their thirties or forties, most with children. Completely believable as low-income families.

When we reached the end of the hallway, the only thing left was an emergency door.

"*Dritt*. I really thought we'd find pregnant women," I said, unable to hide my disappointment.

"The Laytons have to return to their car at some point," Whittaker replied, keeping his usual even keel. "We'll see where they can lead us."

"*Ja*," I mumbled, looking out the small window in the door. "*Fy faen*!" I said, looking around me. "Have you seen any stairs?"

Whittaker shook his head. "No. This place is a single-storey. The roof dormers are part of the facade from the old motel. They don't have windows. It's always been just the one level."

"Then why is there a metal staircase leading to a first floor?"

36

GAS TROUBLE

Sunday 12:30pm

At the top of the steps, I stood facing a hefty fire door without a window. Whittaker clambered up the steel stairs behind me. I tried the handle, knowing it would be locked.

"With your permission, sir?" I said.

He looked at me with a perplexed expression. "Permission for what? We'll never break that door open without a ram."

"I can open it in under twenty seconds," I replied. "No damage."

"We have probable cause. Go ahead, but let me call down to the constables and let them know what we're doing."

"No," I hissed, more firmly than I should have. "Hopefully, whoever is up here doesn't know we're coming unless someone tipped them off. I'd keep radio silence until we see what we have. Sir."

He nodded. "Okay. Go ahead then."

I fished my pick kit from my pocket and avoided making eye

contact with the detective. Fourteen seconds later, I pushed the door open a crack.

"Don't these emergency exits usually have alarms on them?" Whittaker whispered.

"*Ja*. I was waiting for it to go off."

"That wouldn't meet code," Whittaker added.

"It means it's used for access," I pointed out.

Pulling the door farther open, I looked inside down a similar hallway to the apartments downstairs, but with dimmer lighting. At the far end, I could see a reception area of some sort. The corridor was void of people. We entered cautiously, and behind us I resisted the fire door with a hand so it closed slowly and quietly.

We tried the first room on the right, but it too was locked. Same with the one across the hallway. Moving down the corridor, we trod lightly on the linoleum floor, checking each room we came to. They were all locked until we were more than halfway to the reception area. The door to a room on the left opened, and we both stepped inside.

There were no windows, and the ceiling sloped in the outer half of the room, matching the angle of the roof. A dim glow came from a pair of wall lamps to our left, mounted above a hospital bed. Flanked by monitors on wheeled carts, a dark-skinned woman slept soundly. By the curve of the covers, she was either hiding a basketball or pregnant.

We moved out of the room and gently closed the door. From farther down the hallway, I heard a man's voice speaking in a hushed tone. He appeared from one of the rooms with a woman in tow. She wore a nurse's uniform. The man was Rog Hargraves.

The nurse startled when she saw us from the corner of her eye, and Hargraves swung around.

"Bollocks," he muttered, and ran towards the reception before stopping to look all around, weighing his options.

"Damn it, sir, one of us should've stayed downstairs," I yelled.

Whittaker looked at me strangely, but didn't say anything.

Hargraves took the bait, disappearing from our view behind the last room on the left. I snatched up Whittaker's radio.

"Guys, look for a door in the office, quick. It'll probably be a cupboard or disguised as something else."

We moved swiftly down the hallway to the nurse, who stood still, too stunned to move.

"I'll go, sir. Stay with her." I said, tossing back his radio and sprinting for the stairs I knew would be around the corner.

"Okay," I heard Whittaker say with a hint of amusement in his voice.

The stairwell started towards the back of the building before turning ninety degrees right and ending in a small landing on the ground floor. Two options led from there; one into what I'd guessed would be the office, and one outside. The second door was just closing.

Leaping down the final three steps, I landed and shoved the door open with my left shoulder. Lying on the ground outside with a constable standing over him was Rog Hargraves. I quickly stuck my foot in the door jamb before it closed behind me and locked us outside.

"Cuff her too?" the constable asked, nodding towards the office and looking pleased with himself.

"*Ja,*" I replied. "Now get him inside so I can go back upstairs."

The constable put handcuffs on Rog and dragged him to his feet. I held the door while he guided his captive through.

"Yes, sir," the constable said sarcastically as he passed me. "Anyting else I can do for you?"

I rolled my eyes and groaned. "Don't give me shit. I just handed you a collar."

Whittaker had already cuffed the nurse and had her seated in the reception area, which I now realised was a nurses' station. Monitors for each room showed patients in four of the beds, and another room was full of cribs.

"Take a look," Whittaker said and led me to the first room on the road side.

Cribs were lined up in neat rows; five had babies in them.

"I hope one of these is Kendra's," I said quietly. "Poor kid."

"Five babies here, and four expectant mothers," Whittaker commented. "That's nine paydays. What do you think they're getting per child?"

"The message exchange didn't talk amounts. It must have already passed that stage before they gave the Laytons a login," I replied. "My guess would be a hundred grand or more."

Whittaker leaned over one crib and looked at the sleeping child, shaking his head. "Poor kid is right. This is no way to start a life."

"Is it better than the alternative?" I asked, not sure of the answer myself. "I'm guessing the Laytons were about to give one of these babies a pretty nice life."

"Maybe so," Whittaker replied, standing up straight. "But I'd be surprised if they vetted the parents beyond their ability to pay the price. I doubt they're all like the Laytons."

I thought the process through for a moment, voicing the theory as I played it out in my mind. "A young woman comes into the clinic, asking for an abortion. Officially, she's turned down, but Doctor Dickhead then contacts her and offers another solution. Have the baby, stay in my *other* clinic, and I'll pay you to give the child up for adoption. Once she's showing, he brings her here, and after she's given birth, they part ways. He sells the baby through his adoption scheme, and the mother walks away with some cash."

Hearing someone at the door, I turned and saw a young woman standing there with one hand on the door jamb and one on her swollen belly. She stared at me, checking out the uniform.

"Why da police here?" she asked.

I was taken aback and didn't know what to say. How on earth could she think what was going on here was legal in any way?

"What's your name, ma'am?" Whittaker asked politely.

The woman looked back and forth between us, concern

increasing in her expression. "Jeanie," she replied. "What goin' on? Where da nurse?"

"Is everything okay, ma'am? Do you need medical assistance?" Whittaker asked, moving closer to the woman.

"I got da gas pains again," she mumbled. "Nurse gimme someting for dem yesterday."

I looked away and tried not to snicker. Bloating was about to be the least of her problems.

"Let's get you back to your room, Miss Jeanie, and I'll see what the nurse can find you."

Whittaker shepherded Jeanie to her room, and I followed. Once she was bundled back into bed, I showed her a picture on my mobile.

"You know this woman?"

Jeanie squinted at the artist's recreation of the victim. "Dat look like Kendra. She really dead?"

"Is her baby here?" I asked.

Jeanie frowned at me. "Sure. She had her Monday. Din't go perfect, I guess, so she stay overnight. Gone next morning, so I tink she okay."

"You saw about her on the news?" Whittaker asked.

"No TV in here. No phone neither. Den few days ago, I hear dem talkin' 'bout her. Say she found dead, but no one know da girl's name."

"Did you call the police?" the detective asked, glancing at me.

Jeannie looked towards the door and lowered her voice. "I did. He left da mobile at da front desk and I called, but he see me and get all mad. Tell me it none o' my concern and Kendra had an accident."

"Who was that? Who's in charge here?" I asked.

"The doc," she said, looking at me like I was stupid.

"What's his name?"

"He tell us call him Doc, so we do. He from da main clinic on Hell Road. Why you here, now? Dis about Kendra?"

I wanted to scream at the woman. How could she not know she

was part of a baby farm? I held it in and marched out of the room, realising I was steaming more about misreading the good doctor than this woman's naivety.

"Help will be here shortly with something for those stomach pains, Jeanie," Whittaker said, and came out after me.

We walked to the nurses' station, Whittaker talking into the radio as we went. He ordered Central to send more constables, someone from SOCO, Don from TSU, medical staff and ambulances from the hospital, and someone from the Department of Children and Family Services. When he finished, I looked up from my mobile.

"There's a Jeanette Kendrick on the missing file paperwork list, sir."

"I'm sure all these women are on that list," Whittaker replied. "A small piece of good news is the fact that there's only eight files with the contents missing. I hope that means this operation hasn't been active very long."

"Unless Doc only removed the currently active files."

He frowned at me. "Allow me a moment of optimism, Constable."

"Sorry, sir."

Whittaker turned to the nurse who sat forlornly in the chair, staring at the pale blue linoleum-covered floor.

"How long have you been operating here?"

She responded without picking her head up. "Lawyer."

"Seriously?" Whittaker scoffed. "You have the opportunity to be our first and main witness, and you're going to pass up that chance by being obtuse?"

The woman said nothing.

"Ma'am, do you understand how much trouble you're in?" he said, trying again. "We're talking significant jail time. I would start my campaign for leniency right now by helping us if I were you."

"Lawyer," she repeated.

"Please stand up," Whittaker said, his tone tinged with disappointment.

Sirens wailed outside as we marched the nurse down the stairwell to the landing and through the door into the office. My guess had been correct. The door looked like an innocuous supply cupboard in the corner of the room. Whittaker handed the nurse over to the constables in the lobby, and sent the newcomers upstairs to make sure the patients didn't leave and were safe.

The Hargraveses were as tight lipped as the nurse and would say nothing except their demand for representation. After briefing another detective and putting him in charge of the scene, we walked outside into the midday heat.

"What now, sir?" I asked.

"The station," he said, walking across West Bay Road as another police car arrived and more sirens could be heard approaching. "Let's see how cooperative the doctor is willing to be."

"The staff seem to be carefully instructed not to talk. You think he'll be any different?"

"Doubtful," he replied. "But that's my job; persuading him it's in his best interests."

Whittaker's mobile rang as we reached the SUV. "Hold on one moment," he said in greeting and we got in the roasting hot vehicle. Starting the engine, Whittaker waited a moment for the call to switch to the hands-free system.

"Okay, go ahead Vincent."

"We have the Laytons," Weatherford said, "and Ben picked up the guy who dropped them off. Anton Jeffries, according to his ID."

"That's the gigolo guy from the apartments," I said, and Whittaker nodded.

"Thanks Vincent, bring them all to Central, please."

"Will do, Roy."

"Are the Laytons talking?" Whittaker asked.

"They're in mortified silence so far, but I can see they're in panic mode in the back of my car. Want me to separate them?"

"No, leave them together. Hopefully they'll realise helping us serves them best."

Whittaker ended the call and pulled the SUV onto West Bay Road.

"The Laytons may be our best hope," I said as we sped down the street, heading for the bypass.

"I'm thinking there's a contact in the UK who starts the process," the detective replied. "Fingers crossed they met that person face to face."

"And they must have just met with Kirkconnell's partner."

"You think they're a partner rather than someone working for him?" Whittaker questioned.

"The doctor trusted whoever it was to handle the meeting with the fake mother," I replied. "We know it wasn't him as we picked him up."

"Who would he trust that much?"

"Sarika Kumari."

"Yes," Whittaker said thoughtfully. "Agreed."

37

MAKE UP YOUR MIND, BLONDIE

Sunday 1:30pm

Arriving at Central station, we went straight into the interview room where Doctor Conroy Kirkconnell sat at the table. He stood up as we entered the room.

"What's going on, Detective? Why am I being held here?"

"Sit down, Mr Kirkconnell," Whittaker replied, avoiding the man's title of doctor. A title he'd be losing shortly.

"I have a right to know why I'm being detained."

"Please sit down," Whittaker reiterated firmly.

Kirkconnell sat, and we did the same. Whittaker pressed record and introduced each one of us.

"As you've already been told, you're being held on suspicion of facilitating illegal adoptions."

"That's ridiculous! How have you come up with that conclusion, Detective?"

"Because we just raided your maternity clinic above the apartments and arrested your staff."

Kirkconnell stared back in stunned silence.

"How long have you been running the operation, Mr Kirk-connell?"

"My clinic?"

"The one above the Island Dream apartments on West Bay Road."

"I don't know what you're talking about."

"Really?" Whittaker challenged. "We have direct ties between both clinics, patients matching the missing files you tried to cover up, and staff who are spilling all they know in another interview room right now."

The doctor went to speak, but stopped with his mouth agape. Those smouldering hazel eyes didn't look so easy going anymore.

"I want my lawyer."

"Come on, Kirkconnell, you're smart enough to know how this works," Whittaker said, waving a hand at the man. "Give us your partner and the UK contact, and we will take your cooperation into consideration down the road."

Kirkconnell shook his head. "I have no idea what's going on. I want my lawyer."

Whittaker stood. "So be it. The leniency will be granted to someone else. Your loss."

We walked out of the room and Whittaker told the constable outside the door to allow the doctor his phone call.

Continuing to the lobby, we waited for Weatherford to arrive with the Laytons and Anton Jeffries.

"It's a long shot, but why don't I drop by Kumari's residence and see if we get lucky?" I offered. "There's still a chance nobody's warned her."

Whittaker thought it over. "You could take a patrol car from here if there's any left in the pool."

"I'd rather take the Jeep and change out of uniform," I replied. "She'll run a mile if she sees police."

Whittaker nodded. "Okay, but you need someone with you."

"Is Williams working today?"

"I don't think he's on duty."

"I'll see if he'll come in, sir, if that's okay?"

"That's fine, but if he can't, pick up one of the guys at the scene to go with you. We have more than enough people there now."

I ran out to my Jeep and grabbed my gym bag from the back. Looking around, I didn't see anyone close or at least paying attention, so I quickly changed into leggings and a T-shirt.

"Sorry Ridley," I said, not waiting for the temperature needle to come off the stop before driving out of the car park and heading north. I had Kumari's address, which was an apartment in West Bay off Batabano Road, so I headed for the bypass, calling Williams as I wound my way through the back of George Town.

"What shit I gotta bail you outta now?" Williams greeted me.

"Stop playing with your little willy and meet me at the apartments behind Summertime Suites. Come in plain clothes. Sir."

Williams laughed. "Fine. Should I be armed?"

"No. See you in ten minutes. I'll wait by the hotel."

"I need more than…" I missed the rest as I hung up.

That was okay. I always forgot how long it took to get from George Town to West Bay, even on the dual carriageway. It bypassed Seven Mile Beach, but it still ran through Camana Bay and the edge of residential and business areas for much of the way, roundabouts aplenty. Once I was past Snug Harbour, the roundabouts thinned to a kilometre apart, and I pushed the CJ-7 over the speed limit. I knew where all the police cars were, and they were busy.

Five minutes on, I was looking to my left at Jackson's Pond through slight breaks in the trees lining the road, hoping we'd wrap up Kendra Rankin's case today. Less than five days after her murder. A flash of blue caught my eye, and I lifted off the throttle. I didn't have time for distractions, but I found myself braking to a stop by the side of the road.

Hopping the guardrail, I shoved a few branches aside. Sitting in the gravel parking area at the north end of Jackson's Pond was a dark blue hatchback. I rushed back to the Jeep and grabbed my mobile.

"This is Don," the man answered after three rings.

"Did you get a reg plate on the blue car?" I asked.

"Nora?"

"*Ja, ja.* Did you figure out the owner?" I didn't have time for pleasantries, either.

"I got a reg plate, but I wasn't able to look up the owner. I was called out to the illegal maternity place."

"Where are you now?"

"Heading back to the station. Until they get the patients cleared out, I can't mess with…"

"Call me as soon as you get the name of the owner," I interrupted, starting the Jeep. "I need to know now."

Accelerating away, I ended the call and searched for a cut-through I'd noticed the other day. Finding the break in the guard rail, I turned hard left and slowed to first gear. The trees and shrubs swamped the old trail, but the Jeep pushed the branches aside with scraping and scratching sounds. I cringed at the nails-on-a-chalkboard imitation.

"Sorry, Ridley," I muttered again as the CJ-7 rolled slowly down the slope through a thicket of foliage. The old paint was faded, but I dreaded to see the gouges I was adding.

I pushed through into a clearing at the same time I met level ground, and fifty metres to my left was the hatchback. Parking directly behind the car, I couldn't see anyone inside, so I stood on the driver's seat of the Jeep. There was no one in sight.

"*Dritt,*" I groaned out loud. This could be a complete waste of time, giving Kumari a chance to get away. I looked at my mobile, willing it to ring.

"*Faen.*" I jumped out, taking the key with me, and called Williams.

"Change of plan. Go to the apartments we raided on West Bay Road. They're opposite Silver Sands. North side of the building is a trail behind a screen of trees. I'll be coming from the other end of that trail."

"Shit, I was already on Batabano," Williams complained. "Make up your mind, blondie. Who am I looking for?"

"I'll let you know when I know," I replied, breaking into a run. "But it'll be whoever runs away from you."

I shoved my mobile into the waistband of my leggings and picked up the pace. The sun was intense and reflected off the white-grey marl, offering no escape from the brilliance or the heat. Sweat poured down my face by the time I'd crossed the dike and arrived at the clearing before the woods. I paused to look around me. I still couldn't see anyone.

Picking up the pace again, I started down the trail where we'd found Kendra's teeth, turned right alongside the small pond, then slowed once more when I reached the left turn leading to the apartments. I peered carefully around the corner, searching the pathway for signs of the driver of the dark blue car. Overhanging branches threw much of the trail into shade, but the fierce sunlight found its way to the ground in luminous shafts, dancing and moving with the swaying trees. It made picking out details impossible.

I jogged on, the strobing beacons of bright light playing havoc with my vision. Halfway to the trees screening the apartments, my waist vibrated, and I realised my mobile was ringing. Stopping, I caught my breath and answered the call.

"It's Don. The car is registered to the guy from the clinic."

"Kirkconnell?"

"No," he surprised me by saying. I was figuring the doctor had the car in his name, but let his girlfriend, or former girlfriend and current business partner, use it.

"The nurse. Ian Belfrey."

"*Fy faen!*" I'd forgotten about that guy. He's hardly popped up in our inquiry at all. I needed to call Williams. "*Takk,*" I said and ended the call, quickly scrolling through my history to Williams's number.

The trees creaked and the branches waved, allowing light to come and go like a heat lamp on my skin. I heard a crunch of marl and turned just in time to take the brunt of the blow on my shoulder before it glanced off the side of my head.

38

PERSONAL MILESTONE

Sunday 1:30pm

I hit the ground with a thud and felt a stinging pain from my left thigh and elbow. My head was swimming with the bright sun waving back and forth across my blurry vision. Everything ached. Fighting to focus my mind, two thoughts rushed through my head. I noticed black specks of marl amongst the gravel on the trail and thought Rasha was right. It does all get mixed together. The second was illogical but caused a sudden panic; *he's going to bash my teeth out.*

Quickly rolling away from where I'd stood, I covered my mouth with my left arm and blinked against the glare of the dazzling rays squeezing between the foliage above. I tried to shade my eyes and squirm closer to the edge of the pathway, getting away from my attacker and the blinding light.

Finding shade, my vision cleared, and I realised I was alone on the trail. I sat up, checking both directions along the path. I saw no one, and all I could hear was the rustling of branches and the whispering breeze through the woods. Looking down, I saw my leggings were tattered where I'd landed on the rough ground and blood trickled from my forearm from a graze on my elbow.

My shoulder and head throbbed, and gently touching the side of my skull revealed blood on my fingers. I reached for my mobile, but it wasn't tucked in my leggings where I'd left it. I had to find it and call for help. My Jeep pinned his car in, but he would still have a head start.

Before I could look for my mobile, someone wrenched my head backwards by my hair and a thin edge of something cool and sharp rested against my throat.

"Not a fucking word," came the Brummie accent I recognised from the one time we'd met at the clinic. "Turn slowly around and walk into the woods."

"There's no path," I groaned. "I can't fit between all the trees."

"You'll manage. Now go," he barked.

"Why would I do that?" I said, staying still and holding my breath.

"Because otherwise I'll cut your throat right here," he hissed, with his face right next to my ear.

I didn't want to die, and I certainly didn't want to die by having my jugular and windpipe severed. But once in the thick woods I'd be completely at his mercy with no room to escape. Plus, there was only one reason to take me in there - it was much easier to have me walk to my execution than to drag my corpse, leaving an obvious trail of blood.

"Go ahead," I stammered, forcing the words from my mouth. "Make a big mess here, then try to move my body."

The blade pressed harder against my exposed neck and I wondered if there was any chance Williams would show up before I bled out.

"I have a better idea," he growled, shoving me by the fistful of hair he clenched. "You'll be my bargaining chip. Walk." He pushed me in the back with his other fist, which held the knife.

I would gladly move along the trail, even if it was back the way we'd both come. It bought time, and the longer I could stay alive, the more opportunities might present themselves. I noticed my mobile in the weeds by the edge of the trail, its screen shattered. That was okay, I doubt I'd need it anymore. Hopefully, Williams would see it and find the key to my Jeep tucked in a sleeve on the back. Then an idea came to me.

"Wait," I said after a few steps. "My key."

"Fuck your key," he said and punched me in the kidneys.

My knees held, but I fought to catch my breath. "My car is blocking yours," I coughed.

"Where is it?" he snapped.

"With my mobile," I said, and pointed behind us.

I had my back to the man, so I was blindly gambling my life on human nature. He released my hair and took hold of the back of my T-shirt, keeping me in check. If I was wrong, his other hand would thrust the knife into my back. I swung my right elbow with all my strength, pushing from my legs. With his head turned to look where I'd pointed, my bony elbow caught him under his jaw.

His head snapped back, and he staggered, but still had a grip on my shirt, pulling me with him. Completely off balance, I fell, knocking Belfrey the rest of the way to the ground. We both landed with a smack, but landing on top of him partially broke my fall. I felt a searing pain in my right side and saw blood on my shirt.

Rolling away from the wound, I scrambled to my feet and saw the knife in his right hand, dripping red. I stepped in to kick him in the ribs, but Belfrey recovered quickly and whipped the knife hand across his body. I held back just in time for the blade to swoosh past where my leg would have been. In a heartbeat, he was on his feet and switched the knife in his hand so the blade pointed down.

We circled, slightly crouched, arms spread wide, both ready to pounce. I was armed with nimble speed, he with a knife and whatever other fighting skills he possessed. I needed a weapon. Belfrey waved his knife hand back and forth, teasing me to make a lunge. As we turned circles around the narrow trail, I glanced at the edge of the trees, looking for a piece of wood.

Spotting a section of branch I thought could work, I made the mistake of taking my eyes off my nemesis for a moment too long. He stepped in and brought the blade down in a sweeping motion. I leaned back and felt a rush of air past my face and a tug on the front of my shirt. Taking a step back, I kept my feet underneath me, then jabbed at his nose before he could bring the knife up again.

Blood spurted from his face and he stopped in his tracks, his eyes watering. He wiped his face and shook his head, pausing just long enough for me to step to the side and sweep the piece of wood up in my hand. I saw the expression change on his face. He was beginning to panic. He had a blade, but I had better reach with my long arms and a two-foot club in my hand.

Belfrey baited me to swing, knowing the heavy club would take me off balance and I'd be slow to recover. I faked a wind-up and watched him tense in anticipation of his chance to finish me off. When I didn't lunge, he took a step back.

"Tell you what," he said, panting. "Let's walk away before you get hurt. I don't want to hurt a copper."

"You want me to let you go?"

"I'm saying I'll let you go. I've got the knife."

We resumed the slow circling a step apart, both ready to attack or defend.

"I don't want to deprive you of killing a woman. I know you like it."

Belfrey scoffed. "The hell I do."

"Then why did you murder Kendra?"

"Who says I did?" he replied, and I searched his eyes for the truth. He was lying.

Taking half a step forward, I shoved the branch at his face and he reacted by swatting it away with his empty hand. The motion twisted him to his right as his left hand bashed the club down and away, pulling me another half step closer. He saw his opportunity and brought his knife hand sweeping around just as I swung the branch up again, collecting his wrist with a thud on the way. My swing wasn't powerful, but made him stagger long enough for me to bring the club down on his head.

Belfrey teetered backwards and without hesitation I wound up and swung again, this time from the side, hitting him in the left ear. His head jerked violently, his legs buckled, and he tumbled to the ground. I took another step and wound up the heavy branch once more.

Visions of Kendra's disfigured face taunted my mind, and the power of adrenaline and rage pushed me to exact the revenge she would never know. Groaning on the ground before me with blood tinting his hair red, all I could see was a pathetic, greedy man who didn't deserve to live. I heard a voice echoing around the trees, but all I could focus on was the piece of shit below me.

It was unclear to me who were the victims and who were the criminals in much of this case. The Laytons and people like them? I felt sure they would give a young Caymanian a loving, stable home, which the child was unlikely to get from a destitute single mother. Hallie and Jazzy were both smart and resourceful. Most kids from their backgrounds didn't have the tools to make it and wound up incarcerated before they reached twenty-one.

The young mothers? If making poor decisions was a crime, every human being on the planet would be behind bars. Some mistakes are more costly than others, but these women had recognised their lack of ability to care for a child and after being denied an abortion, they'd accepted another path, which in theory worked out for everyone.

But for two people, their position was crystal clear. Kendra was the victim of a brutal murder when I presumed she changed her mind about surrendering her child or crossed Belfrey in some way. And Ian Belfrey, the man at my feet, was guilty as fuck of bringing her young life to an end. I couldn't bring Kendra back, but I could make sure Belfrey shared the same fate he'd inflicted on her.

My fingers dug into the rough surface of the bark, and I gritted my teeth to deliver the final blow, raising the club above my head and aiming for his jaw. But then I paused. A tiny part of me held back and whispers grew louder all around my head. I heard Whittaker and AJ, both calmly telling me to stop. I felt Ridley by my side, reaching up and softly touching my arm until I lowered and dropped the club.

The outside world cleared, and I saw Williams running towards me.

"Nora!" he yelled.

Looking up at him, I smiled. "I didn't kill him."

Williams reached me and checked me over, fussing at the wound on my head. "Are you okay?"

I let out a long, soothing breath. It had taken the help of a group of people who cared for me far more than I cared for myself to temper my rage and keep me on the right side of the line. But ultimately, it was my decision to stop, and I felt quite proud of myself.

"Yeah. I'm good," I said. "As long as some pin-dick lawyer doesn't get this *drittsekk* off on a technicality."

39

ADULTING

My long legs dragged in the sand as my seat swept gently back and forth. Beside me on the next swing was Jazzy. She rocked herself fore and aft, keeping her feet in one spot. We were in the playground at Scholars Park off Birch Tree Hill Road, waiting.

The dried scab on the side of my head felt tight and it took all of my willpower not to scratch it. I'd been lucky. If my shoulder hadn't taken some of the power out of the blow, he would've cracked my skull, like poor Kendra's. I felt fortunate to have an itchy scab and a mild concussion.

Small boobs were a blessing for once. Belfrey's knife had cut my T-shirt and nicked my sports bra, but missed my flesh. The cut on my side where I'd landed on the knife had taken twelve stitches. Any amount farther over would have been a stab instead of a laceration and I might not have got up. The doctor at George Town Hospital congratulated himself on his fine stitch work and swore I'd barely have a scar.

I didn't care. I might as well have some scars on the outside to go with the ones tucked away on the inside.

Ian Belfrey had been behind the whole operation. He referred to himself as 'doctor' at his makeshift maternity clinic above the apartment building, and only the Hargraveses and the two nurses he employed knew his full name. Once his staff realised the house of cards had fallen, they began talking and provided plenty of testimony.

Tying Belfrey to the murder of Kendra was harder, but our SOCO Rasha came through. Although he'd disposed of all his own bloody clothing and the hospital gown Kendra had been wearing and left no evidence at the scene, Belfrey had missed one tiny detail. The locked doors upstairs belonged to rooms not yet furnished for patients, except one.

He'd maintained a bedsit where he could sleep and shower after a long day between the two clinics. The nurse on duty had woken him when she realised Kendra and her baby were not in the ward, and she told us he left to look for her. When she saw him next, he was wearing different clothes and had the baby with him. Rasha and her team scoured the room for evidence of the crime and finally found one bloody fingerprint. Belfrey had scrubbed the apartment clean, except behind the door handle of the refrigerator. He must have opened the fridge to get a drink when he'd returned to the room. The fingerprint was his, but the blood belonged to Kendra Rankin.

Now tied to the murder, the illegal adoption scheme, plus the attempted murder of a police officer, Ian Belfrey's only bargaining chip was his UK contact who brought the adoption customers to him. The London Met picked the guy up and seized his computer, which he'd used to create and update their website. The man in England and Ian were old friends from medical school. I doubted their friendship would survive their jail time.

Belfrey was being deported to the UK to face the charges, as he was a British citizen and only a work permit holder in the Cayman Islands. I wondered if he'd run into Andrew Bentham at the airport, as his work permit and permission to visit the Cayman Islands in the future had been revoked.

I hadn't seen Doctor Dishy Eyes, Conroy Kirkconnell, since the case had been closed, and that was for the best. A relationship kicking off with a first date in the police interview room wasn't destined for success, in my opinion. However, I did feel bad for him, Sarika, and Bee, who were all completely innocent and devastated by Belfrey's deceit.

The Englishman's system was exactly what I'd suspected the doctor of doing. Following up with patients who'd been denied an abortion and offering to buy their babies from them. Marcella Rodriguez was Belfrey's first client, except he performed an abortion for her. After that, she was never pregnant. She and Anton Jeffries were eye candy for the customers to believe they were adopting a beautiful island baby from stunningly good-looking parents who were excited to give their child a loving home.

At $125,000 per transaction, there was plenty of money to pay everyone involved, and if the scheme had continued, Ian Belfrey would have made a mint. His plan was to fill every room in the makeshift clinic with expectant mothers. According to Sheila Hargraves, who wouldn't shut up once she'd starting talking, the next step was paying down-and-out women to *get* pregnant. Anton Jeffries was keenly on hand to perform the male part of the transaction.

The Laytons were mortified when the scheme was explained to them, and devastated they were not going home with a baby. They maintained their story about believing the deal was legitimate, but I couldn't see how they couldn't have been suspicious. Losing a hundred and twenty grand was the penalty for being gullible, and they were sent home to the UK without being charged.

I looked up as a woman walked towards us. Jazzy quit rocking, and I dragged my feet to a stop. My thirteen-year-old friend had finally agreed to meet with someone from the Department of Children and

Family Services, but only in the park where she could bolt if the situation wasn't to her liking. I could tell her tiny frame was already tense, looking around for suspicious people who shouldn't be there.

"Good morning, Miss Sommer. I'm Raylene, and I presume this is Jasmine?" the lady said, staying a few metres away until the girl accepted her presence.

Jazzy squinted at the woman, but didn't say a word.

"I'd like to see if we can help you," Raylene continued.

"Like da last foster home you people *help* me wit?"

"Nora told me there may have been some improprieties. We take that very seriously, Jasmine. I promise you we'll investigate the family. Obviously, you wouldn't be placed with them again, and they'll be in big trouble if what you say is true."

"It true." Jazzy snapped. "And I'm fine on my own. Don't need nobody."

Raylene smiled. "You certainly appear to be doing well for yourself, but I'm afraid it can't continue this way."

"Why not?"

I'd already had this conversation with Jazzy, but apparently she wanted to hear it from someone else. I couldn't blame her. The girl had survived for years off her wits and street smarts. A transition would not be easy.

"Because currently, you're stealing to survive, and when you're caught, you'll go into the juvenile detention system, which I assure you is far less pleasant than living with a family who are happy to have you."

"Gotta catch me first," Jazzy replied, but it was bravado. She knew her time had run out.

"I have a feeling Constable Sommer has turned a blind eye to your ways, but I'm afraid that can't continue to be the case. Of course, we also have to consider your living arrangement and your education."

"My home is just fine, lady."

"I hear you've made quite the place for yourself, but you're squatting on someone else's property. Which again is illegal, Jasmine."

Jazzy sighed and scuffed the dirt with the heel of her shoe. "What you sayin' to do den?"

"I would like to place you temporarily with one of our families who provide a short-term home for children like yourself while we look for your permanent home. We need to evaluate your learning stage and enrol you in school at a suitable level."

"Do I get to choose?"

"Choose your school, dear?"

"Choose da family?"

"The process for finding your permanent home is two sided. We try to match a child with a suitable family, but ultimately, it's the three of you who decide, so yes, you get a say in the matter."

"What if none of dem want me?"

"Then we keep looking. But you're a bright young lady, Jasmine. I don't believe we'll have trouble finding you a family."

I knew families were far more interested in fostering, or adopting, infants or young children over teenagers. It was one thing when your own kid rebels, but quite a different challenge bringing an already troubled teen into the home. Of course, I didn't want to say that in front of Jazzy. "How many short-term foster families do you have?" I asked.

"Not enough," Raylene replied with a smile. "But the ones we have are incredibly kind and patient folks who often have several of our children in their care."

"I'll stay wit you until dey find a family I like," Jazzy said, looking at me.

"That's not how this works, Jasmine," Raylene said, coming to my defence.

"Why?" she rebutted again.

"Because our foster homes have to meet certain criteria."

"What are the requirements?" I asked, unsure why these words were coming from me.

"Twenty-five years old, for starters. Stable environment, with someone present whenever the child is home."

I didn't meet any of those provisions.

"I tink I'll take my chances on my own," Jazzy said, and stood from the swing.

"I'm afraid that's not possible, Jasmine," Raylene said firmly. "I'm obligated to take care of you at this point."

Jazzy looked at me with daggers shooting from her eyes. "You shoulda left me be. Told you nuttin' good come of dis."

"Wait," I said, standing and putting a hand on Jazzy's shoulder. "I have a suggestion."

They both looked at me dubiously.

"Jazzy stays with me for now, which gets her off the street while you can start doing your various evaluations for school and looking for a permanent foster family."

Raylene shook her head. "Miss Sommer, you don't meet the requirements. We can't do that."

"Okay," I responded. "Then let's you and I sit down and watch while Jazzy runs off from here and stays on the street until she's nicked for something down the road. Then she'll bounce around the juvie system where she'll be until her eighteenth birthday."

"That's ridiculous," Raylene replied. "We can stop all that happening if she'll trust me and lets me take care of her."

"Why should she trust you?" I countered. "Her experience of the foster system is shit. Why would you expect her to think you'll provide anything different?"

I noticed Jazzy sat back down, but I remained standing. "If she runs away from me, then I'll wash my hands of the deal and you can do what you want. But how about we start by trusting Jazzy? All you have to do is nothing, except start the process from your end. Tell me where you need her to be, and I'll make sure she's there. Meanwhile, I'll guarantee she's off the street, not stealing from anyone, and we'll figure out online schooling to get her going."

Raylene let out a long breath. "This simply isn't how the system is designed to work."

"Fuck the system. She's on the street because of your shit system," I paused and took a breath. Somewhere in my concussed brain, Whittaker's voice was trying to tell me to be nice. "I'm sure the program is mostly great and full of people who care, but it failed for Jazzy. Now you have an opportunity to make it right. I'm offering to take responsibility for her while you find a permanent solution. A good place to start would be interviewing every kid who you placed with the Bartons. Getting those *drittsekker* out of your system would be a big step in gaining her trust back."

I looked at the kid, and she stared back at me. Her lips curled into the slightest of smiles.

"This arrangement can't go on for long," Raylene finally said.

"You've lost track of her for three years. Now you want to count weeks?"

Raylene sighed again, turning her attention to Jazzy. "Are you willing to stay with Miss Sommer until we can make better arrangements?"

"Okay," Jazzy replied.

"Officially, the file will say…" Raylene stopped herself. "I have no idea what to officially call this, but I'll come up with something." She handed me a business card. "I wrote my mobile number on the back. Call me anytime. I'd like to see you both in one week, at your residence, Miss Sommer."

I nodded. "Sure. I'll have the maid clean up." I winked at Jazzy.

Raylene sighed. "Please don't make me regret this," she said, and walked away along the path.

That meeting hadn't gone even close to how I'd planned. I had no clue what I was going to do with a thirteen-year-old in my shack. Or my life. In the space of a week, I'd not killed a guy who deserved killing and taken a runaway pickpocket into my care. For someone who didn't want any ties or obligations, I'd acted remarkably like a responsible adult. I still wasn't sure I'd done the right thing in either of the two events.

"Do you have a TV?"

"No," I replied, walking towards the exit of the park.

"What about a PlayStation?" she asked, trotting up alongside me.

"No."

"Will I have my own room?"

"No."

"Do you have Pop Tarts?"

"No."

We reached the entrance gate, and I steered her towards the CJ-7.

"Can I drive the Jeep?"

"No."

We both climbed in. "Put your belt on," I told her, and she did so. "Can you swim?" I asked as I pulled onto Birch Tree Hill Road.

"I tink so," she replied.

"What do you mean, you think so?"

"I learnt to swim when I's small, not bin in da water since."

"Swimming is the same now as it was then, so I expect you can still swim."

"Yes den, I can swim."

"Good. I'll teach you to freedive."

"Like hold da breath and swim around?"

"*Ja.*"

"Okay. You hungry?" she asked.

I looked at my watch. It was almost noon. "What do you want?"

"Burger King."

"*Fy faen,*" I muttered. "Maybe I'll drop you back at your little shed. I can't do this."

"You don't like da Burger King?"

"It's shit food."

"I didn't know, I ain't never had it."

"Then why did you say you wanted it?"

"'Cos I ain't never had it."

I turned right on Reverend Blackman Road towards Town Hall, heading for Heritage Kitchen.

"Ever been stabbed?"

"No!" she replied.

"Wanna try that just because you haven't?"

"No," she laughed.

"*Faen.*" I already sounded like my parents. What happened to the goldfish plan?

ACKNOWLEDGMENTS

My sincere thanks to:

My incredible wife Cheryl, for her unwavering support, love, and encouragement.

My family and friends for always being there.

My marvellous editor Andrew Chapman at Prepare to Publish for his diligent work and wise suggestions.

Gretchen Douglas, whom I'd like to welcome to the team with her fine proofreading skills.

Lily at Orkidedatter for her Norwegian advice.

Casey Keller, Craig Robinson, and Alain Belanger for their help with all things Cayman Islands related.

Annalyn Corbin, who won a name contest through my newsletter to have her name included in this story… I swear I didn't plan her character to be quite as she turned out!

Shearwater dive computers for their friendship and support.

The Tropical Authors group for their advice, support, and humour. Visit and subscribe at www.TropicalAuthors.com for deals and info on a plethora of books by talented authors in the Sea Adventure genre.

My beta reader group has grown to include an amazing cross section of folks from different walks of life. Their suggestions, feedback and keen eyes are invaluable, for which I am eternally grateful.

Above all, I thank you, the readers: none of this happens without the choice you make to spend your precious time with my stories. I am truly in your debt.

LET'S STAY IN TOUCH!

To buy merchandise, find more info or join my newsletter, visit my
website at
www.HarveyBooks.com

If you enjoyed this novel I'd be incredibly grateful if you'd consider
leaving a review on Amazon.com
Find eBook deals and follow me on BookBub.com

Find more great authors in the genre at TropicalAuthors.com

Visit Amazon.com for more books in the
Nora Sommer Caribbean Suspense Series,
AJ Bailey Adventure Series,
and collaborative works;
The Greene Wolfe Thriller Series
Tropical Authors Adventure Series

ABOUT THE AUTHOR

A *USA Today* Bestselling author, Nicholas Harvey's life has been anything but ordinary. Race car driver, adventurer, divemaster, and since 2020, a full-time novelist. Raised in England, Nick has dual US and British citizenship and now lives wherever he and his amazing wife, Cheryl, park their motorhome, or an aeroplane takes them. Warm oceans and tall mountains are their favourite places.

For more information, visit his website at HarveyBooks.com.